'A debt to Daphne du Maurier is evident throughout this remarkably assured adult debut.' *The Sunday Times*

'Fans of *The Girls* will love this sweat-soaked, sultry, small town tale full of shadows and lurking dread.' *Red* Online

'Daring, alluring and beautifully atmospheric *******' *Culturefly*

'Beautifully written and utterly captivating . . . and so so dark. I loved it!' Katerina Diamond, author of *The Teacher*

'A must-have.' *Sunday Express*

'Seriously twisted and utterly addictive.' Lisa Hall, author of *Between You and Me*

'Disturbing and beautiful.' SJI Holliday, author of *Black Wood*

'Compelling . . . Engel's portrayal of small-town Kansas truly terrifies. *The Roanoke Girls* shows the devastating power of the psyche in making us believe something wrong can be right.' *Stylist*

'Beautifully controlled horror.' Lucy Mangan, author and journalist

'A controversial read that's not for the faint-hearted.' *Prima*

'Gripping, twisty, dark – what a page turner. One not to miss!' Rebecca Done, author of *This Secret We're Keeping*

'Dark, disturbing and deliciously written, *The Roanoke Girls* pulls you relentlessly into its twisted heart.' Ava Marsh, author of *Untouchable*

'*The Roanoke G_____ _____ t it.' _____ eries* series

3 8015 02542 900 6

'This book is stunning. Stunning but dark, so so dark. Wow.'

Cressida McLaughlin, author of *The Canal Boat Café*

'Utterly gripping, at the end I was destroyed. Highly HIGHLY recommended.'

Liz Loves Books

'This gothic page-turner speeds inexorably toward the kind of devastating revelations readers won't soon forget.'

Publishers Weekly

'A haunting and riveting look at one family's tangled legacy. You won't stop reading until you've unraveled the darkest of Roanoke's shocking secrets.'

Laura McHugh, author of *The Weight of Blood*

'More twists than a bag of pretzels.'

Cosmopolitan US

'Creepy, twisted and compelling. *The Roanoke Girls* crawls under your skin and stays there.'

Harriet Reuter Hapgood, author of *The Square Root of Summer*

'One of the most disturbingly gripping books I have ever read. A family with a dark heart, dissected by Amy Engel and laid out for the reader with astounding skill. I loved it.' Ruth Dugdall, author of *The Woman Before Me*

'An emotionally captivating read.'

Booklist

'This is one of the most unsettling and thought-provoking books I've read . . . a stunning and gripping read.'

Lisa Cutts, author of *Never Forget*

'Wonderfully told, both delicate and sinister . . . undoubtedly clever and memorable.'

Irish Independent

'A twisting, tangled plot that attracts readers from the first page . . . This atmospheric and unsettling tale is recommended for fans of *The Virgin Suicides*.'

Library Journal

'Compelling and thought-provoking.'   Off the Shelf Books

'Will pull on your emotions and leave its mark on you . . . addictive and compelling.'   Shaz's Book Blog

'Electric . . . I adored this book.'   Wordland Reviews

'This book is MAGNIFICENT! I loved every exquisite, sordid and heart-breaking sentence . . . simply breathtaking. A gothic masterpiece.'
My Chestnut Reading Tree

'A crime must-read to devour . . . [the] perfect setting for a gothic mystery full of small-town secrets, lies, and guilt.'   Literary Hub

'It is very rare that I give a book five stars, but *The Roanoke Girls* evoked every emotion in me, and I enjoyed the journey from start to finish.'
Portable Magic

'Dark, disturbing and electrifying, this one moved under my skin and settled there.'   Clues and Reviews

'Engel hits a homerun with this rollercoaster ride through a dark family history and the one devastating family secret.'   *Pulse Magazine*

'The new *Flowers in the Attic* for Generation Z. Engel delivers a haunting and sad story. This is dark. *Very* dark! Uncomfortable and challenging. I might just need therapy! Recommended!'   Northern Crime

'[This] creepy thriller of doomed women is perfect for our times.'
Jenny Boylan, author of *Long Black Veil*

'A highly gripping read: short, fast-paced and completely unputdownable.'
The Misstery

'I've never read another book like this . . . had me hooked till the end.'
Blogging for Books

'A compelling story of psychological suspense.'   Shelf Awareness

Amy Engel is the author of the young adult series The Book of Ivy. A former criminal defense attorney, she lives in Missouri with her family. This is her first novel for adults.

THE
ROANOKE
GIRLS

AMY ENGEL

HODDER

First published in Great Britain in 2017 by Hodder & Stoughton
An Hachette UK company

First published in paperback in 2017

I

Copyright © Amy Engel 2017

The right of Amy Engel to be identified as the Author of the Work has been
asserted by her in accordance with the Copyright, Designs and Patents Act 1988.

A CIP catalogue record for this title is available from the British Library

ISBN 978 1 473 64840 1

Printed and bound by Clays Ltd, St Ives plc

Hodder & Stoughton policy is to use papers that are natural, renewable
and recyclable products and made from wood grown in sustainable forests.
The logging and manufacturing processes are expected to conform
to the environmental regulations of the country of origin.

Hodder & Stoughton Ltd
Carmelite House
50 Victoria Embankment
London EC4Y 0DZ

www.hodder.co.uk

For Brian, you know why

Roanoke Family Tree

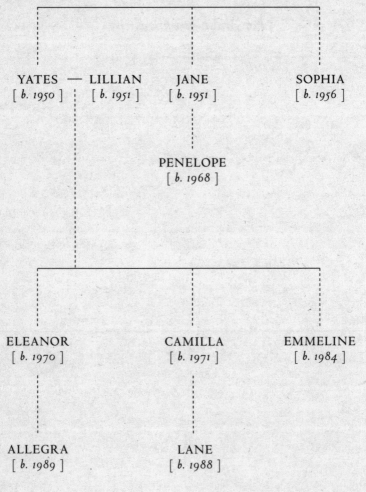

YATES — LILLIAN   JANE   SOPHIA
[b. 1950]   [b. 1951]   [b. 1951]   [b. 1956]

PENELOPE
[b. 1968]

ELEANOR   CAMILLA   EMMELINE
[b. 1970]   [b. 1971]   [b. 1984]

ALLEGRA   LANE
[b. 1989]   [b. 1988]

Look at this tangle of thorns.

—Vladimir Nabokov

Prologue

The first time I saw Roanoke was in a dream. I knew little of it beyond its name and the fact it was in Kansas, a place I had never been. My mother only ever mentioned it when she'd had too much wine, her breath turned sweet and her words slow and syrupy like molasses. So my subconscious filled in the rest. In my dream it stood tall and stately, tucked among a forest of spring-green trees. Its red-brick facade was broken up by black shutters, white trim, delicate wrought-iron balconies. A little girl's fantasy of a princess castle.

When I woke, I started to tell my mother about it. Talking through a mouthful of stale Cheerios drowned in just-this-side-of-sour milk. I got only as far as the name, *Roanoke,* before she stopped me. "It was nothing like that," she said, voice flat. She was sitting on the wide windowsill, knees drawn up into her cotton nightgown, smoke from her cigarette gathered around her like a shroud. Her ragged toenails dug into the wooden window frame.

"You didn't even let me tell you," I whined.

"Did you wake up screaming?"

A dribble of milk ran down my chin. "Huh?"

She turned and glanced at me then, her skin pale, eyes red-rimmed. The bones of her face looked sharp enough to cut. "Was it a nightmare?"

I shook my head, confused and a little scared. "No."

She looked back out the window. "Then it was nothing like that."

Then

The second time I saw Roanoke was a month after my mother committed suicide. She hanged herself from her bedroom door-knob while I was at school. Made a noose of her bathrobe sash and knelt in supplication. Her death showed a kind of dedication, a purpose, I'd never seen from her in life. Next to her she left a note scribbled on the margin of the Sunday *Times*. *I tried to wait. I'm sorry.* The police officers asked me if I knew what she meant, but I had no idea. Wait for what? As if there was ever going to be a good time for her to off herself.

The first few days after she died I spent with the drag queen who lived in the apartment next door. My mother didn't really have any friends and, frankly, neither did I. No one rushing over with hugs and casseroles. As far as potential guardians went, Carl wasn't bad. He let me borrow his makeup. He was kind. And like my mother before him, he wasn't too concerned with the finer points of child rearing. But even if Carl had been willing, I knew the state wouldn't let him keep me.

The social worker assigned to me was an overweight woman named Karen, who had a fondness for faded concert T-shirts and sour cream and onion potato chips. "I don't know why I can't get a job," I told her. "Live on my own."

She shoveled a handful of chips into her mouth, wiped her greasy fingers down Axl Rose's face. "You're not even sixteen."

"Almost," I reminded her. "Three weeks."

"Doesn't matter if it's three minutes. You gotta be eighteen."

"I don't want—"

Karen cut me off, held up a hand. "I found family that wants you."

"What family?" I knew my mother came from Kansas, of course. Grew up in a house that had a name, like a person, like a living thing. But I'd never met any of her family. They never came to visit, never phoned, never wrote. I'd assumed they either were dead or wished we were.

Karen glanced down at the papers on her desk. "Your mom's parents. Yates and Lillian Roanoke. Live just outside Osage Flats, Kansas." She slammed her hand on the desk, making me jump. "It's your lucky day, I'd say." She raised her hand again and held up one finger. "First, they're rich." Another finger went up. "Second, they're already raising a cousin of yours." Karen's eyes fell back to the desk. "Allegra. About six months younger than you. They've had her since she was born, from what I can gather. Third, they want you. Not willing to take you. Want you." She waved the sheaf of paper in my direction. "Already bought you a bus ticket. You leave tomorrow."

It was weird on that bus ride, how the farther we traveled from New York City, the only place I'd ever lived, the only place I'd ever *been*, the more I felt like I was going home. As the crowded cities gave way to wide-open space, flat land and endless horizon, something inside me unwound. And strangely, I wasn't nervous or scared. A lifetime with my mother had given me lots of practice with unpredictability. In her own bizarre way, she had been preparing me for this moment my whole life.

At the bus station in Wichita an old man sidled up to me where I sat waiting on my mom's Louis Vuitton suitcase, one of the few remnants of her life before me.

"Lane Roanoke?" he said, cleared his throat like he was going to hack something disgusting at my feet.

"Yeah."

"I'm Charlie. Work for your granddad. He sent me to fetch ya." He motioned me up and grabbed my suitcase and backpack with the vigor of a much younger man. "Come on then."

I followed him out of the bus depot into sunlight so blinding I thought at first my eyes might burn right out of my head, no tall buildings to block it, no masses of people to hide behind. The heat was different, too, wet and clinging, coating my lungs with moss.

Charlie threw my bags into the back of a rusted pickup, the original bright red faded to the lackluster sheen of an old bloodstain. "Hop on in," he told me, gesturing to the passenger door.

The interior was as hot as I'd feared, even though he'd left the windows down, and I had to resist the urge to hang my head out like a dog. "How far is it?" I asked. "To Roanoke?"

"Couple hours." He made that noise with his throat again and this time twisted his head and spat out his open window.

Wichita seemed empty of people compared with what I was used to, but as the miles unspooled the terrain turned even more desolate. We went long minutes without passing a single other car, only field after field with Charlie pointing out what was growing—corn, wheat, soybean. Occasionally, in the distance, I saw a combine working the land or a cloud of vultures overhead. I'd never known the world could be so quiet. Turned out Charlie wasn't a talker, which was fine with me. He spoke only once more, when we turned off a two-lane country road onto a gravel driveway, passed under an archway with a wrought-iron *R* in the center. "Sorry to hear about your mama. Was there the day she was born."

"Yeah, thanks," I said. Already my mother felt like something that had happened in another lifetime, one I was only too happy to forget. I edged forward on the bench seat, hands curled around the ripped leather, craning for my first glimpse of Roanoke. Unlike my single dream of the place, there was hardly a tree in sight. Instead, oceans of wheat stretched out in all directions, wind surfing along the grain. And there it was . . . Roanoke. Nothing like my imagination. Nothing I could have imagined in a hundred years of trying.

I coughed out a laugh, half-delighted, half-terrified. "That's it?"

Charlie made a noncommittal sound as he brought the truck to a stop in the semicircular drive. Roanoke had clearly started out as something resembling a traditional farmhouse—white clapboard, wraparound porch, peaked dormers. But someone had tacked on crazy additions over the years, a brick turret on one side, what looked like an entirely new stone house extending from the back, more white clapboard, newer and higher, on the other side. It was like a handful of giant houses all smashed together with no regard for aesthetics or conformity. It was equal parts horrifying and mesmerizing.

I slid from the truck, my eyes still bouncing over the house trying to make sense of all the strange angles and materials. It looked like something an insane person would build, or someone who didn't give a shit. It wasn't until I looked at the wide front porch for the second time that I noticed the girl standing there balanced on her tiptoes, as if she was about to fly down to greet me.

"Hi!" she called out, waving frantically with both hands. Her hair was arranged in two long braids, tied at the ends with blue and white gingham bows. She wore cutoff jean shorts and a tank top, but teetered on sky-high red glittery pumps. "Welcome to Oz!" she yelled, flinging her arms wide.

I stared at her, speechless, and her arms dropped. "Jesus fucking Christ," she said with a put-upon sigh, kicking off the shoes. They arced through the air and landed on the lawn near my suitcase. "I was joking. It was a *joke*."

She raced down the porch steps, came to a stop right in front of me. Her eyes flicked over my face, then focused on something behind me. She flapped her hand like a bug was in her way. "Stop lurking. Get out of here, you old coot."

It took me a second to realize she was talking to Charlie, not to me. I watched as he gave her a long, measured stare before he walked away, still hacking. "So gross," the girl said, wrinkling her nose and bringing her attention back to me. She tilted her head and stared. "Well, hell," she said finally. "You're prettier than me." I could tell from her tone of voice that this was a rare occurrence.

"I don't think—"

"No, you are. Don't deny it."

Honestly, I couldn't see much difference between us. She had my dark hair, and the sun caught on the copper highlights exactly the way it did on mine. We had the same long, coltish legs, same willowy frame and big boobs. Although this girl, who I assumed was my cousin Allegra, was showing a lot more in her low-cut tank top than I was in my plain white T-shirt.

Allegra pointed at one of my eyes, her red lacquered nail stopping mere inches from the iris. "You got the Roanoke eyes, you lucky bitch." But she said it with a smile. My eyes were my mother's, ice blue with starbursts of pale green around the pupils. Allegra's were a solid blue, the exact same hue as the cloudless sky overhead.

"I'm Allegra," she said, linking her arm through mine as she pulled me toward the house.

"Lane," I said, allowing myself to be dragged along.

Allegra laughed, high and bright. "Well, duh."

"What about my suitcase?"

"Charlie will get it."

Once through the front door, Allegra let go of my arm and grabbed my hand instead. "I'm so happy you're here. I knew your mom would never move back, but I used to lie in bed and *pray* you'd come home." She squeezed my hand, grinding the bones together.

"Not that I wanted your mom to kill herself, but you know . . . I'm glad it worked out."

I couldn't even formulate a response before she was leading me down a dark hallway, deeper into the house. I wasn't as shocked by her comment, by her almost-crazed energy, as other people might've been. She reminded me of my mother, had the same mercurial spirit. Like she was walking a tightrope between light and dark, joy and sorrow, and all I could do was stand beneath with arms outstretched and hope to make a catch. Or at least that's what I'd done with my mother when I was younger. In recent years, I was more likely to yank away the net just to watch her fall.

Allegra pointed out rooms as we passed: *parlor, living room, formal living room, library, dining room, music room, office, sunroom, down there's the screened porch, up there are bedrooms and a sleeping porch,* but she walked too fast for me to get more than a glimpse of each space. Some rooms were flooded with sunlight, others so dim and dark I'd have sworn it was night outside. Stairwells sprouted at bizarre angles, curving up and down, leading who knows where. The temperature varied from room to room, cold pockets of air-conditioning running smack into walls of heat like the interior of Charlie's truck.

"Where are . . ." I paused, unsure how to phrase it. "Our grandparents?"

"Gran's around here somewhere," Allegra said. "Granddad's probably out in the fields." She led me through a crooked doorway, the floor slanting slightly under our feet. "Here's the kitchen." The room was a hodgepodge, much like the rest of the house. Brand-new stainless-steel appliances kept company with ancient wood floors. The lighting was modern, but the tiles were old, cracked, and held together with grimy grout. It was like someone had lost interest right in the middle of redecorating. The best part of the kitchen was an addition on the far end with a wall of windows and a long plank table lined with a padded bench on one side, chairs on the other. An older woman stood at the counter cutting vegetables. I thought at first she might be our grandmother, but she didn't look up when we entered, and Allegra acted as though she wasn't there, moving around her to lift two aluminum tumblers down from a shelf.

"Purple or red?" Allegra asked me.

"Huh?"

She shook the tumblers in my face. "Purple or red?"

"Oh, I don't care. Purple, I guess."

Allegra danced over to the faucet, filled both tumblers, and shoved the purple one into my hand. I took a sip. The water was ice-cold but tinged with a metallic aftertaste, like drinking through a mouthful of nickels. Allegra watched me over the rim of her cup. Her eyes felt greedy, like she was trying to drink me instead of her water. I set my cup down on the counter.

A woman entered the kitchen from the far side, near the long table. She was slender and delicate with blond hair pulled back in a chignon at the nape of her neck. "Allegra," she said, "where did you put those pearls you borrowed yesterday?"

"I don't know." Allegra flailed one hand in the air. "They're around here somewhere."

The woman clucked her tongue but said nothing more. Her eyes drifted over to me. "You must be Lane."

"Yeah."

She nodded, came closer. "I'm your grandma, Lillian. You can call me Gran like Allegra does." She reached forward and took both my hands in hers, held my arms out from my sides. Her hands were cold, her skin soft and smooth. "Let's get a look at you."

Before this moment I was in possession of exactly two facts about my grandmother. She came from old money on the East Coast, and she was beautiful. I'd always pictured her as some eastern Blanche DuBois, booze-soaked and lipstick-smeared, wandering through her days in a silk nightgown, leaving a trail of cigarette ashes in her wake. This woman was nothing like that. She wore black capri pants and a white blouse, the sleeves rolled up on porcelain forearms. Her hair was glossy, her makeup refined. She didn't look much older than some of the mothers of classmates I'd known back in New York. Her blue eyes weren't cold exactly, but they didn't invite me in, either. She seemed very capable, very calm. The direct opposite of her daughter who raised me.

"I think we'll put you in the white bedroom," she said, dropping my hands. "Allegra, show Lane her room." She left the kitchen as quickly as she'd entered, trailing not cigarette smoke but the faint scent of expensive perfume. If some small part of me had hoped for hugs and loving words, sheer relief at my grandmother's restraint drowned it out. I had no experience with maternal affection, wouldn't have known what to do with it if it was offered.

Allegra pointed to the far corner of the kitchen. "There's a back stairway there. But come this way first. I want to show you something." We exited the kitchen, still without acknowledging the woman working at the counter. But when I looked back over my shoulder, her dark eyes followed me.

"Who was that?" I asked Allegra as we branched off the central hall and went down three shallow steps into a second hallway.

"Who?"

"That woman in the kitchen. The one chopping vegetables."

"Oh, that's Sharon. She's our maid, basically. She does the laundry, cleans, cooks. Her food totally sucks, though. I keep telling Granddad to fire her, but she's been here forever." Allegra stopped in front of a series of framed photographs. "Here," she said, pointing, her cheeks feverish. "Ta-da! It's the Roanoke girls!"

My eyes followed her finger to the biggest frame, golden and gilt-edged. Someone had carved a tiny R♦ into the bottom of the frame, the letters ragged and uneven. The hallway was shadowy, with little natural light, and I had to move closer to see. The frame held a collection of large oval-cropped photographs—two on the top row, four more below, and Allegra on the bottom. I recognized my mother in the middle row but no one else. "Who are they?"

"Us!" Allegra screeched. She stabbed at the top two pictures. "These are Granddad's sisters, Jane and Sophia. Then this row are Gran and Granddad's girls. Penelope. She was actually Jane's daughter, but Gran and Granddad raised her. Then my mom, Eleanor. Your mom, Camilla. Who totally got the best name, by the way." She jabbed me with her bony elbow. "And the baby, Emmeline. We can take a picture of you and put it right here." She tapped the empty space next to her own face, clapped her hands like a little girl at a birthday party.

All of the pictures were black-and-white close-ups, giving them an old-fashioned feel, although even the ones of Granddad's sisters couldn't have been more than thirty or forty years old. They were all taken when the girls were teenagers, except for Emmeline, who was still an infant, which I figured didn't bode well. It was eerie how much they all looked alike, how much they looked like me. As if the Roanoke genes were so strong they bulldozed right over anyone else's DNA.

"Where are they all now?" I asked.

Allegra's pointing finger reemerged. She started at the top, with Jane, and moved down the line. "Jane's gone. Sophia and Penelope are dead. My mom's gone." She paused before lightly brushing her finger over my mother's face. "Your mom's dead, obviously. Emmeline died when she was only a baby. And I'm right here."

"What do you mean, gone?"

"Jane disappeared right after Penelope was born, probably ran off like my mom. I was only two weeks old when she hauled ass out of here." Allegra's tone was matter-of-fact, but her mouth pinched up and her eyes clouded over. She thumped Eleanor's face hard with one knuckle.

"And all the dead ones?"

Allegra shrugged, already bored. "Sophia drowned in the North Fork during the spring floods. She was twenty-something. Penelope fell down the main stairs and broke her neck. Tripped on her nightgown in the middle of the night. She was like our age, maybe a little younger. Totally tragic. Emmeline was crib death. Sharon said Gran didn't get out of bed for six months after. They all thought she was going to waste away. Die of grief."

Hearing their stories turned the faces in front of me from beautiful to tragic. They watched me now with haunted eyes. The only one left was Allegra. And me. I suddenly didn't want a place on the wall. "Wow," I said, goose bumps sprouting along my neck, even in the closed-in heat of the hall. "That's a lot of dead girls."

Allegra did a quick pirouette away from me, her smile a little too wide. "Roanoke girls never last long around here." She skipped along the hall, her voice growing fainter as she moved, like we were standing at opposite ends of a tunnel. "In the end, we either run or we die."

Now

The call comes at three in the morning, that time of night when sleep is so deep it almost feels like death. It takes me at least five rings to surface, swimming up through layers of dreams. "Hello?" My voice is raspy, the vodka I drank before bed still coating the back of my throat.

"Lane? Lane, is that you?"

I hold the phone away from my face, squint at it like they do in the movies, before returning it to my ear. "Who is this?" I ask, although I already know, my stomach bottoming out at the sound of his deep voice.

"It's your granddad, Lane. We need you to come home. Back to Roanoke."

Hearing the word sends an electric shock up my spine, waking me instantly. I shove myself upright, palming hair off my face. "How did you get my number?"

My granddad sighs. I hear the scrape of a chair. "You need to come home, Lane," he repeats.

"Why?"

"Because Allegra is missing."

At the sound of her name, Allegra's words from all those years ago take flight, fluttering around my skull and bouncing off the bone ... *Roanoke girls ... gone ... dead ... dead ... gone.* "I don't ... What happened?"

"She hasn't been seen in a week. The police are looking into it, but they don't have a clue. We need you here." There are voices in the background. "I have to go now. Please come home, Laney-girl." He hangs up on me.

I toss my cell phone away, lower my head to my upturned knees. I stink of alcohol and sweat and my mouth tastes bitter, like I vomited in the night. It wouldn't be the first time. Since I left Roanoke, I haven't spoken to Gran or Granddad, not once. And I've barely talked to Allegra. Never on the phone, just an occasional e-mail, one she always initiated. I scramble for my discarded phone, scroll through my e-mails with shaking fingers. It doesn't take long to find it. Sent nine days ago at 11:42 P.M.

> *Lane, I've tried calling you, but your voice mail is full. I know it's been years, but I really need to talk to you. It's probably nothing. I'm probably crazy (what else is new, right? Ha!). But you're the only one I can talk to about this. Please get in touch. Love, A*

I never called. I never wrote her back.

I leave Los Angeles at sunset, my suitcase in the trunk and a cooler packed with food in the backseat. I barely have enough money to pay for the gas it will take to get all the way to Kansas; I can't afford to buy food, too.

The drive is long and uneventful. I pull over in rest areas for catnaps but never stop for more than a few hours. I try hard not to think beyond the next mile in front of me. It is early afternoon, the sun a blistering ball in the sky, when I cross the state line into Kansas. I murmur, "Welcome to Oz," and my throat tightens painfully.

I arrive at Roanoke without fanfare. It seems like the heavens should open up, trumpets should blare as I turn off old Route 24 and pass underneath the archway across the drive. The prodigal granddaughter returns. Of the ones who left, I'm the first to ever come back. But the house remains silent and still, no cars or trucks parked on the drive or down by the barn. Seeing Roanoke again fills me with a familiar swoop of dread, followed closely by a rush of adrenaline. My head knows this place is no good for me, but my stupid, traitorous heart sings *home*.

I crane my neck, but from my vantage point I can't tell if the house has any new crazy-ass additions. I sit in the car until the heat forces me to move, a tiny rivulet of sweat pooling inside my bra. When I step out, the sounds and smells assault me: grass, wheat, dust, wind, grasshopper and cicada song. It all hits me like a slap, and I take a stumbling step backward, lean against the hot metal of the car until the woozy déjà vu feeling passes. I've been back to New York a few times since I left, and it's never had this effect on me. But one long summer here at Roanoke is somehow imprinted beneath my skin like a tattoo of memories running through my veins.

I leave my suitcase and cooler in the car and climb the wide front steps. The porch swing creaks in the breeze. "Gran?" I call out when I push open the front door and step inside. "Granddad?" Nothing answers except the steady tick-tock of the ancient grandfather clock in the foyer. It still, I notice, fails to keep the correct time.

Every room I pass is empty. In the kitchen a pie crust is rolled out on the counter, a bowl of plump reddish black cherries next to it, but Sharon is nowhere in sight. "Hello?" I say, before giving up and climbing the back staircase to the second floor. All the bedroom doors are closed, and the air in the upstairs landing is thick and sticky. I bypass my old room and head to the hidden stairway at the end of the hall that leads up into the brick turret and Allegra's bedroom. She always loved being up high, even though the room had no air-conditioning and burned like an oven in the summer months.

Her room is not all that different from the last time I saw it, over a decade ago. The bedspread on her antique four-poster has changed from lavender to pale green, and the walls have gone from off-white to a silvery gray. But her floor is still littered with piles of clothes, her vanity table cluttered with makeup and tangles of jewelry. A remnant of her scent—coconut body lotion and musky perfume—lingers. I'm scared to touch anything in case the police haven't been in here yet. I back out slowly, make sure the door is closed the way she likes it.

Back on the second floor I run smack into Gran, who is emerging from the master suite as I round the corner from the turret stairwell. "Lane?" she says, one hand flying up to her throat. *"Lane?"*

"Yeah, Gran, it's me." We don't touch beyond the initial collision, not even an impersonal clasp of hands. Gran has aged a bit since I last saw her, but not as much as I'd expected. Her hair is still blond, her figure remains trim. There's a little softening at her jaw, a new network of lines around her eyes, but she looks impossibly young to be a grandmother to grown women.

"What in the world are you doing here?" She appears mildly irritated at my presence, as if I'm a dinner guest who showed up an hour early and disrupted her careful planning.

For a second I'm dumbfounded, then hit with my own flash of irritation. "Granddad called me in the middle of the night. He said I needed to come home."

Gran's face tightens for a split second. "Oh, your granddad. He always overreacts."

"I don't think being worried about Allegra going missing is overreacting. What happened? I assume the police are involved?"

Gran fans her fingers through the air. "Well, of course they are, although it's completely unnecessary. She'll turn up. Probably took off to Wichita or some such."

I gape at Gran. "For a week? Without calling?" I've been back in this house for less than an hour, and already I feel like I'm losing my mind, the Roanoke reality slithering into place. Where a tornado is a bit of wind or a missing woman is simply out having fun.

"She's an adult, Lane. Just like you. We aren't her keepers."

"But still, Gran, something bad could have happened. She could be hurt or—"

"Don't be dramatic," Gran says. "You know Allegra. I'm sure she's fine."

"Actually, I don't," I say slowly. "I don't really know her at all. I was only here for one summer. And that was a long time ago."

Gran purses her lips, her brow furrowed. "Nonsense." She's already moving past me. "You two are practically sisters."

That's Gran. Still a master of the loaded statement.

When dusk falls I wander downstairs, but the kitchen remains empty, the pie makings spirited away. I poke my head into the dining room but am met with only silence and shadows. Back in the kitchen, I grab an apple and a bottle of beer from the fridge and take them out onto the front porch, where I sit on the top step and watch the night roll in.

A plume of dust rises on the road and a patrol car edges into view, pulls into the semicircular drive, and parks. The deputy inside doesn't seem to be in any particular hurry, so I figure it's not urgent news about Allegra, but I stand all the same, set my beer bottle on the step by my feet. When the car door opens, it's only Tommy who gets out, both hands shoved into his pockets as he walks toward me, stops on the bottom step.

He looks the same as in my memories. Dark brown hair curling slightly over his ears, serious hazel eyes. Some of his second-string quarterback muscle has turned soft—a little thickening at the waist, his face filled out around the cheekbones. But he looks good, solid and strong. His police uniform, complete with handcuffs at his hip and a scuffed silver nameplate over his left breast, suits him, although I never once imagined he'd wind up a cop.

I lean against the porch railing, a slow smile dawning. "You the law around here now, Tommy Kenning?"

"Looks that way," he says, rolling forward on the balls of his feet.

"Damn. Guess that means no more mailbox baseball for us."

"Nope. No shoplifting from uptown, either." Tommy smiles and his teeth are as white as ever. He takes his hands from his pockets and jogs up the four shallow steps to pull me forward against his broad chest. I'm horrified to find myself blinking back tears as I clutch at his shirt. My hands have a hard time grabbing on, the starched cotton slick under my fingers. I let myself sink into him for a three-count beat before I pull away.

"You want a beer?" I ask, avoiding his eyes. "Or is this an official visit?"

"Nope, a beer would be good. I'm off duty. Heard through the grapevine you were back and thought I'd stop by."

"News travels fast."

We settle on opposite ends of the porch swing with our beers and a half-empty bag of pretzels retrieved from my car. "So, what's going on with Allegra?" I ask him. I'm shredding the label on my beer bottle down to nothing, and I force myself to stop.

Tommy jerks his head toward the house. "Haven't they told you anything?"

I raise my eyebrows at him. "You know what it's like around here. Trying to get a straight answer out of anybody . . ." I take a long pull of my beer. "I haven't even seen my granddad yet." I'd expected a flurry of activity at the house, police and search teams and my grandparents frantic and determined. I should have known that's not the way things would work at Roanoke. We are all so good at denial.

"From what we can tell, she up and vanished nine days ago,"

Tommy says in a no-nonsense cop voice. "She had dinner with your grandparents. And your gran saw her late evening when she was heading up to bed. Allegra was settled in on the couch with a movie. She didn't come down to breakfast the next morning, but your grandparents figured she was sleeping in. When they still hadn't seen her by lunchtime, they checked her room. Found her bed not slept in, her car parked in the garage out back." Tommy sighs, scrubs at his face with one hand. "Not a word from her, no trace. Like she disappeared into thin air."

"What about her phone?"

"Left on her dresser."

"Have you checked it? And her computer? What about friends?"

Tommy gives me a weary smile. "We've done all that, Lane. Don't worry. We've done everything there is to do."

"She called me before she disappeared," I hear myself say, my words coming too fast. "E-mailed me, too."

Tommy nods. "I saw that on the phone log. Any idea what she wanted?"

"She didn't leave a message, and her e-mail just asked me to get in touch."

"Did you?" Tommy asks after a slight pause.

"No," I say, looking away. "Do you have a theory yet? About what might have happened?"

"I'm thinking maybe she took off," Tommy says. "She wouldn't be the first one of you to do it."

I'm already shaking my head before he's even done speaking. "She didn't take off, Tommy. She loved Roanoke."

"You might be right. But she wasn't always predictable. Hard to know what Allegra would do."

But I do know. Allegra would never leave Roanoke, not willingly. "What now?" I ask. "What happens next?"

"It's still a missing person case. We don't have any reason to suspect foul play at this point. So we keep looking. We keep digging.

We keep asking questions." Tommy gives my hand a quick squeeze. "Something will shake loose. It always does."

I bark out a laugh, a little harsher, a little meaner than I intended. "You handle a lot of missing persons cases? In Osage Flats?"

Tommy's neck flushes. "Well, nothing like Los Angeles, I'm sure. But we aren't complete idiots out here in the sticks, either."

"That's not what I meant, Tommy." But, of course, it's exactly what I meant.

He waves off my halfhearted apology. "Forget it. Shouldn't have snapped at you. I've had a short fuse lately."

Which is almost enough to make me smile. Tommy's idea of a short fuse is a regular person's infinite patience. I lower one leg, set the porch swing moving with a gentle shove of my foot. "How have things been around Osage Flats since I left?"

"Oh, you know . . . not much changes. Same old, same old. Still not a decent place to eat in town. Della Ward's on her third husband, and Cooper's still fixing engines and radiators."

I breathe past the swift thump in my chest and take a gulp from my beer, wiping my mouth with the back of my hand as a trickle of liquid overflows past my lips. "Cooper's here? I thought he moved to Kansas City."

Kansas City is less than three hours northeast of Osage Flats, but in the time I lived here I met very few kids who'd actually been there. To them it was a Mecca they doubted they'd ever reach, as exotic and unattainable as New York City or Paris. It has always surprised me that Cooper, with his lazy brand of intelligence used mainly for stealing cigarettes and charming the panties off pretty girls, was the one with ambition enough to make the journey.

"Nah. He's been back for a few years now." Tommy gives me a quick sideways glance. "How'd you know he moved away? You two keep in touch?"

"No. Allegra sent me the town update once." In lieu of a newspaper, Osage Flats publishes, and I use that term loosely, a sort of roundup of its residents every six months. The bulk of the entries catalog weddings, births, and deaths, with the occasional success story—the opening of a local flower store or promotion to head cashier at the town grocery—tossed in as an afterthought.

"Oh, yeah." Tommy smirks. "I remember that. Hell, this town will print just about anything and call it news."

"Beggars can't be choosers," I say, and Tommy snorts in agreement.

The blurb Allegra sent me about Cooper was short, only a few sentences. A local-boy-makes-good type of mention, although moving three hours away to work in a body shop wouldn't be considered an accomplishment anywhere but Osage Flats. Allegra wrote: *Cooper Sullivan's hitting the big time! Hahaha!* across the top of the wrinkled page.

Tommy shifts and his handcuffs rattle against the porch swing. "I can't believe you wound up a cop," I say. "When I lived here, you broke the law at least once a day."

Tommy smiles into his upturned beer bottle. "Got it out of my system young."

"How do you like it?"

Tommy shrugs. "Only thing I've ever done, so don't have much to compare it to. Most of the time I like it fine. Lately it's been a little rough."

"Because of Allegra?" I say, not really a question.

"Because of Allegra," Tommy affirms.

"Did you ever . . . I guess you gave up on the idea of marrying her?"

Tommy laughs, although there's not much humor in it. "I must have proposed a thousand times over the years but never could get her to say yes."

If he'd ever asked my advice, I would have told him to save his breath. Allegra was never going to marry him, no matter how many ways he phrased the question. I glance down at the thick gold band on his ring finger, tap it lightly with my thumbnail. "Got tired of waiting, huh?"

"Yeah." Tommy rotates the ring on his finger. "I'm the marrying type, I guess."

"Who is she?"

"Sarah Fincher. She's about a year younger than you, but I'm pretty sure you met her a time or two when you were living here."

"I remember," I say, although I can conjure up only a vague picture of a small, mousy-haired girl who always put a hand up to cover her mouth when she laughed.

"How about you? You married?"

"I was. It didn't take." Tommy stays silent, waiting for me to continue. "He's a pilot. I met him when I worked at LAX."

Tommy seems impressed, in the way only a small-town boy can be by thoughts of the big city, mistaking noise and bright lights for a more glamorous life. I neglect to mention that I was a waitress at the hospitality bar where Jeff and I met. I wore a uniform so short my ass cheeks peeked out whenever I bent over to deliver a drink. Jeff used to joke that it was love at first sight.

"What happened?"

Exhaustion rises up in a sudden wave, and I fight the urge to lie down on the porch swing and close my eyes. "Who knows? What ever happens when people fall apart?" I drain my beer in one long swallow. There's no way I'm telling Tommy the truth, that my marriage ended because I was fucking someone else. Let Jeff catch me in bed with the next-door neighbor, our bodies open and exposed. Good, sweet Tommy would never understand, how sometimes you have to hurt people just to prove that you're alive.

Then

It turned out dinner at Roanoke wasn't served in the light-filled kitchen at the oak plank table. Roanoke dinners were formal, at least in setting, and served in the dining room, a bizarre space right in the middle of the house with no windows to the outside. At one time it appeared there had been, but an addition had been built on in such a way that now the dining room windows gave a view of a dark hallway instead of land and sky. It was like eating in a cave. Sharon set the various dishes out along the walnut sideboard before retreating back to the kitchen. Four places, complete with crystal goblets, linen napkins, and sterling silver utensils, were laid at the table meant for twelve, and I hung back until after Allegra filled her plate so I'd know where to sit.

"Go ahead," Gran said, pointing with her fork to my plate filled with limp green beans, a fishy smelling patty of some type, and a lump of gelatinous tartar sauce. "Your granddad always runs late. No need to wait."

"Yeah, but if she doesn't wait, she'll have to eat *this*," Allegra said. She mimed puking into her plate.

"Oh, hush," Gran said, but without any heat.

"What is it?" I asked.

"Salmon patties," Gran told me.

"Salmon from a *can*," Allegra added. "Watch out for the bones." She pushed back from the table and disappeared through the doorway, returning a minute later with a bottle of ketchup. "It helps if you drown them."

I watched Allegra shake the ketchup bottle over her plate, her generous breasts threatening to spill out of her sundress. It looked like something that would have fit her two summers ago, so short and tight I'd thought at first maybe she was playing another weird kind of dress-up.

A throat cleared, and all our heads turned to the man standing in the doorway. One glance and there was no mistaking my grandfather, Yates Roanoke. Unlike the few details my mother had given me about my grandmother, she never spoke of her father. I'm not sure what I'd been expecting, but he didn't look like any grandfather I'd seen before. He was fiercely handsome. Dark hair with the barest feathering of gray at the temples, skin tan from the sun, tall and broad-shouldered, the Roanoke eyes. The kind of man it wasn't hard to imagine walking into a room and owning every soul inside—all the men would stop talking, while all the women would cease to breathe. I felt a strange burst of pride looking at him, at knowing I was his descendant. If charisma was power, my grandfather was king.

He eyed Allegra and amusement chased its way across his face, never quite settling in a single spot. "That the dress code for dinner now?" he asked, voice mild. "We all gonna start eating half-naked?" He pulled a plate from the stack on the sideboard and began piling it with food. "Go get something decent on."

Allegra stuck out her bottom lip in a pantomime of childish pouting even though his back was turned. "But, Granddad—"

"Girl," he said, still concentrating on the food, "you best do what I tell you."

Allegra slammed the ketchup bottle down on the table, sending a spray of red droplets across the white tablecloth.

"Oh, Allegra." Gran sighed. "Look at the mess!"

But Allegra was already flouncing out of the dining room. I could hear her feet stomping away down the hall. My grandfather set his full plate at the head of the table nearest the doorway and crossed over to where I sat.

"You're Camilla's girl," he said, looking down at me.

"Yeah."

He took my chin between his thumb and forefinger, lifted my face up gently. "You're the spitting image of your mama." We stared at each other, and I would have sworn I'd known him all my life. He felt more like family in five seconds than my mother had in fifteen years. "Glad you're here," he said, let go of my chin, and gave a lock of my hair a quick tweak as he dropped his hand.

"Happy now?" Allegra asked, stomping back into the room. She wore the same tank top and shorts from earlier, still revealing but no longer ridiculous.

"Much better," Granddad said with a small smile that seemed to melt her anger away.

"Sorry about the tablecloth," she said, eyes sliding to Gran. "Do you think Sharon can get it out?"

"I'm sure she can," Gran said. "If not, we'll get a new one."

We ate in relative silence, Allegra and I sending each other pained looks over our plates. I moved my salmon around and around with my fork and barely took a bite. No one asked about my mother or my childhood, and I welcomed not having to speak of her.

"Have you lived at Roanoke your whole life?" I asked my granddad once our dinner plates were cleared and Gran was serving up slices of peach pie.

"Born right here in this house," he said. "Of course, some of the additions came later." He winked at Gran, and she smiled at him, her cheeks blooming little roses of pink. "Having babies always put your gran in a renovating mood."

"I showed Lane the pictures in the hall," Allegra said. "Of all the Roanoke girls."

Granddad smiled at me, his teeth slightly crooked on the bottom. "We need to get a picture of you in there. You fit right in. Look like all the rest."

"Except for Emmeline," Allegra said, and Gran's hand stuttered in the midst of cutting my slice of pie. "Since she was a baby when she died, we don't know what she would've looked like grown."

Granddad glanced at Gran, who kept her eyes on her task, before shifting his gaze to Allegra. "I'm sure she would've been beautiful. Just like all of you."

Allegra leaned forward, resting most of her upper body on the table as she stretched toward me, her red nails skittering across the edge of my plate. "I found parts of my mom's diary. She said when Emmeline died all the sisters had to kiss her at the funeral. Right on the mouth." She lowered her voice to a stage whisper. "She tasted like breast milk and formaldehyde." Allegra wiggled her eyebrows at me. She reached forward and snagged a slice of peach from my pie, sucked it between her lips with a slurping sound. A bead of juice slid down her chin.

"Allegra!" Gran said, her eyes wide. She pressed one hand against her breastbone. "Hush now. That's a horrible story!"

Granddad shook his head, took a giant bite of pie. "Don't know what's gotten into you, girl."

I noticed no one denied it was true.

I thought I would have trouble sleeping in a new state, a new house, a new bed. But even with heat sticking the sheets to my legs and the constant whir of the fan in the window, I fell asleep fast, slept deep and heavy. I awoke early though and was lying in bed watching the sun creep up over the horizon, when someone tapped on my door.

"Yeah?" I called, rolling over onto my stomach and propping myself up on my elbows.

My granddad poked his head into the room, gave me a quick grin. "Hey, Lane," he said. "Thought you might want to come with me out to the barn. See the animals?"

I'd never really been an animal person. We'd never owned so much as a goldfish back in New York, but since I was already awake I figured I might as well join him. "Okay. Give me five minutes."

"Meet you in the kitchen," he said, closing the door softly behind him.

I pulled on a pair of shorts and debated a tank top before finally deciding screw it. It was hot as hell already, and if Allegra and her big boobs could get away with it, I could, too. My granddad chuckled when I walked into the kitchen, his eyes falling to my flip-flops. "We're gonna have to get you some boots. Those aren't farm shoes."

He handed me a giant cinnamon roll wrapped in a paper towel and grabbed a mug of coffee from the counter. "She makes better breakfasts than dinners," he said with a wink when he caught me sniffing experimentally at the roll.

The air outside was just as thick at dawn as it was in the middle of the day, the only slight relief the lack of direct sun. Granddad slid open the big barn door, and we passed into the gloom of the barn, the air hazy with dust motes. A horse whinnied from a far stall in greeting, and a tangle of kittens rolled over my feet.

"Watch where you step," Granddad said, one hand loose on my elbow. "Got these damn cats all over the place." He pointed out each animal by name, three horses, one cow, too many cats to count. "There's a half dozen dogs around, but they don't usually come into the barn unless it's snowing. Goats out back and a chicken coop down the way."

I looked around, the horse in the stall behind me bumping his muzzle against my shoulder. "Is this enough animals for a farm? I guess I always pictured more."

Granddad laughed. "Oh hell, girl, these are all Allegra's pets. Things she got her heart set on and I'm too much a fool to say no." He grabbed an apple from a bucket on the floor and held it, palm out, to the horse behind me, who took it in his big yellow teeth. "This ain't been a real working farm in years."

"What about the wheat?"

"That's just for fun. I like having something to do, still like getting my hands dirty. But oil is what we actually harvest around here."

"Oil?" I pictured that old television show, where the family struck oil in the backyard and ended up rich. It didn't sound as far-fetched now.

"Sure. My dad inherited this land, added to it over the years. More than two thousand acres now, almost all of it fallow. He struck oil when I was young, and that's pretty much all she wrote." The horse chomped down on my ponytail, and Granddad swatted him away. "Your mama never told you any of this?"

"No. She didn't talk about you all much."

Granddad sighed. His face sagged a little, like he'd taken a blow. "Still miss that girl every day. Wish she hadn't taken off."

"Why did she?"

"Scared, I think. Of having you when she was so young, not even seventeen when she lit out of here. But your gran and I would never have made her give you up or kicked her out. Hell, life is complicated. We know that. It wasn't anything to run away over." He smiled. "You better eat that cinnamon roll, then you can help me take care of these animals."

It didn't take long to feed all the animals in the barn, not with both of us working together. After, Granddad took me down to the chicken coop and showed me how to sneak my hand under the fat hens to grab their eggs. He laughed when I squealed the first time, the drift of feathers and the hot, smooth globe of fresh egg so foreign in my hand.

Charlie took the basket of eggs from me, and Granddad led me back to the barn, where we washed our hands in a cracked sink in the corner. He was already easy with me, acted like this was something we'd done a thousand times before instead of only this once. "My social worker in New York . . ." I trailed off, not entirely sure what I wanted to say.

"Yeah?" He kept scrubbing his hands, not looking directly at me.

"She said I was lucky. She said you and Gran wanted me, wanted me to come live here."

My granddad turned off the faucet with a wet hand, grabbed the towel I'd slung back on the hook nailed to the wall. "Ah, sweetheart," he said, "of course we wanted you." He hugged me, quick but warm, and I wasn't sure how to respond, my arms stiff at my sides.

"I'm guessing your mama wasn't much of a hugger," he said as he released me.

I shrugged. "She wasn't much of an anything."

My granddad studied me, and I shifted uncomfortably under his gaze. "Sure sorry to hear that," he said. "I'd hoped for better, for both of you. Our secret, but your mama was always my favorite." He tweaked my ponytail. "But Lord Jesus, she gave me trouble. You gonna do the same?" His eyes twinkled under raised brows.

I thought about it for a second. "Maybe." Paused a beat. "Probably."

I waited for the fallout, but there wasn't any, only another chuckle from my granddad. "All right then. Guess that's fair warning."

As a little girl I'd tried to please, tried to live by the simple refrain my mother repeated like a desperate prayer in my ear: *be good be good be good.* But I'd known even then it wouldn't work, went against something dark inside me. A mean streak that came to the surface more often as I grew. And I thought maybe here, at Roanoke, my being bad wouldn't break anyone. I remembered Allegra's words last night at the dinner table about Emmeline, my granddad's sparkling eyes a moment ago when he spoke of my mother giving him hell. Maybe here it was like a different country, someplace where it was all right to be a little wicked.

Now

In the morning my granddad is sitting on the kitchen table bench, bent over a mug of coffee. I pause in the doorway when I see him, take a second before he notices me. He's aged more than Gran, the gray at his temples spreading up and out. The hands curled around his coffee mug are knotted at the knuckles. He's in good shape, though, no bulge of belly or sagging biceps. The first word that springs to mind at the sight of him is still *handsome*. And when he glances up and sees me, his face folding into a smile, he could pass for a much younger man.

"Ah, Laney-girl," he says. "Aren't you a sight for sore eyes."

It takes me a second to find my voice. "Hi, Granddad." My heart turns over as I slide into a chair across from him.

"Your gran told me you were home. So glad you came. I'm sorry I didn't track you down last night."

"That's okay." I take a muffin from the platter in the middle of the table, break off a tiny piece. Blueberry juice stains my fingers. "Tommy Kenning came by. Said they haven't found anything new on Allegra."

Granddad nods. He has hollows under his eyes, and he missed a patch of whiskers on his left cheek when he shaved. "Tommy's doing all right by us. Keeping us informed."

"What do you think happened?" I ask, eyes on my hands.

He doesn't answer for so long that I raise my gaze, surprised to see tears hovering on his lashes. "I don't know," he says finally. "She seemed fine. Not a thing wrong that I could tell." He shakes his head. "I've gone over the day or two before she disappeared a thousand times. Can't find anything out of the ordinary. She seemed fine," he repeats. He's not an old man, only in his midsixties, but he sounds like one now, lost and confused.

"Well, you'd be the one to know." I wait a beat, holding his eyes. "I mean, assuming you were still screwing her."

The house pulses around us, an awful, ticking silence. All the air sucked from my lungs, the room, the entire world. My heart is jackrabbiting in my chest, my palms and underarms slick with sweat. I have broken an unspoken rule; in this house we talk around, not about. But I can't pretend anymore, at least not with him, not inside these walls.

My granddad cocks his head at me, his face slowly waking up, his gaze curious. Like I'm an intriguing new treasure he's anxious to get his hands on, crack open, and sift through with eager fingers. "You always did promise to give me hell," he says, the corners of his mouth curling into a grin.

My own mouth responds in kind before I even know what's happening, and I bite down on the insides of my cheeks to stop the movement. That's all it takes, two seconds and the lift of his lips and he's managed to turn me into his coconspirator. I realize that the distance I've put between us, both in miles and in years, matters not at all. Because behind the secrets and the horrible truth, under the shame and anger that beat like a heart, there still lives a terrible kind of love.

"We were talking about Allegra," I remind him, voice sharp.

The smile fades from my granddad's face. "I love her," he says. "If that's what you meant."

"No," I say. "That wasn't what I meant at all." I put the piece of muffin in my mouth. The sweet cake turns to sawdust on my tongue.

I doze away most of the day, naked and sweating under my thin cotton sheet. The sun through the curtains casts filmy yellow shadows against the walls. It gives the illusion of being trapped in a moist, warm cocoon, and I feel drugged and fuzzy, my limbs still heavy with sleep, when I finally drag myself out of bed and get dressed.

I splash my face with cold water in the bathroom, and I'm wandering back to my room when the phone on the hall table rings. No one else picks up so I grab it, anxious for news of Allegra.

"Roanoke residence."

"Hey, Lane. It's me, Tommy."

I lean back against the wall, hit with sudden dizziness. "Allegra?" I ask.

"Oh, no . . . no." Tommy clears his throat. "Nothing new to report. Sorry."

"It's okay." I blow out a slow breath. "What's up?"

"Listen, Sarah and I are going to Ronnie Joe's tonight for a drink. Want to join us? Sarah's dying to see you again."

I wonder if the lie burns on his tongue. "I'm pretty beat still from the drive. Maybe another time."

"Come on, Lane. It'll get you out of the house. Get your mind off things." He pauses. "Some other old friends might show up, too." We both know exactly who he's talking about without either one of us having to say the name.

"I don't know, Tommy."

"Oh, come on. It's just a couple of drinks."

I give in, only because I don't have the energy to argue, and an alcohol stupor is exactly what I need. "Okay, fine. When?"

"In a few hours. Around eight?"

"Yeah, sounds good. I'll see you then."

The inside of Ronnie Joe's is about what I expected, but I can't suppress a flash of disappointment at the cheap plywood bar, the aging girlie calendar tacked to the wall, the slack faces poised over mugs of beer. When we were teenagers, we anticipated the day we'd be old enough to enter this tired brick building crouched at the end of Main Street like a stray dog waiting to be kicked. As with so many things in life, the reality isn't worth the wait.

The place doesn't exactly fall silent when I walk in, but there's a tightening of the air. My presence disturbs some delicate balance honed over years with no new faces making an appearance. The men sit higher on their barstools, watching me from the corners of their bloodshot eyes. The women bristle. If they were cats, the fur along their spines would be standing on end. Allegra would've loved the reactions. She always thrived on this type of attention, the breathless satisfaction of being the biggest fish in a very small pond.

They're sitting at a table near the back, under a glowing Bud Light sign, and Tommy motions me forward with his hand. The neon gives his skin a sickly green cast, highlighting the shadows beneath his eyes. The tall man across from Tommy keeps his back to me, doesn't turn around even after Tommy waves.

I thread my way between the close-packed tables, whispers following me as I move. "Hey, Cooper," I say when I reach the table. My voice comes out desert-dry.

Cooper looks up at me, not bothering to straighten from his relaxed slouch, his spine melting into the wooden chair. "Hey there, Lane," he responds in his gravel-deep drawl. "Long time, no see."

His hair still falls into one eye, but it's darkened to the color of winter wheat, just a few strands remain streaked with youthful gold. His body is as lean as ever, but the muscles in his arms are harder, veins standing out against his tan skin. A cigarette dangles negligently from the corner of his mouth, and when he plucks it out, I notice that he's never had his chipped front tooth repaired—a souvenir from a drunken fight. His golden brown eyes study me with plenty of fire but very little warmth. He is still, after all these years, the most beautiful person I've ever seen.

I gesture to the shot of whiskey in his hand. "Any more where that came from?"

Cooper grins and the dimple in his right cheek flares to life. He used to call that dimple his insurance policy. If all else failed, flash the cheek dent. "There's always more liquor around here. It's the one thing we've got plenty of," he reminds me.

"Lane, glad you could make it," Tommy cuts in, formal in his nervousness. "This is my wife, Sarah."

"Hi," I say, holding out my hand. Sarah takes it limply in hers like I might be trying to pass her something unwanted in my palm. She is slight, overpowered by a mass of light brown curls she's tried to tame with a white fabric headband. She lives in the vast, overpopulated territory somewhere between plain and cute, with the kind of face you can never fully recall afterward, every feature blurry around the edges. "I'm sorry about your cousin," she says. "I'm sure everything will turn out fine."

"Well, that's reassuring," I say, pulling out a chair at the end of the table. Sarah's eyes drop away, her cheeks burning. Tommy gives me a warning look that I ignore.

"So"—Cooper takes a lazy swallow of his drink—"how've you been since you ran away from here?"

"I didn't run away."

"You didn't?" Cooper raises his eyebrows. "Could've fooled me."

He doesn't give me a chance to respond, scraping back his chair as he heads to the bar. Tommy, Sarah, and I sit in uncomfortable silence until Cooper returns moments later with a round of shots in his hands and an hourglass redhead by his side. When they sit, she positions herself under his arm, his hand dangling dangerously close to one plump breast. He doesn't introduce us.

"Are you the one who went to California?" the girl asks. She stinks of cheap perfume and bubble gum.

"Yeah, that's me," I say, downing my shot with grim determination. The whiskey hits my empty stomach with a hard thump, and sweat blooms along my hairline. My cheeks flush with heat.

"What's it like?"

I think of California, with its endless blue skies, sunny days, and perfect temperature, how the seasons bleed into one another with no way to mark their passing. The unearned bounty becomes a kind of narcotic so that you wake up one morning and realize ten years have come and gone and you have nothing to show for it. "It's different."

"Cool. Different." The girl gazes at me as if I've said something profound, and Cooper rolls his eyes.

"I could have told you that much," he says. I can't tell if he's more disgusted with her or me.

"What do you do in California?" Sarah covers Tommy's hand with hers as she speaks. I must make her nervous, looking so much like Allegra, the one Tommy really wanted.

"Whatever I can. Kind of hard to find jobs with only a GED." I shrug. "Waitress, cashier, receptionist."

"Aren't those all code words for stripper?" Cooper asks. He gives me a sideways twist of his lips, a sly smirk full of bad intentions. This is the Cooper most people know. The one who hides behind snide comments and shit-eating grins. Once I knew a different side of him. But I'm not surprised it's this version who's shown up tonight.

"Clever," I say and give him my own tight smile in return. He blows smoke in my direction, and I wave it away. "No one smokes anymore," I tell him.

He glances down at the smoldering cigarette between his fingers as if it begs to differ.

"No one smart," I amend.

"Well, you know us dumb hicks," Cooper says, deepening his drawl. "Always behind the times. Thank God you're back, so we can get caught up."

I open my mouth to respond, but the redhead cuts in, leaning across the table toward Tommy but looking at me. "Hey, I heard someone thought they saw Lane's cousin hitchhiking out on Lone Tree Road."

The whole table freezes, Tommy's gaze flying to mine. "Just a bunch of stupid kids spreading rumors, Lane. Looking for attention. But we checked it out. It was nothing."

"She wouldn't need to be hitchhiking," Cooper says. "She had her own car."

"Allegra did lots of things she didn't have to do," I remind him. "Just for the hell of it."

Tommy shakes his head. "No, it wasn't her. Remember Beth Van Horn?" He doesn't wait for me to nod. "It was her oldest girl. Somebody saw the long dark hair, jumped to conclusions."

"The whole thing is totally tragic." The redhead makes sad puppy-dog eyes to prove her sincerity. She pauses to light a cigarette, and I smirk at Cooper. "And like no offense or anything since we don't know what happened to her yet . . ." She glances at me before continuing. "But what if we have a serial killer here?" She gives an exaggerated shudder. "It's like a horror movie. I swear, I can hardly sleep at night."

Tommy's eyes swing from Cooper to me and back again. He raises his eyebrows and Cooper shrugs. "Um . . . one missing woman doesn't mean we have a serial killer at work," Tommy says.

"It sure could," the girl argues. "Osage Flats's very own serial killer." She makes it sound like a potential tourist draw. Hell, for all I know, maybe it would be.

"Actually, that's the definition of *serial*," Cooper informs her. "More than one."

The girl frowns, her head tilted to the side. "What?"

"Never mind." Cooper sighs, tapping ash from his cigarette into the already full ashtray.

"This whole town is completely fucked up," I mutter under my breath and catch the twitch of Cooper's mouth out of the corner of my eye. He rakes a hand through his hair, pushing it off his face in a gesture so familiar it makes my throat ache. His hands are bigger than I remember and, unlike in our youth, his fingernails are clean now, no half-moons of black. But the deep lines of his palms are still permanently stained dark with grease. Once I went to church with that grease smeared across my breasts. My skin hummed all day under my thin cotton bra.

"You still working at your dad's garage?" I ask. It's a stupid question, but it's something to say that doesn't feel dangerous.

"My garage now."

"Did your dad retire?" I picture Mr. Sullivan, who always looked older than the other fathers, with his sloping shoulders and hard paunch of belly. I don't think I ever saw him smile.

"Nope. Died. Last year."

"How?"

Cooper plucks a piece of errant tobacco from his tongue. "Heart attack," he says, voice mild like he's talking about the weather.

"Oh. Sorry," I say, because something seems required, even if it's not heartfelt.

Cooper nods, and for the first time all night he holds my gaze for longer than a moment. All the old, confused emotions tangle together in my gut, a heavy knot of pain.

"How's your sister? Is she still here in town?"

Cooper looks amused as he taps a fresh cigarette from his pack on the table. This type of small talk was never our area of expertise. "No, Holly's in Kansas City. She has been for years."

"I heard you were in K.C. for a while."

"For a while. Wasn't for me."

The redhead leans into our conversation. "I'm getting us another round. Then maybe you can tell me more about California." She holds out her palm, and Cooper fills it with cash, barely glancing in her direction.

"Looks like your date is more interested in me than you," I comment when she's out of earshot.

Cooper grunts, his arm grazing mine as he drains the last of his drink. "No big loss. I've already been around that block one too many times, checked out all the major landmarks."

Sarah leans over and swats Cooper's free hand. "Don't be nasty!"

"Sorry," he says, but I can tell he doesn't mean it. I lower my eyes and run my thumb in absent circles on the tabletop. Slowly conversation starts up around me as the redhead returns with a bouquet of shot glasses. I drink mine with whiskey-numb lips, my gaze catching Cooper's as I swallow. A small, secret smile tugs at the corner of his mouth, telling me he's not fooled. He knows the truth—knows little Lane Roanoke likes his brand of nasty just fine.

Jane

(*b. 1951, left Roanoke 1968*)

They were born on the same day, exactly one year apart. Him first, her after. Not twins, but they might as well have been. They were always treated like a set. Yates and Jane. Jane and Yates. Always a *they*, a *we*, never two separate people. Sophia came five years after Jane. She was an afterthought to more than their parents. All Jane really remembered of Sophia's childhood was her high, pleading voice, *"Wait for me!"* They never did.

Sometimes Jane tried to pinpoint when it started, but there wasn't a single moment she could look at and say, *There, right there was the beginning.* By the time he kissed her it was already done. That kiss felt like the thousandth step, not the first. She thought maybe it started from the time they were born. The two of them and two thousand acres. All that childhood curiosity combined with all that isolation. There was no one else for them to play with, talk to, fixate on. And even if there had been, would it have mattered? Would any other boy have been as handsome as Yates? Would any other boy have looked at her like every word out of her mouth was gold, like every move she made hung the moon?

She was fourteen the first time they had sex, in the hayloft in the barn, hot and sweaty and neither of them feeling any shame. It felt like a natural progression of all the things they'd done before: catching frogs and riding horses, laughing on the sleeping porch after dark, sharing ice cream on sticky summer days, whispering secret dreams for the future, kissing behind the barn, his warm hand under her blouse. Yates and Jane, always together.

She wasn't even sure if she loved him, as much as they were fused. Like he was an extra appendage, a part of her that could never be severed. A single heart beating between them. The two of them lived in a bubble of their own making. Other people might see the dark edges, but they saw only the gilded center. But then Jane got pregnant. And something inside her grew along with the baby. The idea that she wanted more than this farm, this endless blue sky and flat horizon. The idea that maybe there was something beyond this place. But she didn't even have to ask to know he would never leave. He loved Roanoke. If Jane owned half of Yates's heart, Roanoke held the other half, and it was never letting go. But the truth was, Jane didn't think she owned her half outright anymore. Because Yates loved Sophia now, too. Not the same way he loved Jane. Not yet. But she could see it whenever Sophia walked into the room, the way Yates's eyes sparked, a little flash of heat.

Jane stayed until the baby was born, though. Suffered through their mother's thin, pinched lips when her eyes fell on Jane's growing belly. Endured their father's nightly dinner table sermons about sin and hellfire. Yates held her hand during labor, cradled their daughter's tiny body in his still teenage arms. Jane let him name her. Penelope. It wasn't a name Jane would have chosen, but she wouldn't be the baby's mother for long, so it didn't matter.

She left in the night, without a note or a good-bye, her body still bleeding from Penelope's birth. If given the chance, he probably could have convinced her to stay. So she made a clean break, ran down the driveway and hitchhiked her way south. No more Yates and Jane. Just Jane. And she was free.

Then

In the few days I'd been at Roanoke, my gran had been more of a passing presence than a permanent fixture. She swept past me in the hall, admonished me to put on sunscreen when I was out by the barn, snapped her fingers at Allegra and reminded her to clean up her mess in the kitchen (a directive Allegra ignored). But beyond those quick interactions and nightly dinner in the dining room, I'd seen her hardly at all.

So it took me by surprise when I found her sitting on my bed, a pile of fresh laundry stacked next to her. "Come in, Lane," she said with a clipped smile, when I hesitated in the doorway. "I want to talk to you." She patted a spot on the bed, and I sat, curling my feet up underneath me, the laundry between us.

Once she had me where she wanted me, Gran straightened the seam of her pant leg, plucking away invisible lint. "Lord, it's hot in here. We can get you a window unit. The fan isn't much help."

"It's okay. I kind of like having the windows open." In New York when we'd opened the windows it had smelled of exhaust and stale Chinese food from the restaurant below us. Here the air was fresh and hot and green.

"You and Allegra. I don't know how you girls stand it." She

fanned her face briefly. "Anyway, I wanted to ask you about your mother."

"Oh." I'd known at some point one of them would want more details about my mom and our life, but I'd figured it would be my granddad. It wasn't that it was difficult for me to talk about my mother. More that I had nothing to say, nothing anyone in their right mind would want to hear.

"I know it probably seems impossible to you because she was your mother, but she was my little girl once," Gran said. Her voice remained steady, her eyes dry, for which I was thankful. "I was only twenty when she was born. Nineteen when I had my first one, Eleanor. Not as young as Camilla was when she had you, but still mostly a child myself."

"You and Granddad got married young."

Gran smiled. "Very young. I was eighteen. He was only a year older. Oh, my family threw a *fit*." She slapped her leg with one hand in emphasis. "We were in St. Louis visiting my mother's aunt and I saw your granddad across the lobby of our hotel. Knew right then and there I had to have him." She laughed, leaned her head toward me. "I was a willful thing, at least when it came to Yates."

"Did you move here right after you got married?"

Gran nodded. "It took some getting used to. After Boston. All this space. All this . . . nothing." Her voice drifted off and her eyes followed. It took her a few seconds to find her way back to the story. "But I had Penelope to look after. Your granddad's niece."

"Allegra told me about her. She said you and Granddad raised her."

"Yes, we did. Until her accident. She wasn't even a year old when we got married. Our own started coming right after. Sophia, your granddad's youngest sister, was here to help me, at least, until . . ."

"Allegra said she drowned."

"Well, Allegra's certainly been filling you in on the family history." Gran smoothed a strand of hair off her face, tucked it into her tidy chignon. "I'm sure you know then, that your mother ran away before you were born. We never knew much about what happened to either of you after that. Your mother didn't make it easy for us to keep in touch. And eventually, we gave up trying." Gran sighed. "I always wondered about her, though, about how she turned out. Was she a good mother?" Gran touched the back of my hand with one manicured fingernail.

"No," I said. "Not really."

Gran nodded, like that was the answer she expected. "Were you close?"

I had no idea how to answer her question. How could I be close to someone who barely spoke to me? Someone who I strongly suspected hated me more than she loved me? But at the same time, my mother was as much a part of me as my blood or my skin. Sometimes I swore I felt her vibrating through my bones. "I don't know," I said finally. "She was my mother."

"Tell me something about her," Gran said, twisting toward me. It was the most interest she'd shown in me since my arrival. "Your strongest memory."

I scrolled back through images of my mother, almost all of them tearstained. "She was sad," I said. "She cried a lot."

Gran closed her eyes for a moment, gave my hand a quick pat before opening them again. "Is there anything you want to ask me? About your mother?" She voiced the question reluctantly, like she owed me a debt she wasn't sure she knew how to pay.

I scooted closer on the bed. Gran put her hand on the laundry to keep it from toppling over, or maybe to keep a barrier between us. "Actually, I wondered about my father."

"What about him?"

"She never talked about him. Do you know who he is? If he still lives in Osage Flats? Did she tell you his name?" I leaned toward Gran, my words spilling out of me.

"Lane." Gran sighed. "He could have been anyone. Anyone. Your mother wasn't exactly . . . discerning."

"Oh." My shoulders sagged even as I resisted the urge to pound my fists against the bed. My mother had dragged my father along with her to the grave. One more in a long line of answers she'd denied me.

Gran stood. "Get this laundry put away, why don't you, before Sharon takes exception."

Once she was gone, I flopped back on the bed, let my laundry unspool around me. I'd lied to Gran. Not about my mother crying all the time. That part was true. But my most vivid memory of my mother was one I would never share willingly. It wasn't the type of recollection to be passed around, touched and fawned over. We'd been lying on her bed in our apartment, on our sides, facing each other. I was ten. She was tracing my face with her fingertips, and I remember being happy. Happy she was paying attention to me, focusing solely on me without tears or trepidation. "Right now," she whispered, "you look exactly like your father. I loved him so much." I thought maybe she was finally going to tell me some detail about him, but before I could ask a single question her hand trailed lower, around my neck. She squeezed. Gently at first, so that I didn't wrench away as fast as I should have, then harder, her nails digging into my skin. "It makes me want to hurt you," she said, voice calm and eyes wild. By the time I broke away, two of her fingernails had pierced my skin. Blood pearls set in a necklace of bruises. Later, when she locked herself in her room, weeping and pulling at her hair, I stood in front of the bathroom mirror and tried again and again to re-create the look on my face in the moment before she'd hurt me. Tried to find the expression that reminded her of my father. But no matter how I contorted my features, only my mother's face stared back at me.

"Get your ass out of bed," Allegra yelled, slapping at my legs with both hands. "What are you doing anyway?"

I rolled over onto my back and covered my face with a pillow. "Taking a nap. Don't people nap in Kansas?"

"Not when there's stuff to *do*," Allegra said, yanking the pillow off me and tossing it to the floor. She peered into my face. "Are you like depressed or something? About your mom?"

I shook my head. "No. Not really." And it was true. I didn't miss my mother the way I should have. Her death felt more like relief than sorrow. She had slipped away into oblivion, where she'd wanted to be all along. We were finally free of each other.

"Then come on," Allegra said. She pulled me up by one arm.

"Where are we going?"

"Into town." Allegra frowned at me. "Is that what you're wearing?"

I glanced down at my cutoff shorts and plain T-shirt. "Yeah. Isn't Osage Flats like ten miles away?" I looked out at the cut-glass sky, not a single cloud in sight. "We're going to get heatstroke walking that far."

"We're not walking," Allegra said. "Hurry up!"

I slipped my feet into a pair of flip-flops and stood still while Allegra tied my T-shirt into a knot at my waist, ran her hands through my sleep-tumbled hair. "Perfect," she said. "You look freshly fucked. Here, put this on." She handed me a tube of lip gloss. It left my lips tacky and tasting of strawberry.

"We need to get you some better clothes," she said as she skipped down the main staircase. "Everything you have is like bargain basement crap."

I wasn't offended. My clothes *were* crap. "I don't have any money," I told her. "My mom wasn't exactly rolling in it."

"You don't need money." She grabbed my hand and pulled me down the front hall and through a series of rooms I was still learning my way around. "Quick detour," she said over her shoulder. She stopped in the office, in front of our granddad's large cherrywood desk. She opened the top left-hand drawer and pointed at a black zippered envelope. "Credit cards. Get on the computer. Buy what you want. That's what they're for."

I hesitated. "But only for emergencies, right?"

Allegra snorted. "Sure, if you consider an urgent need for a dozen crop tops an emergency."

"Is there a limit? I mean, I can't order whatever I want, can I?"

"I don't see why not. I do." Allegra bumped my hip with hers. "Seriously, Lane, that's why Granddad leaves them there. For me. For us." She glanced down at her phone. "Oh shit, come on, we're late!"

We racewalked down the drive, Allegra urging me to hurry up. "But don't run. We don't want to be all sweaty!"

"What the hell are we doing?" I asked. Despite her warning, beads of sweat were already trickling down my back. There was no wind today, the air stagnant and wet against my skin.

"Getting a ride!" Allegra said. She stopped where the driveway intersected with Route 24. "They'll be here soon." She gathered her hair into a messy knot on top of her head. Her giant gold hoop earrings flashed in the sun when she turned to me. "How do I look?"

"Gorgeous," I told her honestly, and she smiled. "Who are we getting a ride from?"

"You'll see."

I looked behind me at Roanoke. When strangers drove past and saw it in the distance, they probably thought it was an insane asylum. The idea made me smile. To me it looked like a ship, strong and unsinkable, afloat on a wild sea of wheat.

Allegra pinched my forearm. "Here they come!"

A small silver car crested the rise to the north. Allegra waved, and the driver gave a quick tap on the horn. The car pulled into the driveway and stopped beside us, kicking up a tornado of dust, which left me coughing.

"Hey, handsome," Allegra said, leaning into the driver's side window.

A teenage boy with dark hair smiled back at her. He looked out of place in the tiny car, his broad shoulders spanning the width of the driver's seat. "Hi, pretty girl. Need a ride?" he said. From the interior of the car someone muttered, "Oh, for God's sake," and I turned my face away to hide my smile.

"Lane, get over here," Allegra said. "This is Tommy Kenning."

"Hi," I said, giving him a brief wave.

His eyes sparkled as he grinned at me. "Hi. I've heard a lot about you." He hooked a thumb toward the passenger seat. "And this is Cooper Sullivan."

I bent down a little to see into the car. The boy in the passenger seat glanced over at me, his blond hair blocking one eye. He raised a single finger off the open window frame in greeting.

"Get in the back, Cooper," Allegra demanded. "I want to sit up front."

"Fuck off," Cooper said. "You wanted a ride, you get in the back."

I tried to pull open the passenger door on the driver's side, but it wouldn't budge. "Sorry," Tommy said, craning his neck toward me. "That door doesn't open. You have to go around."

"Are you and Tommy dating?" I whispered to Allegra as we skirted the back of the car.

"Kind of." Her grin was smug. "He's totally in love with me!"

"How old are they?" I asked, not worried, just curious.

"Eighteen. They graduated a few weeks ago." She opened the car door and mouthed, "An older man," at me before collapsing into giggles in the backseat.

I couldn't help but laugh. "Scoot over, crazy girl," I told her, prodding her with my knee.

"So, you been into town yet?" Tommy called back to me once we were on the road.

"No. This is my first trip."

"I hope you're a fan of disappointment," Cooper drawled. I caught his eye in the side-view mirror, and a fever blush spread across my cheeks. But I didn't look away, made sure Cooper dropped his gaze first, a little smirk dancing on his face.

We parked at the end of Main Street, Tommy's car one of the only vehicles on the entire stretch of road. "Where is everybody?" I asked, as we all climbed out of the car.

"Who knows?" Cooper said. "Probably in their trailers cooking up meth."

"This is the downtown?" I couldn't believe a place so quiet and empty could be the center of town.

"Uptown!" Allegra said. "We call it uptown. Like, get me some milk when you go uptown."

From what I could tell, "uptown" consisted solely of a collection of ragtag stores: a small grocery, a walk-up hamburger stand, a secondhand clothing store, and a five-and-dime with strips of faded flypaper hanging in the windows. The majority of the storefronts we sauntered past were empty, faded For Lease signs propped in dust-streaked windows.

"Down there is Ronnie Joe's," Tommy said, pointing to the far end of Main, two blocks in the distance. "Local bar," he said in response to my questioning look. "And across from it is The Eat."

"Our version of a fine dining establishment," Cooper said. "Where you go when you really want to impress the ladies." Somehow we'd ended up walking two by two, Tommy and Allegra holding hands in front, Cooper and I behind, a careful wedge of space between us. The sidewalk shimmered under the relentless prairie sun, and we all gravitated to the thin strips of shade the store awnings provided.

"And that's Cooper's dad's gas station," Allegra said, "down past The Eat. Last thing you pass on your way out of town." Allegra let go of Tommy's hand and turned, walking backward. "Maybe someday, if you're really, *really* lucky, it will all be yours, Cooper."

I glanced at Cooper, expecting anger, but he only continued to tap a cigarette from the pack he'd pulled from his back pocket.

"Maybe," he said, flipping the cigarette between his lips. "We can't all be little rich girls."

"Oh, screw you!" Allegra said, whirling back around. She grabbed Tommy's hand and pulled him forward, away from us. Cooper grinned around his cigarette and held out the pack to me. "Want one?"

I used to smoke sometimes back in New York, huddled in alleyways with girls from school who were never my friends but pretended to be. "Sure," I said. Cooper cupped his hand around the cigarette to light it while I held it to my mouth. His hand brushing against mine sent sparks cascading into my belly, and I sucked in too fast, choking on the smoke.

"Easy," he said, amused. "You inhale the smoke, not the whole cigarette."

I glared at him, and he laughed, a dimple appearing in his right cheek. I wondered what it would feel like to rest the tip of my finger inside it.

"Come on, you slowpokes!" Allegra yelled from the corner. "I want to show you something, Lane!"

When we rounded the corner and caught up with Allegra and Tommy, they were standing in front of a dilapidated old house with a familiar-looking turret on one side. "This is what Gran modeled the brick addition on," Allegra said. She was hanging on to the chain-link fence surrounding the house, her fingers and toes hooked through the metal, sandals abandoned on the sidewalk. Signs were posted along the fence warning people to keep out. The house looked like a strong wind would topple it, send it crashing into a pile of matchsticks. "Isn't it cool?" Allegra said.

I looked at the boarded-up windows, the sagging front porch, the patches of rotted wood, not sure what to say. If Roanoke was an insane asylum, this place was a haunted house, vengeful ghosts lingering in all the shadows. "No one's lived here for years," Allegra continued. "Not since like 1960."

"Nineteen seventy," Cooper corrected.

"Whatever. Anyway, the lady who owned it was called Madame Wright. She was a loon." Allegra kept her eyes on the house as she talked. "She gave illegal abortions in her basement."

"I don't think that's true," Tommy said.

"It's true," Allegra said. "Granddad told me they found tons of teeny tiny baby bones in her backyard well after she died." Allegra glanced back at me, smiled. "Too bad she was before your mom's time, Lane. We could have gone digging for the bones of your brothers and sisters."

"Jesus Christ," Cooper said. "What the fuck is wrong with you?"

It took me a minute to understand what Allegra was saying, my brain sifting the words until they made sense. "She was only sixteen when I was born," I said finally.

"So?" Allegra said. "Just because you were her last, doesn't mean you were her first. You were just the only one she didn't have yanked out and thrown away." Allegra turned and looked at me. Her face fell. "Oh, don't be upset, Lane," she pleaded, hopping down from the fence to fold both my hands between her own. "It's not like my mom wasn't knocked up a bunch of times, too. The Roanoke girls are fertile." Her smile was all glee and excitement. "We get pregnant every time we spread our legs."

"Better be careful there, Tommy," Cooper said.

"Shut up," Tommy muttered, his eyes downcast and his neck flushed red.

Now

I wake with a pounding headache, my tongue whiskey-thick and stuck to the roof of my mouth. I may be in a different state, but the outlines of my life are depressingly familiar. It's only late morning, but the sun already roars in through the sheer curtains, making me realize how gentle the sunshine was in California. There, it bathes you. Here, it smacks you across the face. I heave myself upright with a muffled groan and swing my legs out of bed. The floor underneath my left foot feels uneven, and I glance down, find ALLEGRA + LANE gouged into the wood. I rub the message with my big toe, remembering the morning Allegra carved it there, still in her nightgown, one of Sharon's strawberry muffins clasped in her free hand. The memory gives me an idea, and I shift back onto the bed and grab my phone from the nightstand, look up the number of the police department. The receptionist puts me straight through to Tommy, who answers around a mouthful of food.

"Oh, hey, Lane," he says once I identify myself. "How're you feeling this morning?"

"I've been better."

He chuckles. "One shot too many?"

Or maybe three too many, but that's not information I need to share with Tommy. "Listen," I say, "do you remember how Allegra used to carve words into things? And sometimes little pictures?" Tommy doesn't respond, and I forge ahead. "Like if she was into a band, she'd carve the name into the top of her dresser. Or if she was in a good mood, she'd leave a heart on my doorjamb. Did you look for anything like that in the house? Maybe she left a message before she disappeared?" Hearing it out loud sounds even crazier than it did inside my head. I'm about to say forget it and hang up, blame it on the leftover booze in my system, when Tommy steps into the silence.

"She scratched *dick* on my dashboard once when she was pissed at me." His voice is full of laughter and a dazed kind of wonder. "Shit, how could I have forgotten that?"

"I'd pretty much forgotten it, too," I tell him. "But I was thinking maybe she left some sort of clue behind."

Tommy sighs. "Sounds pretty far-fetched to me, Lane. It would be a lot easier to leave an actual note."

"You're probably right, but can I look? Is it okay if I go through her room?"

"Sure," Tommy says. "We're done in there. But if you find anything, it comes straight to me. Got it?"

"Got it."

I roll out of bed and race up to Allegra's room. The summer I lived at Roanoke, I found Allegra's handiwork scattered throughout the house. The R4 on the picture frame was only the first of many. ЅLUT carved in inch-high letters on the bottom of what had been her mother's bedroom door; a tiny sun etched into my headboard; ЅWEAT left on the ladder into the hayloft; LΘVE gouged across the corner of our granddad's desk. I asked her about it once, and she only shrugged, said sometimes she had thoughts she needed to get out of her head. I think she liked the mystery of it, the inherent drama of knife against wood, the image it left in all our minds of Allegra drifting through the house leaving a trail of word confetti behind her.

I start with her bedside tables, move on to her bed, but find nothing other than the wear and tear of daily life. Her dresser yields only a tiny cluster of stars on the front of a drawer. I run my eyes and hands over her closet doorjamb, feeling more foolish by the second. Already my tank top is soaked with sweat, the air in the room barely moving even with the window fan on high. I sink onto the padded stool in front of Allegra's vanity, eyes roaming over the knots of jewelry and piles of makeup. I slide it all carefully to one side, still searching. Maybe Allegra gave up her strange graffiti in the years I was gone. Or maybe she confined it to other parts of the house, places where it was more likely to be discovered.

I use my forearm to listlessly shove the junk on Allegra's vanity to the opposite side. I've lost interest in the task already, anxious to go downstairs, where at least the temperature is set to bake, not broil. The freshly uncovered top of the vanity reveals all manner of beauty product stains: spots of spilled perfume, cloudy swatches of hairspray residue, a sweep of sparkling champagne eye shadow streaked across the wood. I run my fingers over the eye shadow, golden glitter sticking to my skin, and like a blind person reading braille, I feel the bumps and ridges of letters under my fingertips. I swipe the rest of the eye shadow away from the vanity top with the flat of my hand, lifting up from the stool to get a closer look.

RUN LANE

The breath freezes in my chest, goose bumps pinpricking my neck and the backs of my arms despite the stifling heat. My knees give out, and I sit back down hard on the stool, my jaws clacking together at the impact. RUN LANE. It's impossible to know when the words were written. It could have been a decade ago. Or in the days before Allegra disappeared, hands frantic to leave this message, hoping that if I somehow ended up back here, I wouldn't be dumb enough to stay.

I look up, catch my own pale, eyes-too-big reflection in Allegra's mirror. *Run Lane.* As if I needed Allegra to tell me that.

After a shower, I eat a late lunch on the screened porch—a limp tuna sandwich from a platter Sharon left in the fridge. I wash it down with a couple of beers and watch my granddad loading hay into the barn with Charlie, who is so stooped over with age I'm surprised he's not laid up in a nursing home somewhere. Sweat pours off both of them, and my granddad works with a kind of single-minded ferocity, like the hay is responsible for everything that's gone wrong.

When I'm done, I carry my plate and empty beer bottles back into the kitchen and pull up short in the doorway at the sight of Sharon. I've eaten her food, seen evidence of her in the kitchen, but haven't come face-to-face with her yet.

"What's for dinner?" I ask. She's peering into the fridge and rears up, almost smacking her head on the freezer door, at the sound of my voice. "I'm hoping not salmon patties."

"You scared me!" she says. She's thicker through the middle, her hair completely gray now, cut in an unflattering bowl around her head. Her dark eyes accuse me of all manner of sins. She tosses a bag of green peppers and a package of hamburger onto the counter. Oh goodie, stuffed peppers.

I lean against the doorjamb and watch her grab a knife from the butcher block, go to work on a pepper. "I bet you're loving this, right? Allegra gone."

Sharon's mouth thins. "I'm not going to pretend I miss that little bitch."

"Nice," I say. "Maybe the police should be talking to you." I cross to the sink and set my plate and beer bottles inside with a clatter.

Sharon shakes her head. "Wherever Allegra's gotten to, she did it on her own." She pauses in her slicing to glance over at me. "I hope you're here to help your gran, not stir up trouble."

"Meaning what, exactly?"

"Not one of you girls have ever done right by your gran. Everything that woman's done for you all, put up with . . ." She shakes her head. "Shameful."

My cheeks burn, although why I feel chastened is a question I'm sure a good therapist would love to get ahold of. Sharon laughs, a hoarse little cackle, when she sees my face. "What? Did I hurt your feelings? Are you going to tell on me? Tattle to your granddad and get me fired?"

"No," I say. "We both know you're not going anywhere, no matter what I say. You know too much, right?"

Sharon gives me a disapproving cluck, goes back to the peppers. The longer I stand there, the stiffer her shoulders get. I linger before drifting even closer, let my fingers riffle through the various papers stuck to the fridge with plain silver magnets. Sharon's grocery lists, Gran's volunteer schedule, a take-out menu from The Eat. And peeking out from the edge of the menu, I spy the curly loops of Allegra's handwriting. Her actual writing is bigger and bubblier than the carvings she leaves on solid surfaces, but still instantly recognizable to me.

I lean closer, shift the menu aside, and run my fingers over the words written in blue ink on a wrinkled piece of white paper. *Turkey, bananas, saltine crackers, cornflakes.* And last on the list, *vodka,* underlined twice. My heart twists along with my lips. I blink back the sting of tears.

"When did Allegra leave this grocery list?" I ask Sharon.

She barely glances at me, waves her knife through the air. "Not long before she flitted off. Didn't see much point in buying things for someone not around to eat them."

I ease the list out from underneath its magnet without really knowing why. It feels like the closest I've gotten to Allegra since I've been back, as if her essence is embedded in this forgotten scrap of paper, and I don't trust Sharon to keep it safe. I flip the paper over, hoping, maybe, for some more personal message. But it's just a drugstore receipt from Parsons, a larger town about forty-five minutes from Osage Flats. I'm about to stuff the list in my pocket, when I notice the date. A month ago, not all that long before Allegra disappeared. What was she doing in Parsons? What did she buy? The receipt doesn't list the item, only the price: $14.99. I fold the receipt carefully and put it in my pocket.

I call Tommy and tell him I'll drop the receipt off at the police station, more from a need to get out of the house than any pressing desire to go back into Osage Flats. By the time I arrive, he's gone out somewhere. I leave the receipt at the front desk in an envelope marked with his name and *URGENT* in all caps.

Last night I only got as far as Ronnie Joe's, didn't venture any farther down Main Street, so today I creep along the main drag. I've been away for almost eleven years. A lifetime anywhere else, in this world that moves forward at lightning speed. But Osage Flats is one of those places that never appears to change, at least not in any way that counts. Driving down Main Street I still recognize every face I see, even if I've never met the person wearing it before in my life: the overworked mother with too many kids and not enough money, her hand itching to slap; the bar regular heading to Ronnie Joe's for his first drink of the day, figuring it has to be five o'clock somewhere; the gaggle of high school girls sauntering along hoping for trouble, with skirts too short and expectations too low. It's the type of place where you can easily believe Obama was never elected, women never earned the right to vote, and gays still hide in the closet. That nothing has ever moved forward and nothing ever will.

I pull into a parking slot in front of the secondhand clothing shop. The outfits in the front window are at least ten years out of date. But I didn't bring much with me when I left L.A., foolishly hoping I wouldn't be here long, and I need some additional clothes.

The bell above the door makes a sad little chime when I push inside. Like every secondhand store the world over, this one smells of other people's sweat, the scent overlaid with a heavy dose of lavender air freshener, which only makes it worse.

Too late, I notice Sarah Kenning thumbing through the rack to my right. She spots me before I can sneak out. "Hi, Lane," she says. Her smile is so painfully polite it might as well be outlined in frosting.

"Hi, Sarah. Thought I'd check out what's new uptown."

"Not much, unfortunately. We lose businesses right and left."

"Hmmm . . ." I say, my gaze running over the half-empty racks of clothes. Everything looks tired and worn. The thought of wearing any of it depresses me. The only other person in the store is the elderly woman behind the counter, who eyes me suspiciously over her glasses. As if I'd want to steal any of this crap.

"I guess this isn't what you're used to," Sarah says. She's holding a floral print dress I wouldn't be caught dead wearing. "I mean"— she flushes—"being a Roanoke and all."

I shake my head. "That was another lifetime."

"You know, it's thanks to your grandparents we have even these stores left."

"How's that?"

"They're very generous, always doing what they can," Sarah explains. "The whole town relies on them."

"Oh, yes," I say with a roll of my eyes, "they're quite the philanthropists."

Sarah's unsure what to do with my statement. Her smile blinks on, then off, then on again, like a malfunctioning string of holiday lights. I walk deeper into the store, flick halfheartedly through the racks. From the selection, it appears ninety percent of Osage Flats's female population weighs more than three hundred pounds. No wonder Sarah snagged that dress when she saw it.

"Aren't these adorable?" Sarah asks, and I turn to see her holding up a pair of tiny pink overalls.

My insides clench, swift and sudden, surprising me. "I guess," I say. "I'm not exactly the maternal type. Do you and Tommy have kids?" Tommy always wanted a family, ever since I first met him. Traditional images filled his vision of the future: a wife, a house, a big family laughing around the kitchen table. Cooper used to tease him about it, told him he was worse than a girl.

Sarah puts the overalls back on the rack. "No," she says. "No kids. Not yet. We're trying, but we're having a little trouble." It's obvious from the look on her face that the trouble is more than little. I can't help but think of Allegra, the fertile Roanoke girls. If she was Tommy's wife, they'd probably have a houseful of kids already. And if I'm thinking it, I'm sure Tommy's thought it, too.

"So," Sarah says, pulling a smile onto her face. "Cooper and you used to date, way back when?"

I give a short, sharp laugh. "I wouldn't have called it dating, exactly. Less going out to dinner. More end result." More fucking up against every available surface, if we're being technical. The truth is actually more complicated, but this is the version I tell myself.

"Oh . . . yeah . . . okay," Sarah says. "Right." She's trying hard to play along, but I can see I've shocked her. It's been a while since I've met someone this innocent. I would bet good money she was a virgin the first time Tommy took her to bed. And that was probably on their wedding night.

We continue to stroll through the racks for a few minutes. Sarah finds a sweater to add to her dress, but I don't see anything interesting enough to warrant the lifting of a hanger.

"Any word on your cousin?" Sarah asks, as I'm turning to leave.

"No, not much. Doesn't Tommy talk about it?"

Sarah shakes her head. "Not really. He keeps things pretty close to the vest." That doesn't sound like the Tommy I remember. She pauses, looks away. "When it comes to Allegra, at least."

"Oh."

"I know he still loves her," she says, her voice barely a whisper, forcing me to move closer to hear. "I know he'll always love her more than he loves me." When she looks at me, her eyes are tear-bright and broken.

This is where a better person would tell her a gentle lie. Say *no, he doesn't love her anymore . . . you're everything to him . . . Allegra was a long time ago.* But this is me we're talking about, and I've never been mistaken for a better person. Not even once.

Sophia

(b. 1956, d. 1976)

The water was colder than she expected. The night air was mild, scented with river grass and the faint tang of rotten things decaying on the bank. But the water rushing over the top of her bare foot was frigid. She'd planned on wading in slowly, but now thought she'd have to simply plunge in. She wasn't sure she could brave the cold by inches.

In contrast to the water, the tears on her face were warm, salty against her lips. She wondered if Yates had noticed yet that she was gone. She hoped he was worried. She hoped he spent the night traipsing through fields, calling her name, his voice ragged and worn out come morning. She entertained a romantic vision of him weeping over her pale, waterlogged body. She hoped, when all was said and done, that he suffered.

All her life, from the first moment she could actually remember being alive, he had been there. For so long just the outline of a boy, one she was always trying to catch. Their parents would laugh, talk about how much she idealized Jane, when all the while it was Yates she really wanted. He mesmerized her with his smile, his gaze, his handsome face. She lived for the moments when she earned his undivided attention.

And for a while, he had actually been hers. Jane gone. Their parents dead in a car crash, buried in the tiny family plot beside the house. Yates and baby Penelope her sun and moon. Her only family in the world. And they were enough. More than enough. Yates thought so, too, at least at first. She knew he did, could remember the exact look on his face when he'd bring the baby in to snuggle between them on cold winter mornings, his hands tangling in her hair across Penelope's sleeping body.

But now he had a real wife and his own beautiful, dark-haired daughters. He didn't need Sophia anymore. He had a whole house full of girls who worshipped him. She'd told him so, in another one of their one-sided fights—she smashing dishes and screaming curses while he spoke in that calm, deep voice she usually loved. He'd denied it, claimed he loved her as much as he loved Lillian, as much as he loved Penelope and Eleanor and Camilla. As much as he'd ever loved Jane. And it may have even been true. But Sophia didn't want to share. She'd rather have nothing than some tiny, pathetic sliver of him. She wouldn't live on the sidelines. At least dead, she would be the one he mourned, the one he'd always wonder if he might've been able to save. She would have a spot all her own.

She plunged forward into the river. The current was strong, sucked her into the mud-clogged depths as easily as a slender branch, arms flailing, feet swept out from underneath her. She had only a single moment of blind panic . . . *wait . . . WAIT!* . . . his name a wet scream in her throat, before the dark water closed over her head.

Then

"Laney-girl, get down here!" my granddad's voice boomed. He didn't sound upset, but I still worried I'd done something wrong. Maybe he'd gotten the credit card bill. I'd waited a week after Allegra told me about the cards before I got up the nerve to use one of them. And then I couldn't stop, my finger clicking, adding clothes to my shopping cart like a crack addict getting her fix. Spent over a thousand dollars in less than an hour . . . clothes, makeup, jewelry. All the things I'd ever wanted and never had. When the first shipment of boxes showed up and Charlie stacked them outside my bedroom door, I was so sick to my stomach I had to go lie down. But no one ever said a word beyond Granddad commenting he liked a top I wore one day and Allegra rolling her eyes and muttering *fucking finally* when she saw me in my new clothes.

"What?" I called, racing down the main staircase. Already my stomach was braced for a fight, my mind rattling with arguments in my defense.

Granddad waited at the bottom of the stairs, holding a large box wrapped in shiny silver paper, an elaborate black bow on top. He smiled up at me as I came to a stop a few steps above him. "Know your birthday isn't for a couple of days yet, but wanted to get you this. I'm a big believer in spoiling." He winked at me when I didn't move. "Come on, girl, get on down here."

I couldn't remember the last time anyone bought me a present. With my mother birthdays usually consisted of a card from the kiosk on the corner and a carry-out pizza if we could afford it. A couple of years she didn't remember at all. I sat down on the bottom step, and Granddad put the box on my lap. He was grinning like he'd won the lottery; he looked so excited I worried he might rip the paper off himself before I could do the job.

"Pretty bow," I said, fingering the silky ribbon.

"Your gran helped with that part," Granddad said. "I'm not much use at girlie stuff." He smoothed a hand over my hair. "Go on, then," he said, voice gentle. "Open it up, honey."

I kept my eyes on my task as I unwrapped the box, scared if I didn't I might do something stupid, like cry. Once I had the ribbon unwound and the paper taken off, I lifted the lid. Nestled inside was a pair of cowboy boots. Expensive medium-brown leather, hand-tooled aqua roses up the side. I lifted one out, spun it in my hand. The fresh leather scent tickled my nostrils.

"Told ya you needed farm boots," Granddad said. "Saw the pattern and thought they looked like my Laney-girl." He pulled the second boot from the box. "Beautiful and a little unusual. I told 'em the flowers needed to be the same color as your eyes."

I looked up at him. "You had them made?"

He laughed. "Well, hell, girl, course I did. Roanoke girls don't wear boots from the five-and-dime!" He put the boot back in the box, and I replaced the one I held, too. I slid the box off my lap and stood on the step, not quite sure what to do with myself. My granddad solved the problem by pulling me forward, and after an awkward hesitation I wrapped my arms around his neck. He smelled like hay and sweat and a hint of spicy cologne.

"Thank you," I whispered. "I love them."

He gave me a tight squeeze, his broad palms warm against my

back. When he kissed my cheek, his stubble burned. "Happy birthday, girl. I love you."

My actual birthday fell on a Friday, which Allegra said was perfect because we were going to party. But first, she said, we had to get through the family dinner. Sharon grudgingly asked me earlier in the week what I wanted to eat, and Allegra coached me to request brisket and mashed potatoes. When I told Allegra I didn't even know what brisket was, she said to trust her, it was the one meal even Sharon couldn't manage to fuck up too bad.

And the brisket was edible, we could say that at least. Unlike the salmon patties, or ham loaf, or the other variety of horrors Sharon had inflicted upon me since my arrival. After dinner, there were more presents: a bottle of perfume from Gran (which Allegra sniffed and promptly declared old lady), a promise of driving lessons from Granddad, complete with my own car at the end if I could manage to drive without hitting anything, and a cell phone from Allegra, so I could "join the fucking twenty-first century." Granddad swatted her hand for cussing at the dinner table.

Allegra grew quieter as the evening went on, so that by the time they were singing "Happy Birthday" over a German chocolate cake, her lips were barely moving. When dinner was over, Allegra changed into a low-cut top, traded her flip-flops for high heels, and we met on the front porch.

"Gonna be hard to walk down the drive in those," I told her.

"I'll manage," she said, taking off ahead of me.

I stopped. She didn't. "What's your problem?" I called after her.

"If you're coming, you better haul ass!"

I thought about going back to the house, but I didn't want to spend my birthday alone in my room, Gran and Granddad holed up somewhere in the house. It was inevitable Allegra and I would fight eventually, but I was pissed she'd picked today.

I figured Tommy's silver car would be waiting for us, but instead there was a powder-blue minivan idling at the end of the drive. A high-pitched squeal came from the car, the driver flashing the lights at the sight of us. Allegra screamed in return and took off running, wobbling on her high heels. When she reached the car, the driver tumbled out, and they jumped around in a circle, hugging each other. Allegra's friend was tall and stick-thin, with limp blond hair growing in dark at the roots. Her eyes were outlined in black eyeliner, her lips painted a garish red.

"Oh my God, oh my God, oh my God!" Allegra yelled. "I've missed you *so* much!"

"I *know*," the girl she was hugging yelled back. It was a wonder they both weren't deaf already. The girl glanced over at me. "Who's that?" Her eyes raked me, head to toe.

Allegra waved a hand in my direction. "Oh, just my cousin, Lane."

"Hi." The blonde smirked, bumping her shoulder against Allegra's. "I'm Kate."

"We were best friends in school," Allegra told me.

"Yeah, until you dropped out," Kate accused.

"I didn't drop out!"

"Dropped out, home-schooled. Same difference," Kate said, laughing when Allegra gave her the finger.

"Are we going or what?" I asked.

"Get in the back," Allegra said without looking at me. She climbed into the passenger seat. Kate and Allegra talked the entire way into town, both of them pretending I didn't exist. I stared out the side window and tried not to care. I wanted to ask them where we were going, but refused to give them the satisfaction.

I expected a hidden-away bar catering to underage drinkers or someone's old farmhouse, but we drove right into Osage Flats, took a left off Main, and pulled into a parking lot next to the town park. There were still a few families using the playground, which consisted of huge metal slides and a couple of rickety-looking swing sets. Through the deepening twilight, I could see a carousel nestled in the trees on the far side of the park and a small group of people milling around in front of it.

Kate and Allegra got out of the car without a word to me and took off across the grass, their arms intertwined. I followed behind, my heart rate speeding up when I recognized Cooper's golden hair in the distance. I'd seen him a few times since the day we met, and it was always the same: sweaty palms, thundering heart, my eyes meeting his before skittering away, only to bounce right back again five seconds later.

"Hey, happy birthday!" Tommy said when we reached the carousel. He handed me a beer and folded me into a one-armed hug. A small, mousy-haired girl hovered behind him, but Tommy seemed oblivious to her presence, all his attention focused on Allegra.

"Thanks," I said. Allegra was still ignoring me, giggling into Kate's shoulder and batting her eyelashes at anyone who looked in her direction. "Does the carousel work?" I asked Tommy, pointing with the neck of my beer bottle.

"Oh, sure," he said, tearing his eyes away from Allegra. "It's only a nickel a ride. But it shuts down after dark. We'll have to come back sometime during the day."

I found a spot on a blanket someone had laid out in the grass and sat, content to watch the party unfold around me. The only people I knew were Tommy, Cooper, and Allegra, and I didn't have much interest in meeting anyone new. My anger at Allegra buzzed under my skin, and I drank more than I should have, taking whatever was passed to me in outstretched hands and swallowing without question. It was the first time since coming to Roanoke that I felt homesick and alone.

For most of the night, Cooper and I never got within twenty feet of each other. But I knew where he was every second, my awareness of him nothing I could control. I watched Kate flirt with him, stroking his arm and tipping her face up to his, some of her lipstick migrated to her front teeth. I smiled into my beer bottle when he twisted away from her, left her standing there without a backward glance.

The night air was hot and still, fireflies blinking all over the park like tiny beacons. I looked up at the stars, so many more than back in New York, and the world spun. I lay back, closed my eyes, tried to anchor myself to the earth. When someone dropped down beside me, I didn't open my eyes. I felt the brush of skin against my arm. The smell of motor oil and sweat, the cool scent of soap, one too many cigarettes burned my nose.

"Hey, Cooper," I said, voice husky with alcohol and want.

"How drunk are you?" he asked with a little laugh.

"Pretty damn drunk," I said, smiling.

"You're sixteen now, need to learn how to hold your liquor."

"I can handle it," I said. "I'm not a baby."

I turned my head, careful and slow, and opened my eyes. He was lying on his back next to me, looking up at the sky. His profile was flawless, the kind of face that would've been on a movie screen if he'd been born somewhere else, into a different kind of life. He shifted his head to look at me, our eyes meeting in the dark. "Nope," he said. "Definitely not a baby."

His hand brushed against mine, so feather-light it could have been a mistake. I stayed still, prayed he'd do it again. His fingers smoothed over my hand, spreading my fingers, sliding back and forth on the skin between. It felt dirtier and more dangerous than it should have, everything inside me turned hot and liquid. My eyes fluttered closed, my heart beating in my throat.

Allegra's voice cut through the night, screaming and laughing, loud enough my arm jumped. Cooper moved his hand away, sat up, and I did the same, the world shifting back into hazy focus. "What the hell is she doing?" I asked. It was hard for me to form words, my lips numb and my body undone.

"Acting like a psycho," Cooper said, his voice deeper than usual. He lit a cigarette and sucked hard on the filter.

Allegra stood on one of the carousel horses. A white one with a pink mane. She balanced on one foot, her high heels long gone. Tommy stood below her, hands lifted to her hips, whether to keep her from falling or just as an excuse to touch her, I couldn't tell. "I'm queen of this whole town!" Allegra yelled. "I'm everyone's favorite! I'm the best!" She laughed, but her face crumpled. She slid down sideways onto the horse's back, landing on her butt. She wrapped her legs around Tommy's waist, her hands knotted in his hair. I could hear her sobbing, Tommy's voice soothing her as he rocked her body slowly.

Cooper sighed, tapped his ash onto the ground. "You know your family's fucked up, right?" he asked. "Like, seriously screwed."

I thought of my mother, the days she spent curled naked on the bathroom floor, her eyes glazed over. "Yeah," I said. "I know."

Cooper stared at me, reached over and ran the backs of his fingers down my cheek. After he walked away, I could still feel him there, right between my thighs.

The next day Allegra came to my room before breakfast, slid between my sheets with a glass of ice water in her hand. "Here," she said, voice raspy, "drink this. It'll help your hangover."

I pushed her hand away. "You probably need it more than me." She'd ended the night passed out in Tommy's backseat, and I'd dragged her upstairs after he dropped us off.

She curled some of my hair around her finger. "I'm sorry, Lane, really." Her mouth twisted up, a tear trailing down her cheek. "I get stupid sometimes. I can't help it. I'm such a bitch. I don't even like Kate, she's a complete loser."

"Whatever," I said. "It doesn't matter to me." I started to turn my back on her, but she grabbed my shoulder.

"No, wait, *listen,* please. It was hard . . . watching you get the attention at dinner. I know . . . I know . . ." She held up a hand as I started to speak.

"I guess that explains this," I said, voice still tight. I flicked my fingers toward ENVY scratched into the leg of my bedside table.

"I did that before we left for the park," Allegra said. "I know I acted dumb and selfish last night. I've wanted someone here with me forever, and I'm glad it's you. But for a little while yesterday, I really wanted to bash your face in." She wrinkled her nose. "Sorry."

I stared at her and burst out laughing, brought my knees up to my chest and rolled a little side to side. "You are totally nuts."

"I know, right?" She giggled. "Certifiable." She sucked a piece of ice into her mouth and set the glass aside. "Do you forgive me?" she asked, the ice wedge tucked into her cheek.

"Yes," I said, surprised to find I meant it. Already, I couldn't stay angry with her for long.

Allegra smiled at me. She pushed the ice out of her mouth halfway, held it between her teeth, leaned over and ran it across my lips. I opened my mouth, and the ice slipped inside, cold from the glass, warm from her tongue.

"There," she whispered, patting my lips with her fingers. "Now we're sisters again."

"Come on," my granddad said. "I want to show you something." It was still early morning, Gran and Allegra asleep inside the house and Charlie out back taking care of the eggs I'd brought up from the chicken coop. My stomach growled and my new boots were rubbing a raw spot at the back of one ankle, but I heaved out a sigh and followed him around the barn to a low wrought-iron fence surrounding a scraggly patch of grass. "You know what that is?" he asked.

"Um, yeah," I said. "A cemetery. I see it every day."

"Not just any cemetery," Granddad said, unfazed by my sarcasm. He put a hand on the gate but didn't open it. "The Roanokes are buried here." He glanced at me, pointed to a gravestone in the far corner. "Your mama's over there. Thought you might want to go pay your respects."

I took a step back. "She is?" There hadn't been a funeral in New York, and no one had told me what had happened to my mother's body after she'd been whisked from the apartment on a sheet-covered stretcher. I'd never thought to ask.

"Of course she is," Granddad said. "It's not how I wanted her to come home. But at least she's finally back at Roanoke." He took his hand off the gate and cupped my cheek, the scent of iron lingering on his fingers. "And now we have you, Laney-girl. Makes me awful happy seeing your face every morning."

Just as when he'd told me he loved me, his words warmed a space inside of me. But it wasn't a comfortable kind of heat. It burned my stomach and throat like acid I had to expel. I jerked my head away from his hand. "I don't think my mom would like being in there," I said. "She hated this place."

My granddad studied me. "You trying to hurt me?" he asked, as I squirmed under his gaze. I shrugged, kicking at the dirt with the pointed toe of my boot. "That's not like you, Lane. What's the trouble?"

I crossed my arms, kept my head down, remembering all the awful things I'd said to my mother near the end. "You don't even know me."

"I think I do," Granddad said, voice gentle. His warm fingers closed around my chin and pulled my face up until our eyes met. "I don't know how things were between you and your mama, although I've got a pretty good idea. But there is nothing you could ever, *ever* do that would make me stop loving you." He eased his hand away. "You understand?"

I didn't. I had no frame of reference for what he was telling me, no real belief that anyone had ever loved me, let alone that they'd never stop. "What if I kept saying horrible things to you?" I asked. "Unforgivable things?"

Granddad shook his head. "Ain't no such thing. You're a teenage girl, figure ugly's gonna come out of your mouth more often than not. You should've heard some of the things your aunt Eleanor used to say to me. Lord Jesus, that girl had a mouth on her. But if she walked up this driveway today . . ." His eyes took on a wistful sheen, the smile he gave me tinged with sadness. "I'd welcome her back like none of it ever happened."

"What if I broke the law?" I said, plowing on, not knowing how to believe him. Not knowing if I wanted to.

Granddad's gaze was amused now, his eyes dancing. "That's what lawyers are for." He rested one hip against the wrought-iron gate. When I didn't speak, he made a rolling motion with his hand. "Go on, let's hear it all."

I cast around for something that might push him over the edge. "What if I got knocked up?"

Granddad laughed. "Wouldn't be the first time a teenage girl turned up pregnant around here."

"What if I murdered someone?"

"I'd help you bury the body," he said without missing a beat.

A giggle burst out of me, a sound I'd heard a thousand times from other girls but couldn't remember ever having made myself. "What if I ran away?"

"I'd be waiting right here to hug you tight when you decided to come home."

I raised my eyebrows, smirked in his direction. "What if I wrecked your truck?" I hadn't missed the way he babied his truck, always keeping it clean and never letting Charlie drive it.

Granddad pushed away from the gate, threw both hands into the air. "Well now, that right there's a deal breaker. Wreck that truck and it's all over." He reached out and tugged lightly on the end of my ponytail.

Another round of giggles bubbled up, and Granddad smiled, gave an exaggerated sniff of the air. "Is that bacon I smell?" he asked. "Lord knows we'd better hurry up and get in there before Sharon burns it." He winked at me, and we walked back to the house side by side, his arm a welcome weight around my shoulders.

Now

There's a search for Allegra set for 10:00 A.M. in one of the fallow fields close to town. The location makes no sense to me, as if the police simply tacked a map of Osage Flats to a wall and threw darts at it randomly to determine points of interest. I already know it's a waste of time, but it's something to do that makes me feel like I'm doing something. If not bringing me one step closer to finding Allegra, at least proving I haven't given up on her yet.

The day is hot, the sun white and blazing, burning through the stagnant air. There's no good place to park, so I leave my car pulled over on the weedy verge, the driver's side tires resting on the road. The only sound is the buzzing of insects, the hum of grasshoppers in the fields. If you wanted to hurt a woman, this would be as good a place as any, with only the wide, blank sky as witness.

About twenty people show up, and Tommy spreads us out in a line, tells us to walk shoulder to shoulder, eyes on the ground. He looks even more exhausted than the last time I saw him, the shadows under his eyes darkened from lavender to deep purple. "You should get some rest," I tell him. "You look terrible."

"Thanks," he says with a strained smile.

"You know what I mean."

I end up walking next to a tall blond woman. Her body looks young, but her face is a horror show, all pockmarked skin and sunken eyes. "Hey," she says, staring at me. "Aren't you Allegra's cousin?"

"Yes." I look at her more closely, recognize the dyed hair and overzealous use of black eyeliner, her lipstick morphed from red to frosted pink. "Kate?"

"Yeah, Kate Levins. Man, it's been ages."

"Uh-huh." I return my eyes to the ground. "You're still friends with Allegra?"

There's a pause. "Not really. Not for years." When I shade my eyes with a hand and squint at her, she gives me a small smile. A few of her teeth are missing, the rest stained yellow. "We kind of drifted apart."

"Why was that?"

"Oh, you know . . . life. For a long time, I thought it was your fault. After you came to Roanoke, Allegra didn't care much about the rest of us."

"That's not true," I say, but know I'm lying. From the beginning, Allegra clung to me, a manic burr attached to my side. I became a partner in all her teenage crimes. The other Roanoke girl—the only one who could potentially understand. It's only now, looking back at that summer through the long lens of time, that I realize how desperately she needed me to read her clues and how I missed them all.

"I'm not mad," Kate says. "I always knew Allegra and I weren't going to be friends forever. I'm not an idiot. But it was fun while it lasted." She stops to pick up a plastic grocery sack, crumples it in her fist to make sure it's empty before letting the wind take it again. "You know, I always thought someday she'd marry Tommy and have one of those beautiful families you see in magazine ads, and I'd tell my kids, hey, I used to be friends with them." She laughs. "Stupid, right?"

My eyes find Tommy, walking ahead of us. The back of his khaki uniform shirt is drenched with sweat and his shoulders hunch forward. Today he looks older than his years, defeated. "Not so stupid," I say. "You have kids?"

"Yeah, four of 'em."

"Wow, four. Your husband's from around here?"

Kate huffs out a laugh. "No husband."

I remember Kate the night of my sixteenth birthday, the way she hung on Cooper, desperate for his attention, chasing after a boy who made no secret of his disdain for her. It doesn't surprise me at all to find out she's already had four kids. Each one living proof that for at least a single night someone chose her.

"I still can't believe Allegra never married Tommy," she says. "Guy like him wanted me . . . shew, I'd be on that like white on rice. Good job, nice-looking, sweet." She shakes her head. "And the way he followed after her. Good Lord, you'd think she walked on water. Never could do any wrong. Cheated on him, treated him like shit, and poor guy always came back for more."

"She didn't cheat on him," I say. At least not in the way Kate means.

"Well, came pretty damn close then," Kate says. "Disappearing all the time, doing *stuff*."

I'm not going to waste my breath arguing with her. The summer I lived here Allegra might've been a lot of things, but a two-timer wasn't one of them. She was always a one-man woman, God help her. "Tommy loved her," I say.

"Yeah." The way Kate says the word makes clear her opinion on the usefulness of love. We walk a few beats in silence. "And she had that thing, you know, whatever it is makes men stupid over you," Kate says. "Like moths to a flame." Out of the corner of my eye I see her look at me. "You've got it, too."

"I seriously doubt it." Sweat slithers down my neck, staining the top of my T-shirt.

"No, you do. I remember when you moved here. Cooper Sullivan had never had any trouble taking what I offered, but then you showed up and it was like nobody else existed. I could have taped a Free Ride sign to my vagina and he still wouldn't have gone for it."

I laugh, a shocked squawk, and Tommy turns around to glance at me. "I don't know what you're talking about," I say.

Kate gives me a sly once-over. "Sure you do."

We stop talking after that, wilting under the brutal sun. According to Kate, it hasn't rained in Osage Flats in weeks, since long before I returned, and the dust we kick up settles in my throat, a fine gauze of dirt lacing across my tongue. My mouth tastes like dead things, barren and dry.

We walk for hours, but we don't find any evidence Allegra ever came this way. Our searching eyes uncover not a single sign of her.

After the fruitless search, I'm heading back to my car when Tommy jogs up beside me. "You up for a late lunch?" he asks. "Taco Tuesday at The Eat. Cooper usually comes, but he can't make it. He's got a car that has to be fixed by this afternoon."

I ignore the way my stomach flips at the mention of Cooper's name. "Sure. I'll meet you there."

The Eat looks exactly the same as it always has—beer-stained tablecloths and dusty plastic flowers on every table. A string of fairy lights, half of them burned out, rings the front window. Someone's sad idea of romance. Once upon a time this place had a real name, but no one can remember it now. I'm sure there are still a few people around town willing to engage in pointless argument over what it used to be called. For everybody else the giant neon EAT sign outside is good enough.

When I arrive, Tommy's already at a table against the wall, his back to the room where he can watch the entrance. I don't know if that's a cop reflex or if he wants to be able to spot me as soon as I walk in the door.

"Tacos?" I ask, pulling my chair over the scuffed wood floor. "This town's going cosmopolitan on me."

"You know Osage Flats," Tommy says. "Always up on the latest trends."

The waitress approaches our table with a smile for Tommy, made bigger with the liberal application of plum-colored lipstick. Her auburn hair is pulled into a loose bun, stray tendrils sticking to her neck. Her name tag, embroidered on her uniform shirt in dark green thread, reads BRANDI. She eyes me with curiosity and something close to disappointment. "The usual?" she asks.

"Yeah and a Coke," Tommy says.

Brandi glances at me again. "Where's Cooper?"

"He's busy today. Said he'd be here next week."

"Well, tell him I said hi."

"I'll have a taco and a beer," I butt in, not waiting for her to ask.

"It's Taco Tuesday." She says the words slowly, like I'm short a few brain cells.

I look at Tommy for an explanation. "It's buy one, get one free."

"Oh, then two tacos, I guess." I'd rather have two beers, skip the food altogether, but I manage to keep that thought to myself.

"How's it going out at Roanoke?" Tommy asks, once Brandi's left the table.

"It's like being in the Twilight Zone," I tell him. "Like I never left. Which is scary as hell."

Tommy looks down at the table. "I tried to get Allegra to move into town. Thought maybe I'd have a better chance at convincing her to marry me if she wasn't living there. But she wouldn't even consider it." He glances up at me. "She says Roanoke is in her blood."

"It's in all our blood," I say. "Like an infection." My laugh sounds more like a sob, and I drop my eyes, a blush sweeping across my face.

Brandi comes back with our drinks, sloshing a small puddle of Coke across the worn tablecloth as she sets them down. My beer is barely cold, but I don't complain. Tommy slurps down half his Coke before he even unwraps his straw. "Goddamn, I hope this caffeine works fast," he mutters.

"Been working long hours?"

"Yeah. On Allegra's case. And then yesterday, on top of everything else, I had to call Family Services to take custody of some kids. Mom let her new boyfriend use them as punching bags." He rubs at his temples with one hand, thumb and middle finger stretched wide. "I don't get it. How a mother can choose some man over her own children? Yesterday wasn't even terrible in the scheme of things. Some bruises, a black eye. But you wouldn't believe the shit I've seen, Lane. The things mothers let men do to their kids. The things mothers will turn a blind eye to." He shakes his head, blows out a long breath.

It takes work to keep my face impassive, my tone light. "Oh, you might be surprised at what I'd believe."

"Okay, enough," Tommy says, slapping the table with both palms. "I'm depressing myself." He peels the paper off his straw. "You seen Cooper again since the other night?"

I raise my eyebrows at him. "Very subtle. And no, I haven't."

"You oughta talk to him, Lane. After you left, he—"

"Stay out of it, Tommy. It's none of your business."

Tommy's eyes frost over. "The hell it isn't. You're the one who dragged me into it. If he ever found out—"

I hunch forward, lower my voice. "I'm not going to tell him. Are you?"

"Hell, no," Tommy says. "I'd like to keep my best friend and my face intact, too."

"Then stay out of it," I repeat. "Besides, Cooper and I stopped having anything to talk about a long time ago."

Tommy's gaze is sad, like I'm a child who's disappointed him. "If you really believe that, Lane, you're kidding yourself."

I gulp down my beer, eyes on the ceiling. Tommy stirs his Coke with his straw, ice rattling against the glass. I grasp desperately for a change of subject. "Did you find out anything on the receipt I brought in?"

Tommy shakes his head. "Not yet. One of the clerks working that day thought maybe she remembered Allegra, but couldn't provide any details. They have surveillance tape, though. They're pulling it and sending it to us, and we'll go through it, see what we can find."

Brandi returns for a second time with our plates balanced on one arm, so quickly I know the food came straight from a microwave. Four tacos for Tommy, two for me, served with a soupy glop of beans. With one glance I know I'm not going to be able to eat it. It doesn't seem to bother Tommy, who digs in with gusto, his first bite of taco littering his plate with cheese and wilted lettuce.

"I wouldn't get your hopes up, though," he says, "about the receipt. It's probably nothing."

I take a bite of taco. The shell is cold and stale, the meat gummy with tomato paste. I chew and chew until I can manage to swallow without gagging. "I know," I say finally. "But it's worth a shot. I owe her. I can't go back to California and forget about her." I've done that once already.

Tommy's eyes narrow, his brow furrows. "Owe her for what?"

A vision of Allegra, hands clutching mine, her face streaked with tears—*don't leave me don't leave me*—flashes across my mind. I close my eyes. My feelings for Allegra were never complicated. It didn't matter if she acted crazy or made me angry or smothered me with devotion. In my whole life, she was the only person I simply loved. And I left her anyway.

"For everything," I say. My bite of taco sits in my stomach like a piece of jagged glass. For being the one who got away.

Penelope

(b. 1968, d. 1982)

Her hands were shaking with excitement. It took her three tries to get the soft pink lipstick on her mouth without smearing it. She blew out an unsteady exhale, debated pinning her hair up versus leaving it down, long and dark around her shoulders. The only thing she was one hundred percent sure about was the nightgown. White and sheer and innocent-looking. It was too long, dragging along the floor when she walked, but that only made it more romantic.

She'd been working up her nerve for the last week. Ever since he'd kissed her in the kitchen, his strong hand cupping the back of her head. She'd been shocked; who expects their first real kiss to be from their thirty-two-year-old uncle? But she'd kissed back once she'd felt the curl of heat in her belly, his fingers sifting through her hair. It had been so exciting. Forbidden and sexy, like something in one of the romance novels Sharon was always reading. Way better than the sloppy half-kiss she'd gotten from John Perkins on the last day of school.

Uncle Yates had been the one to pull away first, voice rough and breathless. He'd told her they probably shouldn't, even as his lips moved against her neck. But in the end he'd left it up to her, traced the line of her cheekbone with his index finger and told her she had to make the choice. He was her favorite person in the entire world— what choice was there to make?

And tonight was the night. She knew he was down in his study, and Aunt Lillian had gone to bed early with a migraine. Eleanor and Camilla were occupied up in the turret room, giving each other makeovers. They'd invited Penelope to join them, but she'd told them she was too old for that baby stuff. Pissing them off guaranteed they'd leave her alone for the night. Besides, it was true. She was fourteen now. Time to grow up.

She dabbed Love's Baby Soft perfume behind her ears the way she'd seen Aunt Lillian do with her bottle of Chanel. One more deep breath and she slipped out of her bedroom into the dark hallway. She didn't turn on the light, liked the way the moon from the window lit her up, catching on the ends of her hair. Her heart surged, lips and fingertips almost numb with nerves. She didn't bother to lift up the nightgown as she raced down the steps, white cotton swirling around her toes.

Then

"Brake, girl, brake!" my granddad yelled, throwing a hand forward to catch himself against the dashboard of his truck as I slammed my foot down and we shuddered to a stop.

"Sorry," I said. "Oh my God, I'm never going to be able to do this."

My granddad laughed, wiped his brow theatrically. "That was a close one. Thought that fence had seen its last day." He reached over and patted my knee. "Takes practice is all, Laney-girl. You'll get it. Go on now, try again."

Granddad had insisted that I needed to learn to drive a stick shift, said once I had that mastered an automatic would be a cakewalk. But he probably already regretted it as we bucked and stalled out along the old cattle road behind Roanoke. We both might need neck braces by the time we were done.

"Did Allegra have this much trouble?" I asked. Allegra was not yet sixteen, but it turned out everyone in Kansas learned to drive early. Not like in New York City, where half the adult population barely knew how to drive a car.

Granddad shook his head, chuckled low in his throat. "Let's just say there's a reason this truck has a brand-new front end. Girl can't drive to save her damn life. Always in such a hurry to get where she's going, she never keeps her eyes on what's right in front of her. Told her she had to wait a few months before we give it another go. Otherwise, I might have a full-blown heart attack."

I laughed and pressed down too hard on the gas, sending us lurching forward. "Ease up, girl," Granddad said. "You ain't stomping a killer spider. Wanna be gentle with it."

I managed to drive a few miles going progressively faster, switching from first to second, second to third, without stalling out. "I'm doing good!" I crowed. The smile stretching across my face felt unfamiliar to me, like my skin belonged to a different girl.

My granddad looked over at me, grinning. "You sure are. Now eyes on the road, speed demon."

When we reached a gate across the road, Granddad told me to stop, and we both hopped out to open it. "So," he said, as we worked together to pull the gate clear, a small plume of dust boiling up at our feet, "you and Allegra been going into town a lot."

It didn't sound like a question, so I didn't say anything. "You're not in any trouble, Lane," Granddad said. "I know it can get pretty boring out here. You girls need a little excitement." He pointed at me. "Just not too much excitement."

"Yeah," I said, nodding.

"Allegra still seeing that Tommy Kenning?" Granddad tilted his head up to the sky. It seemed like he was always watching the clouds, waiting for rain, which hardly ever arrived.

"I guess," I said. "Yeah."

"He's a good enough kid," Granddad said, as we climbed back into the truck. "Don't know if he's strong enough to handle Allegra, though. She needs someone ain't gonna take her crap."

"He's really nice to her." I felt protective of Tommy for some reason. Maybe his kind eyes, the way he always tried to include me, acted like I'd been at Roanoke all along instead of being a new addition to be regarded with a touch of small-town suspicion.

"I'm sure he is," Granddad said, head angled toward the window, eyes still on the sky. "What about you?"

I inched the truck forward, proud when I didn't grind the gears as I shifted. "What about me?"

"Nuh-uh, don't do that. Don't get smart." It was the first time he'd used his stern voice with me, and although my heart stumbled in my chest, I felt a flash of defiance, too. "You know what I'm talking about."

"I'm not dating anyone," I said. "If that's what you mean." Granddad waited. "I kind of like Cooper Sullivan," I admitted in a begrudging half-whisper, heat racing up my neck into my face. *Like* seemed a weak word for what I felt when I saw Cooper, at once both too childish and not big enough. He hadn't touched me since that night at the park, but plenty of nights I'd touched myself in the heat of my bedroom, pretended my own slick fingers were his.

Granddad cracked out a laugh. "That little pissant? Jesus, girl, you sure know how to pick 'em." He laughed again.

"What's wrong with Cooper?" My hands tightened on the steering wheel. I sat up a little straighter, squared my jaw.

"Don't go getting all het up now. Nothing wrong with the boy. But he's a wild one, from what I hear. It's not entirely his fault, though. He got stuck with a real jackass for a daddy. Man doesn't know anything but beating the tar out of his own wife and kids. I heard Cooper whipped his ass, though, soon as he got big enough." Granddad pointed to the left, indicating we should start heading back to the house. "Shows he's got balls and a backbone. Two good things in a man. Guess you could do worse."

I was quiet the rest of the drive, mulling over what Granddad had said. Cooper never talked much about his family, other than an occasional mention of his younger sister, Holly. What would it have been like to grow up in a house where you had to tiptoe for fear of being hit? Other than the one time she'd tried to choke me, my mother had never hurt me. Not physically. Her hate didn't burn hot;

it was wholly indifferent. There were some days growing up when I'd have a moment of panic, wonder if I even existed because it had been so long since my mother had acknowledged my presence. The only time she paid attention to me was when she was slipping over the edge, scrabbling for someone to save her. But that wasn't passion; it was only desperation. A part of me was jealous of Cooper's injuries, craved the hard slaps and angry fists. The heat that caused such damage.

I pulled up in front of the garage and stopped smooth, letting out a tiny whoop of delight at the achievement. "Good job, Lane," Granddad said. He patted my bare leg, gave my knee a warm squeeze.

"Thanks."

As we walked to the house, the light changed, turning to the pale purple promise of evening. I glanced over at my granddad, and for a split second it didn't even require the work of imagination to picture how he'd looked in that hotel lobby the day Gran first saw him, the moment when she knew he had to be hers. The setting sun silhouetted him, and his eyes glowed, his dark hair lit up in a golden halo. I smiled at him, and he winked, flashed me a quick grin.

"Lord Jesus," he said, tugging on my ponytail, "the Roanokes sure do make some beautiful girls."

I blushed, secretly pleased. I caught movement in an upstairs window, craned my neck and saw Allegra staring down at us. I waved up to her, grinning, still riding the high of my driving lesson. She looked at me with flat eyes, turned away without waving back.

When I went out on the screened porch after dinner, Charlie was sitting on the back steps, one of the hound dogs lying at his feet. "What are you doing?" I asked, sinking down beside him. I knew Allegra didn't like Charlie, but I had no idea why. He wasn't chatty, no one would ever mistake him for friendly, but he'd been kind to me so far.

Charlie reached down and pulled something dark from the dog's belly, flicked it away. "Pulling ticks," he said. "Dogs get covered in 'em." He grabbed another tick between thumb and forefinger. "Secret is to pinch 'em down low. Otherwise, they're liable to explode on ya." The words were barely past his lips when the tick, swollen to the size of a large raisin, burst between his fingers, splattering blood.

"Oh . . . God . . . gross." I groaned. "That's so disgusting." For a second I thought Sharon's beef Stroganoff might make a second appearance on the porch steps.

Charlie glanced over at me. "You got a weak stomach for a farm girl."

"Yeah, well, I've only been a farm girl for a month," I reminded him. "It's gonna take a lot longer than that for me to get used to ticks. Especially the exploding ones."

Charlie grunted, twisted his head away from me, and spat just as my granddad rounded the corner of the house. "You coming?" he asked Charlie. "That horse's shoe ain't gonna fix itself."

Charlie gave my granddad a long look. "Be there when I'm done," he said.

I couldn't get a good read on my granddad's relationship with Charlie. They spent the better part of every day together, and clearly my granddad trusted Charlie with his farm and his family, but they didn't appear to like each other much, a thread of tension underlying all their interactions.

Once my granddad disappeared into the barn, Charlie got back to work on the ticks. I tried not to watch, but my eyes kept wandering in that direction. "Have you worked at Roanoke a long time?" I asked.

"Yup," Charlie said. "Came to work when your granddad was small, maybe four or five. I was sixteen, desperate for a job, and your great-granddad hired me on."

So Charlie had been at Roanoke for almost fifty years. I knew he had a little apartment above the garage, unlike Sharon, who lived in town. No family of his own. "You never thought about leaving?"

Charlie cleared his throat. "Not much." The tips of his ears flushed dark red, but his face stayed expressionless. "Been here so long now, can't imagine anywhere else."

"You said you were there at the hospital the day my mom was born, right?" Somehow I couldn't picture Charlie pacing the halls of a hospital, taking a celebratory cigar from my granddad's outstretched hand.

Charlie shook his head, tossed away another tick. "Roanokes aren't born in hospitals. Not unless something goes wrong. They believe in home births." He tilted his head toward the house behind us. "All of them born right here."

"Really?"

"Really." Plucked. Flicked. Spat. "Probably wouldn't have made it to a hospital with your mama anyway, she came so fast. Like a greased pig flying out of a chute. Your gran barely had time to squawk."

I laughed a little at the image, and Charlie smiled, his teeth tobacco-stained.

"I actually had to help catch your mama. Doctor didn't make it in time." He put a foot down gently on the dog's belly. "Stay still, boy," he said. "Ain't done yet." He turned his head to look at me. "She was a pretty little thing, barely even cried."

I snorted. "Well, she made up for that later."

Charlie gave me a sharp look. "That's your mama you're talking about. Got no idea what trials she went through before you came along. Could be she had good reason for tears. Show her some respect."

I ducked my head, cheeks burning. I thought about walking away, but Charlie kept talking, his voice softer. Maybe his version of an apology. Either way, I wanted to hear this story.

"I remember holding her. She fit in the crook of one arm," he said. "Your gran kept asking, 'Is it a boy? Is it a boy?'" Another tick burst in his fingers, and I lifted my gaze.

"She wanted a boy?"

"Yup. Hoped Eleanor would be one. With your mama she prayed and prayed. By the time Emmeline came along, she was pretty much desperate. Even tried some of those tricks they talk about in books." From the tone of his voice it was clear what he thought of that type of nonsense.

"I guess Granddad was disappointed, too?" My chest ached a little at the idea that for all his love and pride Granddad secretly wished at least one of us had been a boy.

A pause. "No, I wouldn't say that. Your granddad was happy as a clam with all you girls. Didn't care one bit he never had a boy." Charlie shooed the dog away, stood up. "Truth is, don't think he ever wanted one." He walked down the porch steps, wiping his blood-stained fingers on his jeans as he went.

The hamburger stand on Main served two flavors of ice cream, vanilla and chocolate. Both soft-serve and always so close to melting that if you didn't eat fast you'd be left with a bowl of ice cream soup within minutes. A better choice, relatively speaking, was the ice slush, four flavors: orange, cherry, grape, and lime. Allegra always picked cherry because she liked the way it stained her lips red, but I preferred the lime, even though it left me with a green tongue.

"You want anything?" Tommy asked Cooper, pulling his wallet from his back pocket.

"Nah, I'm good," Cooper said. "Unless they've started selling a beer slush I don't know about."

There were a couple of old plastic picnic tables in the parking lot behind the hamburger stand, but there was no shade and even at six o'clock it was too hot to sit.

"Wanna walk over to the park?" Tommy asked, his arm slung around Allegra's shoulders.

Cooper shrugged. "Sure."

"Sounds good to me," I said.

The park was virtually deserted, those empty hours between the afternoon rush of kids and the evening's restless teenagers. We rode the carousel a few times, more for the relief of wind through our sweaty hair than out of any desire to spin around in circles. After the carousel, Tommy and Allegra disappeared into the trees, the sound of her laughter drifting out from between the green branches.

I stood there awkwardly, not sure what to do. I definitely didn't want to hang around with Cooper and listen to Allegra and Tommy have sex. "You ever go down the slides?" I asked him.

Cooper smiled. "Not for a long time. We used to bring wax paper when we were kids, really get up some speed."

"Come on," I said, grabbed his hand before I could overthink it, and pulled him across the park.

My granddad had told me the park slides were original, dating to the 1940s—jagged-edged metal behemoths towering more than twenty feet above the ground. They would never be allowed in a new park. Just looking at them made you think of broken limbs and nasty cuts, old rust flecks buried beneath the skin.

"I'm not sliding down that," Cooper said, pointing at the tallest slide with his cigarette.

"Why not? You too cool?"

"Definitely."

I laughed, handed him my slush. "Well, I'm going."

"Knock yourself out."

I scrambled up the ladder, not realizing how high I was until I got to the top, vertigo hitting as I looked down at the ground. I grasped the railing with both hands. "It's high," I yelled.

"Yeah," Cooper yelled back. "No shit."

I knelt down and touched the metal, warm from the heat of the day but not hot enough to burn me. I swung my legs onto the slide, took a deep breath, and shoved off, hands held above my head. The descent was swift and steep, so fast I didn't have time to slow myself down before I shot off the end of the slide, the back of my head smacking into the metal.

"Oh, fuck," I heard Cooper say. He dropped down next to me on one knee, his hand curving behind my head. "Are you okay? Lane?"

I struggled to breathe, the air knocked out of me, silver starbursts exploding in my peripheral vision. "I'm okay," I wheezed, finally, pushing myself up on my elbows.

Cooper didn't move, still cradling my head. "When I said 'knock yourself out,' I didn't mean literally."

I laughed and then winced. My head ached. My shorts and legs were covered in a layer of dirt, and I was pretty sure I'd scraped the hell out of my back, too. "This is not my finest moment," I told him.

"Oh, I don't know." Cooper rubbed his thumb gently over my neck, and even though it throbbed I didn't want him to stop. "Gracefulness can be overrated."

I shoved at him halfheartedly. "Stop making me laugh. It hurts my head."

"Yeah?"

"Yeah."

"What about this?" He leaned over and pressed his lips against my collarbone, moved to the tender juncture between neck and shoulder, ended right below my ear. "Does this hurt?" he whispered against my skin.

"No," I breathed out as he raised his head to look at me. My neck felt like it was made of Jell-O. If not for his hand cupping the back of my head, it might have fallen off and rolled away.

His eyes shone gold, a sheaf of blond hair drifting across his forehead. I reached out and pushed it back, kept my hand there to pull him forward. He kissed me for real then, there in the dirt at the base of the slide, and my mind flew away, circled up into the summer sky and left only my greedy body behind. Later, when I tried to remember every second, it came to me in fragments. Cigarette and lime. Teeth and tongue. Pleasure and pain.

Now

Allegra finally learned to drive well enough to merit her own car, if the shiny black Range Rover in the garage is any indication. Even in the shade of the garage, the interior is steamy, and my bare legs stick to the leather almost immediately. Besides her room, this is the only other place Allegra has sole dominion. If she was going to leave a clue as to where she is, maybe this car is where she put it. I start with the dash, move on to the doors, the console between the seats, search for anything written on the visors. Nothing. I push the driver's seat back as far as it will go and crouch down in the footwell before crawling over to the passenger side. I crane my neck to look under the seat and see only a few shriveled french fries.

"What're you doing, Lane?" my granddad asks from the open driver's side, and I jolt upward so fast I smack my head on the dashboard. He hisses in a breath through his teeth. "Gotta be careful there, girl."

I'm frozen in place, as if watching from a great distance, as he reaches out, catches a lock of my hair between his fingers. At the very last second I come alive, jerking back just as he gives my hair a gentle pull. My scalp stings, and when I look up, a few long, dark strands dangle from my granddad's grip. He spreads his fingers, and the strands waft away in the humid air.

"What're you up to?" he asks again as I lever myself up to sit on the passenger seat.

"Nothing, really," I hedge, but like when I was a teenager, he waits me out, leaning into the car, arms folded and braced above his head. "I'm checking if Allegra left any sort of message out here. You know how she always—"

"Carves up things she doesn't have any business ruining?" he finishes for me, a smile on his lips.

"Yeah," I say. Of course he wouldn't need a reminder of Allegra's quirk. He's lived with her every single day of her life. He probably has her memorized by now.

"Police already checked her car, Lane."

I shrug. "Can't hurt to give it a second look."

"Find anything?"

"Not yet."

Without asking if I want company, he swings into the driver's seat, puts both hands on the wheel. He gives it an affectionate pat. "She loves this car. Can still barely drive worth a damn, though."

"How many've you had to buy her?" I ask, and my granddad shakes his head. "You don't want to know," he says. I turn my face to the side so he won't be rewarded with my smile.

Neither one of us speaks, and heat snakes under my hair, forces sweat from my pores. "I worried about you, missed you, every second," he says as I'm reaching to open the passenger door and escape. "Every single second you were gone."

I know his warm gaze is a trap, designed to make me feel like the most special girl in the world, but it's still almost impossible to tear my eyes away. "You didn't need to worry," I say, voice tight. "I did fine." I'm having a hard time breathing in this enclosed space, my chest aching with the effort. I have to get out of this car, out of the garage, back into the open air.

When I risk another glance at him, he nods, face somber. "I can see that. Do you want to tell me about it?"

"No," I say. In truth, I don't have many clear memories of the time immediately after I left Roanoke. A Greyhound bus, miles of highway, the first view of Los Angeles—flat and sprawling and cloaked with a dirty blue sky. I spent the first two nights sleeping on the streets, clutching my suitcase like a shield against my body. At the forty-eight-hour mark, I thought about calling my granddad and begging to return to Roanoke. I was working up the courage to do it when a man who ran a shelter for homeless teenagers happened to stop into the McDonald's where I sat hunched over a Diet Coke. He convinced me to give the shelter a shot, and I lived there for a while, then took off again. I had trouble with roots. Still do. Always trying to stay one step ahead of my past, my granddad, Roanoke.

And look how well that turned out.

I haven't talked to Charlie since I've been back, so I climb the rickety steps on the side of the garage and knock on his door. A window air-conditioning unit hums next to me, dripping cold water in a puddle at my feet on the narrow landing.

"Lane," Charlie says, when he opens the door. His smile is brief and shows only a hint of tobacco-stained teeth, but the slight gleam in his eyes tells me he's glad to see me.

"Hi, Charlie."

He steps back, opening the door wide, and I walk inside. I've only been in Charlie's apartment once before. An early September day that burned like July. I don't remember much about it, actually, other than my tears and Charlie giving me a handkerchief from his back pocket to dry them. I never made it past his living room.

He gestures me toward the tiny table in his kitchen. The floor is cracked linoleum, the seams dark with years-old dirt no amount of scrubbing will ever get clean. The whole room is worn, run-down appliances and tired paint. "You should have my granddad fix this place up," I tell him.

Charlie spits into the cup clutched in his hand. "Suits me fine." He pulls out the chair across from me, sits with a slight grunt. His overalls are stained with prairie dust, and he gives his face a quick swipe with his handkerchief. I wonder if it's the same one he loaned me all those years ago.

"I don't have the money I owe you," I tell him.

"That wasn't a loan. It was a gift."

"Blood money?" I ask and feel like shit when Charlie winces, the color draining from his face. As if I have any right to accuse Charlie of wrongdoing. As if I'm any better. I run my thumb along the aluminum edge of the table. "I hope you didn't get in any trouble over giving me the money, back then."

"Nah," Charlie says, leaning back in his chair. "I know how to keep a secret."

"Yeah." My eyes find his. "Me too."

Charlie hooks his thumbs into the straps of his overalls. "Not gonna lie, Lane. Hoped I'd never see you again."

I cough out a laugh. "No offense, Charlie, but I kinda hoped that, too."

"You're here for Allegra, I take it?"

I nod. "Granddad called me."

Charlie unhooks one hand to lift his chaw cup for a spit. "He should've left you well enough alone."

"No," I say, surprising myself. "I'm glad he called. I want to help Allegra if I can."

Charlie sighs. "I don't think there's any helping Allegra. All that's gonna happen is you're gonna end up hurting yourself. Allegra should've gone with you. Would've been better for everyone. Especially her."

"How was she?" I ask. "After I left? All these years? We didn't talk much."

"She was Allegra," Charlie says, the tone of his voice betraying all the complicated emotions between them. "Mouthy, willful, sad. Once that Tommy Kenning got married last year, she wilted a little bit. Like she might've been sorry he got away."

"She never would've married him, though."

"Nope," Charlie agrees. "But maybe she liked knowing the option was there. Like a life raft. Once he tied the knot, it was over. I don't know Tommy all that well, but he seems like the type takes marriage serious."

"He is," I say, remembering Tommy spinning the gold ring on his finger. "So how was she lately, the last few weeks? According to Gran and Granddad, she was the same as always."

Charlie gives my words some thought, his gaze distant. "Nothing jumps out at me," he says finally. "But I'm the last person on earth she'd talk to, so I don't have any details." He snorts out a laugh, ends with a hawk into his cup. "I know you want to do right by Allegra. But make sure you're doing right by yourself, too. This place is no good for you. You shouldn't stay. At least not for long."

I stare at him, so much a part of Roanoke it's impossible to imagine it without him, even though he doesn't carry the family name. "Why'd *you* stay?" I ask.

"Penance." He keeps his eyes on the cup as he speaks. "For a wrong I did someone a long time ago. I stayed and did what I could to help you girls." His hand tightens around the cup. "I don't expect you to forgive me, Lane. I know that's too much to ask. But I did as much as I was able. It still wasn't enough, but I tried."

"I know that, Charlie," I say. "And for what it's worth, I don't expect to be forgiven either."

I don't know if dinners at Roanoke have become less formal in the years since I've been gone or if it's Allegra's disappearance that's caused the lack of gathering around the dining table. Whatever the reason,

I've been back at Roanoke for more than a week before Gran corners me in the upstairs hall and tells me dinner will be served at six o'clock. It's clear she expects me to attend. It shocks me a little that she wants us all gathered in one spot. I can't imagine anything good will come of it.

I'm the first to arrive, and I stand in the doorway while Sharon brings in platters from the kitchen. Her back tenses at the sight of me, but she doesn't make eye contact. I could offer my help to save her from making multiple trips, but I don't. "It looks appetizing, as always," I tell her, then hate myself for being childish.

After she's gone, I take a plate and scoop up some mayo-heavy potato salad and a piece of withered chicken. I skip the orange Jell-O salad studded with shredded carrots and pineapple. I told Jeff once about the endless variety of Jell-O salads served in the Midwest, but from the way he laughed it was clear he thought I was joking. Green Jell-O embedded with chunks of canned pear wasn't part of Jeff's worldview.

Gran arrives as I'm sitting down in my old spot, and Granddad walks in last like always, making an entrance.

"Laney-girl," he says. "I sure do love seeing you at this table again."

I keep my eyes on my plate, cutting my chicken into tiny, manageable bites. "I don't know how she can ruin chicken," I say. "It's like she's doing it on purpose. Even I can cook chicken."

No one answers me. Allegra's absence looms over the table, like she's hovering above us, taking up more space than she ever did actually sitting here. Every time I raise my eyes, all I can see is her empty chair.

"Tell us about California," Gran says. "Allegra said that's where you were living." Obviously Granddad has thrown it to Gran to try to find out more about my time away from Roanoke. Gran looks as thrilled with the assignment as I suspect I do.

"Not much to tell. It's California. Ocean, sunshine, traffic. I wasn't hanging out with the A-listers or anything."

Granddad and Gran exchange a look. "And you were married?" Gran asks, taking a dainty bite of potato salad.

"Briefly."

"No children, I take it?"

Something rolls over in my stomach. "Nope. Guess Allegra and I are the end of the line for Roanoke girls."

My granddad's gaze falls away. Gran sips her water. The room is very quiet, so quiet I can hear the grandfather clock ticking from the front of the house. So quiet I can't stand it.

I drop my fork with a clatter. I'm never going to be able to eat anything anyway. "How did things work around here after I left? Did you three all share a bed? Or was there a schedule? Tuesdays and Thursdays with Gran? Monday, Wednesday, Friday with Allegra? Or was it random? Did you draw straws?"

"Lane," Granddad says.

"What?" I turn to him with wide eyes, my voice falsely innocent. "It's only us here. Can't we talk about it?"

"You're ruining my dinner, Lane," Gran says, calm as ever.

"Oh, so it's okay that it happens, right?" I say. "But talking about it, that's crossing the line."

The only answer is the scrape of forks against china, that goddamn clock ticking in the hall. My hands are trembling in my lap, and I feel Allegra rising up in my throat, wanting to burst out. She deserves to have someone speak for her when she's not here to speak for herself. "How about Allegra?" I ask. "Is she an appropriate topic? What does everyone think happened to her?"

My granddad lifts his eyes to mine, fork filled with food halfway to his mouth. "I have no earthly idea."

I swing my gaze away from him, toward Gran. "What about you? Any theories?"

Gran wipes the corner of her mouth with her napkin, sets it carefully beside her plate. "I think she ran away. Same as her mother, same as her aunt." She pins me with her cool blue gaze. "Same as you."

I nod. "Well, for starters, I don't think what I did can actually be called running away since you all knew I was leaving. Second, Allegra's twenty-six years old. She's kind of beyond the 'running away' stage." I make overly dramatic air quotes to illustrate my point. "Third, that's a lot of girls bolting for the door around here over the years." I stare back at Gran. "That doesn't give you any pause?"

"You all make your own decisions," Gran says. "It's got nothing to do with me."

I laugh, the sound echoing wildly in the cave of a room. "Oh, wait, you're being serious?" I ask, when my laughter fades away. "Sorry, I assumed that was your attempt at a bad joke."

"Stop it now, Lane," Granddad says, the same stern voice he used on me when I sassed him as a teenager. "That's enough."

Rage boils up from the pit of my stomach, mixing with outrage in my throat. "It's not enough!" I say, my voice loud, just this side of yelling. I push back from the table, chair scraping against the floor. My knee hits the table leg and my glass falls over, water seeping across wood. "Allegra is gone. She's gone! And both of you are sitting here like everything is normal! Like this whole place isn't *fucked*!"

My heart feels close to bursting, tears prickling the backs of my eyes. I brace myself for some kind of reaction, a slap maybe, or a *get out of our house*, but Gran simply places her napkin back into her lap, irons it flat with her hand. "There's no need to be vulgar," she says.

Granddad puts his elbows on the table, lowers his head into his hands. "Nothing around here is right without her," he says, voice muffled. "Without Allegra."

"News flash," I tell him. "Nothing around here has ever been right."

After dinner, I drive into town and pick up a six-pack of beer at the tiny grocery store. Most of the shelves are only half-filled, as if this is a third-world country instead of America's heartland. I find the lack of choice somehow comforting. The flickering fluorescent lights snap and buzz overhead, competing with the static twang of a country song playing from a small radio up front.

In the single checkout line the cashier stares at me with eyes as dull and worn as old pennies. Her bottle-black hair shows at least three inches of nondescript brown at the roots, the ends crunchy with cheap hairspray. "You a Roanoke?" she asks.

"Yeah," I say and wish it weren't true.

"Huh," she grunts, apparently all she has to say on the subject, which is a relief.

The interior of my car is already hot when I emerge, even though the sun is close to setting. I've been trying to ignore the red gas light glowing on my dash, but I'll have to face it—him—sometime. There's still only one place to go in Osage Flats if you need gas. A single filling station, situated at the end of Main, right before it becomes County Road 7. A metal sign, riddled with BB gun holes, hangs from a pole out front. SULLIVAN'S. The big garage bay door is open, and a couple of cars are parked inside, their guts spilled out onto the oily floor. I slide my car up next to the rusty pumps, probably the last two in America not yet replaced with a newer model. They both list slightly, like magnets repelling each other. The white-on-black numbers flip over with tiny clicks as I fill my tank.

Once my tank is full, I pick my way across the torn and rumpled concrete, thick weeds poking through every crack. A large black Lab resting near the garage entrance watches me without moving, his tail beating a random greeting against the ground.

I step past the dog into the garage bay. It takes my eyes a moment to adjust to the gloom. Other than the two mutilated cars, the garage is empty. I cross to the tiny, windowless office and poke my head inside. It's like sticking my head into an oven; the heat makes my eyes water, stings the tender lining of my nose. A stack of worn tires leans drunkenly against the wall, and various car entrails are scattered across the grease-stained floor. The only sound comes from a small metal fan, each blade coated in dust, whirring in the corner. The remains of someone's long-ago breakfast, a partially eaten doughnut and a Styrofoam cup of coffee, litter the surface of a card table with a folded-over newspaper wedged under one rickety leg.

"Hey, Lane," Cooper says from behind me. I turn, and he's leaning against the front counter, wiping his hands on a stained rag. We stare at each other, and the years fall away. He could be eighteen again, in his jeans and dirty white T-shirt, the boy I used to know.

I clear my throat, hold up my crumpled bills. "I owe you for gas."

He nods, points at my face. "How'd you get the sunburn?"

I touch my nose with my fingertips, wincing at the throb of tender skin. "Oh. I went out on the search for Allegra a couple of days ago."

Cooper clicks his tongue between his teeth. "Waste of time," he says.

"It can't hurt."

"Can't help, either."

"I don't see why not," I say, already feeling my blood pressure rise. I should have risked running out of gas. "It's better than sitting around doing nothing."

"Doubtful. What are you now, some kind of half-assed Nancy Drew?"

"For your information, I wasn't the only one out there. Ran into your old friend Kate Levins." I smirk at him. "She had some interesting things to say about you."

Cooper tucks the rag into his back pocket, blows out a dismissive breath. "I'm surprised she could talk around her meth pipe."

"Yeah? From what Kate said, there was a time you two were pretty close."

"We fucked once or twice, back when we were kids," he says. "Is that what you're getting at?"

"I'm not getting at anything," I say. "Poor Kate was another notch in your belt, huh?"

Cooper smiles, but his jaw is tight. "I never was quite the manwhore you wanted me to be, Lane. Sorry to disappoint you."

My heart trips against my rib cage. "Are we engaging in revisionist history now?"

Cooper glances away, rakes his hair off his forehead. "No. Just saying it was easier for you if I was a bastard, so you made me into one anyway."

"Oh, I think you did a pretty decent job being a bastard all on your own. You didn't need any help from me."

"That's how you want to play this?" Cooper shakes his head. "We both know I acted exactly the way you wanted me to, Lane. I was always dancing to your tune."

I toss my money down on the counter and walk out, pull away in a screech of tires. A few miles outside of town I jerk to a stop on the side of the road, slam my hands into the steering wheel, and scream, so loud and long my throat burns when I'm done, like something's clawing for a way out. I soothe the ache with a beer and then a second and a third, choking a little in my haste. I wipe tears from my cheeks with the palm of my hand, trying to forget who I am and where I came from. Trying to forget what it means to be me.

Back at Roanoke, I plummet into sleep, my thoughts black and tangled. I dream of the Roanoke girls, lost and broken. Staring eyes and crumpled bodies. Jane. Sophia. Penelope. Eleanor. Camilla. Emmeline. Allegra. They are calling for me, begging me to help them. I search and search, but never find a single one.

Eleanor

(b. 1970, left Roanoke 1989)

I t took her an hour, all the hot water, and almost a whole bar of soap to scrub Charlie off. The worst part wasn't the memory of his hands on her breasts, his breathy grunts, the stupid, scrunched-up face he made when he came across her belly. The worst part was how easily he gave in. She'd had such faith in him. In the Charlie who taught her how to shoe a horse and skip rocks in the pond. The Charlie who let her ride next to him on the tractor all afternoon and never asked a single question, somehow understood when she needed to get away. She'd been utterly confident when she'd told her dad it would never work. Charlie would never do it. But her dad had only grinned, quick and sharp, his fingers tracing lazy patterns on her bare back. "He'll do it," he'd said. "Because he's not perfect, no matter what you think. He's only a man. And you're irresistible." And then he'd proven it to her in the exact same way he'd been doing since she was fourteen.

It turned out he was right. Of course he was. If there was one thing her father knew well, it was man's baser appetites. At first, Charlie had looked at her like she was on fire, backed away, flush up against the wall of the barn when she yanked her top over her head, and Eleanor's heart had soared. He *was* different, wasn't going to let her down like everyone she'd counted on before him. But within seconds she could see the want slinking into his eyes, his protests not quite as strong as his reaching hands. Mouth saying, *no, Eleanor, honey, no,* but what was below his belt saying something else entirely. And her heart had broken. Flown right out of her chest in a thousand splintered pieces. Because, in the end, Charlie was the same as everyone else. Weak and dirty. A bitter, brutal disappointment.

They'd ensured Charlie would never talk. Would never breathe a word about what went on out at Roanoke. Because she'd made him part of it, with naked skin and thrusting hips and ten minutes he could never take back. Charlie was ruined now. And so was she.

Then

For the most part, Allegra and I were able to avoid farm chores. I still woke up early and helped Granddad with the animals, but afterward I'd roll back into bed and sleep until Allegra stumbled in around ten with mugs of coffee, one of the few decent things Sharon could manage to make.

But today Granddad told us we had to help stack hay in the barn. "Oh my *God!*" Allegra moaned. "That's like pure *torture!*" She threw herself onto the couch.

"Stop your drama, girl," Granddad said, but he was smiling. He pointed at me. "You girls go put on something you don't mind getting dirty and meet me outside."

"*Dirty* means covered in sweat and animal crap," Allegra told me as we dragged ourselves upstairs. It was already well over ninety degrees, the day clear and sizzling with heat.

Granddad opened both sides of the barn, but no cross breeze blew, the air still and soupy. Within minutes, I was soaked with sweat, bits of hay sticking to any exposed skin. We settled into a rhythm: Allegra heaved a bale of hay to Granddad, who tossed it up to me where I stood on the ladder, and I pushed it over the edge into the hayloft above. "Once we get 'em all up there, you girls need to stack 'em against the wall. Neat. Not just ass over teakettle like last time. You hear?" he said, looking at Allegra.

"I hear." She sighed. "At least I have Lane to help now." She paused to wipe sweat off her face with her gloved hand. "Where the hell is Charlie anyhow? Isn't this like his *job*?"

"Day off," Granddad said. He gave a grunt as he tossed me the hay bale. I caught it, but had to steady myself against the ladder with one hip when it threw me off-balance. "Whoa, Laney-girl," Granddad said, his hand grasping me behind the knee. "You all right?"

"Yeah, I'm fine."

"Seems like Charlie should be here, is all," Allegra continued. "Pretty convenient day to go missing."

"He didn't go missing. Man's entitled to a day off once in a while."

"I don't see why," Allegra said. "We basically pay for his whole life."

"Mind your own business, girl," Granddad said, in the tone that meant he was done with her bullshit. "Last I heard, you weren't in charge around here."

Allegra huffed, but kept her mouth shut.

"Why don't you like Charlie?" I asked her.

" 'Cause he's a creeper." Allegra gave an exaggerated shudder. "And nosy as hell."

"I don't even know what a creeper is," Granddad said with a laugh. "But I'm pretty sure Charlie isn't one."

I turned and pushed a hay bale into the loft. "You don't act like you like him, either," I told my granddad. When I turned, he was looking at Allegra, something swift and unreadable passing between them.

"That's not true," my granddad said, easy, and it was almost enough to make me think I'd imagined the look.

"Seems true," I muttered, annoyed at being left out of something, some Roanoke past I wasn't a part of.

"Well, I'm his boss. He's my employee. Hard to be friends, really.

It's enough he does what I say, works hard. Doesn't need to be more than that." Allegra had her head down, working on dragging a hay bale in Granddad's direction. "Why don't you girls cut on out of here?" Granddad said. "You've done enough for one day."

"I thought we had to stack them in the hayloft," I reminded him.

"Nah. You shown Lane the swimming hole yet?" he asked Allegra.

"No." She still wasn't looking at either of us.

"What are you waiting for, girl? Go on, you two, get out of here. Go have some fun."

Turned out the swimming hole wasn't in reasonable walking distance, tucked away on the back-side of what Granddad considered "Roanoke proper," right before the fences ended and acres upon acres of fallow fields began. I drove Granddad's truck, bouncing over ruts while Granddad's warning that the truck better come back exactly as it'd left rolled around inside my head.

"What do you think he'll do if I wreck it?" I asked, jaw clacking after another hard bump.

"Kill you," Allegra said. "Jesus fucking Christ, do you have to hit *every* rut?"

"I can't see them! The grass is too high."

"There! Right there!" Allegra screeched. "Stop!"

We climbed out of the truck, dragging towels and a small cooler from the bed. Sharon had offered to make us lunch, complete with a sour look on her face, but Allegra had rolled her eyes, said we'd handle it. "At least then we know it'll be edible," she'd said in a voice designed to carry.

I expected the swimming hole to be something closer to its name. A small, muddy hole in the ground. But it was big and the water looked surprisingly clear. It was so quiet out on the prairie I imagined I could hear the grass baking in the sun.

Back at Roanoke, I'd told Allegra I didn't own a swimsuit. It wasn't one of the many purchases I'd made since moving in. "We don't wear swimsuits, stupid," she'd said. "Why bother?" And now, out here with only the wind and sun and sky for miles, I saw her point.

"Strip it," Allegra said, pointing to my shorts and tank top. "We're going in!"

I pulled my tank top off over my head, unclasped my bra and threw it aside. "Is it cold?"

"I fucking hope so!" Allegra kicked off her shorts and underwear and ran for the water.

I followed right on her heels, screaming as I jumped. The water was more lukewarm than cold, but still felt amazing against my sweaty, itchy skin. I came up spouting, Allegra treading water next to me. We played like children, even though we were on the cusp of growing up, freed because there was no one watching us. We found a fat bullfrog in the mud and tossed rocks to watch him jump. We dunked each other and played endless games of Marco Polo, then ate the peanut butter and jelly sandwiches and pretzels we'd packed earlier, washing them down with a couple of beers we'd snagged from the fridge when Sharon's back was turned.

"I'm going to be so fried," Allegra said, pressing her fingers into her shoulder.

"Me too."

Allegra glanced over at me, set her beer down in the grass, and stuck her chest out. "I think my boobs are bigger than yours. A little."

I looked down, then over at her. "Maybe."

"But seriously, though, isn't it weird how much we look alike? I mean, head to toe? I bet if you blindfolded Tommy and Cooper and had them feel us up when we were naked, they wouldn't be able to tell us apart."

I choked on my beer, foam burning my nose. "Cooper and I have only kissed, so it would be kind of an unfair test for him."

"But one I'm sure he'd enjoy," Allegra said, wiggling her eyebrows. She leaned back on her elbows, not shy at all about flaunting her naked body. "Did it make you all tingly inside when he kissed you?" she asked.

"Pretty much." I tried not to grin and failed.

"Oh my God, I love that feeling," Allegra said. "Like your heart's about to beat out of your chest and you want him naked and smashed up against you." She lay back with a sigh, stretched her arms above her.

I turned my head away, watched the wind ripple across the surface of the water. I knew exactly what feeling she was talking about, the one I got when Cooper touched me. The one that made me realize my body was really in control and, in the end, I would do whatever it demanded of me.

"Wanna know a secret?" Allegra asked, her voice a whisper only slightly louder than the breeze. She was still lying on the ground, her eyes closed.

"Sure."

"Even if it's the worst secret in the world? Even if it's terrible?" Her eyes opened, found mine across the small space between us.

"What? You actually love Sharon's cooking?"

She didn't smile, not even a slight curve of her lips. "Actually, it's the best and worst secret. Both at the same time."

"I have no idea what you're talking about."

Allegra nodded. Her eyes looked sad and very old. Older than Gran, older than the world. "It's the secret of all the Roanoke girls," she said. "It's what makes us special." I noticed she was pinching herself, the tender skin of her forearm sacrificed between her nails.

I reached over and touched her hand, pried her fingers apart. "Stop," I said, as gently as I could. Like I was talking to one of the horses when they were acting skittish. "Tell me."

She looked at me, and I waited, tried not to breathe. I could hear the blood swooshing through my head, the rapid pulse of my heart.

Allegra opened her mouth, and I tensed. She sat up, my hand falling away from her arm. When she smiled at me, sudden and wide, it didn't reach her eyes. "Last one in is a rotten egg!" she yelled right in my face, making me jump. I watched her run away from me, her long legs bicycling against the sky before she dropped into the water.

I got up and stood on the edge of the swimming hole. "What was that?" I called. "I thought you had a secret."

Allegra laughed. "I do. You're a rotten egg. Now get back in here!"

"Allegra . . ."

She dove, her body a pale arrow beneath the surface. I hesitated and then dove after her, the water green and sparkling against my closed eyelids. We stayed until almost dinnertime, ended the day floating on our backs and watching stray white clouds skim across the sky.

For better or worse, Roanoke was a house you could get lost in. There were days I'd lose track of Allegra or my granddad or Gran for hours at a time, like the house had swallowed them up and I wouldn't see them again until it was ready to spit them back out. But it worked to my advantage also, when I wanted to be alone. There was always a nook or cranny, a whole tucked-away room, where I could retreat if I needed the relief of quiet. Sometimes Allegra disappeared at night, took off alone with Tommy or vanished after dinner not to be seen until morning, when she would shrug off my questions about where she'd been. On those nights I usually curled up with a bowl of popcorn and a movie in the living room, or sat out on the screened porch and watched the fireflies come out, listened to the sounds of the country: cicadas and coyotes, owls and distant train whistles. I didn't mind those nights alone, Gran and Granddad hidden somewhere inside the big house. Sometimes I even slept on the old wicker couch on the screened porch, woke in the morning with a stiff neck and cramped legs.

Tonight I drifted downstairs after dark, Allegra gone who knows where, to do who knows what. I was too restless for a movie, and my bedroom was too hot for sleeping. I settled onto the couch on the screened porch, tied my hair up on my head, hoping for some relief from the heat. The backyard was dark, the moon only a sliver in the sky. My heart tripped in my chest when I saw something move, a black smudge against the blacker background.

"Hey, Lane," Cooper said from the darkness, his drawl more pronounced, somehow, when I couldn't see him. "Want some company?"

I sucked in a breath, stood up and pushed open the door to the screened porch. "What are you doing all the way out here?" I asked.

Cooper climbed the steps to the porch. He let his hand linger at my waist as he moved past me. "I hadn't seen you in a few days," he said. "Figured I'd visit."

"Tommy's been working nights a lot," I said, motioning him to the couch. Trying like hell to pretend this was a normal occurrence and my heart wasn't flipping and flopping inside my chest like a hooked fish. "And Granddad won't let me drive the truck into town yet. We've been kind of stranded."

"Where's Allegra?"

"Who knows? Maybe with Tommy?"

Cooper shook his head. "He's working tonight."

"Oh, well then, I don't know." I sat down on the couch sideways, facing him. He smiled at me, tucked a stray strand of hair behind my ear. I waited for him to kiss me, but he reached behind him and pulled a flask from his back pocket instead. "Want some?"

"What is it?"

"Vodka."

"Sure." He passed me the flask, and I unscrewed the lid and took a swallow. It burned on the way down, and my stomach boiled when the liquor reached its destination. Cooper took his own swallow, set the flask on the floor at our feet.

"What've you been up to?" he asked me. "How's your head?"

I blushed and was glad of the darkness. "It's fine. That was days ago."

"I know, but you conked the hell out of it."

"It's not funny," I said, when I saw the flash of his teeth.

"It's a little funny," he said, "now that it's over and you're okay." He held up his hands for protection when I leaned over to swat at him.

"Yesterday Allegra and I went to the swimming hole," I told him. "You ever been there?"

He nodded. "Once or twice. Not for a few years. The weeds still grab your ankles while you're swimming?"

I laughed. "A little bit, but it didn't bother me." Without permission, my mind turned to Allegra and the secret she'd almost told me, the one she swore later had been only a joke.

"What?" Cooper asked, giving my toe a tweak where it rested next to his thigh.

"Nothing, I just . . ." I reached down and grabbed the vodka, took another big gulp. "You said my family was fucked up."

Cooper ran a hand through his hair. "Yeah, well, all families are fucked up."

"No, but . . . you meant it when you said it about mine."

He looked at me, rested his hand on my bare ankle. "Yeah, I meant it."

"But what is it? What makes us so messed up?"

Cooper shook his head. "I can't answer that for you, Lane. I don't know. But I do know that Allegra . . . I know you love her, but she isn't right."

"I'm part of this family," I whispered. "My mom was, too. Which means I'm probably as fucked up as the rest of them."

There was a long pause, so long I thought he might not speak at all. "My dad used to beat the shit out of me. My mom and sister, too. For anything, for nothing." He leaned to the side and lifted the edge of his T-shirt, took my hand and ran my fingers along his warm skin. "Feel that?"

"Yeah," I breathed, the feathery scrape of scar tissue under my fingers.

"Cigarette burns," he said. "That was the last time he ever touched any of us. About a year ago. The next time he tried, I beat him until he couldn't stand up, blood fucking everywhere." He dropped his shirt, but I didn't move my hand away. "My mom and sister finally pulled me off him, but I wanted to keep going." His eyes glowed in the faint moonlight. "I wanted to kill him."

"Cooper . . ."

"We're all fucked up, Lane, one way or another. It's only a matter of degree."

I didn't hesitate, leaned over and pulled him on top of me, hands working under his shirt, lifting it up and away. His mouth was hot and wet against mine. His tongue tasted of the bitter sting of alcohol. I spread my legs, made room for his body between them. His weight pressed me into the couch, and I buried my face in his neck to muffle my moans as we rocked against each other.

All my life, the advice I'd received about sex was simple: *Don't. Don't let a boy take advantage. Don't let him touch you. Don't give it away. Don't be a slut. Don't. Don't. Don't.* Back in New York, there'd been one boy I'd fooled around with a few times after school. Nothing major, just kissing, one fumbling foray under my shirt. I hadn't even liked him much, had been curious more than anything. Testing the limits of my own boldness. But he always backed off before we went too far, more scared than I was of what came next.

But unlike that other boy, when his moment came Cooper didn't falter or back away. He didn't feel guilt for claiming something that did not belong to him. He took it without asking, as though it was meant for him all along, and I was glad to give it up—to finally be rid of the burden of deciding what kind of girl I would become.

Now

Leaving California, I had a vague hope that I would roll into Kansas and Allegra would show up a few days later, laughing at everyone's worry. We'd all chastise her, she'd give a lame apology, and I'd be back in L.A. in less than a week. That's not the way it's worked out, of course. And now I can't go back until I know what's happened to her. I wait until nine o'clock California time, a respectable hour for a Saturday morning, to make the call.

The phone's picked up after three rings, Jeff's perky new wife on the other end.

"Hi, Maggie," I say. "It's Lane. Can I talk to Jeff for a minute?"

She pauses, sets the phone down with a clunk. I hear the murmur of their voices. I haven't called Jeff in over a year, not since I moved into a smaller, cheaper apartment and needed to know if he wanted his old armchair. He didn't.

"Hello, Lane," Jeff says, when he comes to the phone. "What's up?" His voice is brisk, not rude but not friendly, either. It's hard for me to fathom we once slept in the same bed, saw each other naked, whispered together in the dark. Hearing his voice now brings only a tired sadness. When I first met Jeff—ten years older, safe, and respectable—he felt like salvation, a way to stop running from one crappy job, one run-down apartment, to the next. Except marrying him was just another kind of running, a fact I was too stupid to figure out until later.

"Sorry to bother you. Apologize to Maggie for me." I've met Maggie only once; she's a streamlined brunette whose good looks owe more to the magic of money and makeup than to actual beauty. But there is no denying she's a better match for Jeff. Hell, anyone would be.

"Yeah, okay," Jeff says. "What is it?"

"Listen, I had to leave L.A. in a hurry. I thought I'd be back by now, but I'm kind of stuck here."

"Where's here?"

I take a deep breath. Jeff knows only the vaguest outlines of my time in Kansas, my mother's family. I don't think I ever said the names Roanoke or Allegra to him. "Kansas. I have a cousin who's in some trouble."

I can hear Jeff processing the information, probably deciding whether it's worth it to say something shitty about all the secrets I keep. In the end, he's more mature than I would be in his place. "What do you need?"

"I need to pay my rent for next month. Could you cover it and I'll pay you when I get back to L.A.?"

Jeff laughs. "Seriously? Can't you send them a check?"

"I could if I had any money in my account," I snap at him. "I don't exactly have a job at the moment."

"Then how are you planning to pay me back?"

I close my eyes, grit my teeth. "I'll figure something out. Do me this favor, please?"

"Don't you have anyone else you can call?"

"No." I know he's thinking about our former neighbor, the one I fucked a dozen times before Jeff finally caught us.

"You're a real piece of work, you know that?" Jeff says. I wonder if he thinks he's telling me something I don't already know. I hear a drawer slam, the rattle of pens. "Fine, give me the address and the amount."

"Thanks," I say.

"One time, Lane. I'll do this one time."

"I appreciate it. I wouldn't ask if I had another choice."

"You always have choices, Lane," Jeff says, weary. "You just keep making the wrong ones."

I'm passing the late afternoon in a heat stupor, sprawled out on the front porch swing, when Tommy pulls up to the house in a cloud of dust.

"Hey, Tommy," I call, once he's out of the patrol car.

"Lane." His voice is formal, and I bolt upright, my hand rising to shade my eyes so I can see him better. "Is it Allegra?" I ask, my heart suddenly beating triple time. Pale dots dance in my vision from sitting up too fast. "Did you find her?"

"No," Tommy says. He's climbing the porch steps, one hand out like he's trying to calm me down. "But there is some news." He looks toward the front door. "Are your grandparents here?"

"Yeah. Let me go get them. Or do you want to come in?"

"I'm fine out here."

I scramble into the house, calling for my granddad and Gran. I'm breathless by the time I make it back out to the front porch, my grandparents trailing behind me. "Tommy's here," I'm telling them. "He says he has news about Allegra."

"What is it?" Granddad barks, and Tommy shoots me a look.

"Don't go getting your hopes up. It's not big news," he says.

"Well?" Gran says. "Go on."

"We got the surveillance tape from the drugstore in Parsons, and Allegra was there a few weeks before she disappeared."

"What in the world would she have driven all the way to Parsons for?" Granddad asks, the same question he's had on a loop since I told him about the receipt I found.

"Well, from the video we were able to pinpoint which clerk rang Allegra up, and the videotape helped refresh her memory." Tommy tugs at his uniform collar, where a thin line of sweat has darkened the fabric.

"And?" I ask.

Tommy looks at me, shifts his gaze to my grandparents, who are standing behind me. "She bought a pregnancy test," he says. The words hang in the air for a minute, before landing with a sharp thud.

"Oh, sweet Jesus," Granddad says. When I turn around, he's sunk onto the porch swing, his head dipping low.

"A baby?" Gran asks, voice quiet, the color drained from her face.

"We don't know for sure," Tommy says. "No way to know what the result of the test was. But it's another piece of the puzzle. Another thread for us to pick away at."

"Did the clerk say anything else?" I ask.

"Only that Allegra was friendly, but not very talkative."

"What now?" My voice sounds like it's coming from somewhere outside my body. Maybe Allegra and I aren't the last Roanoke girls after all.

"We keep doing what we're doing," Tommy says. "Asking questions, searching. Maybe this information will help knock something loose." He walks over to my granddad and shakes his limp hand, gives my gran a quick pat on the shoulder. "I'll be in touch," he says.

I follow him down the porch steps, all the way to his car. "What do you think it means?" I ask him.

"I don't know yet." He scrubs at his face with one hand, stubble rasping against his palm. He looks beat down, even worse than on the day of the search, eyes bloodshot and skin pasty. "But babies tend to make the girls around here run. Your great-aunt, your aunt, your mo——"

I interrupt him before he can finish the list. "I already told you she wouldn't have left Roanoke." I want to imagine Allegra sunning herself on a beach in Florida or strolling the busy Chicago sidewalks. But she was tied to Roanoke, maybe tighter than any of the rest of us. It's impossible for me to envision her anywhere but here, especially if she had a baby on the way.

"It's just a theory, Lane." Tommy opens his car door, puts one foot inside, his arm balanced on the roof. He looks at me over his shoulder. "If she was pregnant, I wish I'd known," he says, not quite meeting my eyes, a dark flush working its way up from underneath his collar.

My heart skips a beat, then gallops against my ribs. "Why? Why would it have mattered to you?"

He doesn't answer, folds himself into the patrol car and starts the engine. "Tommy . . ." I put both hands on the edge of his open window as if I can hold him there, force him to talk.

Tommy glances at me, and something flares in his eyes: sadness, alarm, shame, guilt. I can't pinpoint the emotion before he looks away. My fingers tighten on the window, even as Tommy puts the car in drive.

"I've gotta go, Lane," he says.

I lift my hands, watch him glide away.

Just as there's only one gas station in Osage Flats, there's only one place to go for car repairs: Sullivan's. So when my car won't start, and doesn't respond to Granddad's and Charlie's attempts to jump it, I know who I have to call.

"My car won't start," I tell Cooper when he answers the phone, my voice flat.

"I'll swing by after work and see what's wrong with it."

"You don't have to come yourself. You can send someone else."

"I'm the only one here right now. You want to wait until tomorrow?"

I sigh. "Can't I have it towed there?"

"Sure, if you want to pay fifty bucks for the tow job." He's definitely enjoying this.

"Fine. Stop by when you can."

It's after seven when he arrives, although there's still plenty of daylight left. I'm sitting on the front porch waiting for him.

"Took you long enough," I say, as he swings out of his truck. He's parked behind my ancient Honda on the semicircular drive.

"Contrary to popular belief, I actually have a life that doesn't revolve around you, Lane," he says. "Keys?"

I toss them to him, and he scoops them out of the air with one hand. "I already said it won't start."

My voice must sound angrier than I realized, because he says, "Easy, tiger," holding up both hands in surrender. "I'm just checking. That's why I'm here, remember?"

When he climbs back out of my car, I give him a smug look. "Told you."

He shakes his head at me as he moves around to the front of the car and lifts the hood. "It's probably your battery."

"My granddad and Charlie already tried to jump it."

"From the looks of this thing, you need a new one." He glances at me through a panel of wheat-gold hair that's fallen to cover one eye. I ignore the sick drop of my stomach, like an elevator plummeting toward the ground. "Lucky for you, I brought one with me." He pulls the old battery from my car and sets it on the drive. "You got anything to eat?"

I raise my eyebrows at him.

"I skipped dinner to come out here. Would it kill you to make me a sandwich?"

"It might," I say, but I stand up.

"And a beer," he calls after me once I'm through the front door.

I take my time making two ham sandwiches. I remember Cooper likes his with mustard and extra cheese, hold the mayo. It's funny the things your mind clings onto, even when you'd rather forget. A distinct memory of the last time I made him a sandwich flashes through my head and I try to shake it out, try hard not to picture us in his parents' kitchen—green walls, white curtains—the house quiet and empty around us. He'd come up behind me at the counter and kissed his way down the back of my neck, put his warm hand on my stomach to pull me closer.

When I push out through the screen door, plates balanced on one arm and two bottles of beer clutched in my fingers, Cooper is leaning back against my car, the hood still open.

"When's the last time you had your oil changed?" he asks, taking his plate and beer from me.

"I don't know. It's been a while. Why?"

"I'll go ahead and do it now."

I cross back to the steps and sit down, putting some space between us. "You don't have to do that."

Cooper takes a huge bite of his sandwich. "Thanks," he says, holding up the rest.

"Welcome." The cold beer tastes good. Even with dusk coming on it's still muggy; my shirt sticks to my back and my skin feels heavy with moisture. We eat in silence, each staying on our side of the yard, as though someone's run an invisible piece of tape down the center, a line not to be crossed. As always, I'm hyperaware of him, feel every shift of his body without having to see it.

"Where are your grandparents?" he asks. "Awful quiet around here."

"Isn't it always? But they're in town tonight. Having dinner at The Eat."

Cooper nods. "Your granddad came in for gas last week. He was pretty broken up about Allegra."

I take a careful sip of beer. "Well, she is his granddaughter. And she's missing."

I can't read the look Cooper gives me. "Yeah? He didn't seem all that worried when you up and disappeared."

"That was different. I didn't disappear. They knew I was leaving. I said good-bye." I take my mind in both hands and steer it away from that morning, from those last minutes right here on this porch.

"Not to everybody, you didn't," Cooper points out.

"No," I admit, "not to everybody."

Cooper waits until I look at him before he speaks. "I may not have been the perfect guy, Lane, but I deserved better than that."

"What do you want me to say, Cooper?" I shrug, struggling to keep my voice even. "I left. I didn't tell you. I can't change it now."

Cooper stares at me for a long moment, then sighs, sets his empty plate on the ground, and pulls a pan and a dirty rag from the back of his truck.

"Really," I protest, "you don't have to change my oil. I can bring the car in some day this week."

"It's okay. I'm already here."

"What? No hot date with the redhead?" I say, going for teasing but not quite reaching it. "Or Brandi?"

"Nope," he says, sliding under my car. "Not tonight."

I sit on the porch, nursing my beer and watching him work. It's the far edge of twilight when Cooper loads his equipment back into his truck, slams my hood down. "You're all set," he says and crosses the yard. He stops a few feet from where I stand by the steps.

"Do you want to come in?" I ask. "Have another beer?" I don't even know exactly why I'm asking, only that I don't want him to leave yet. I'm not ready to watch him drive away.

"I wouldn't mind another beer." He moves closer, his eyes shifting to Roanoke. "But how about out here or around back? That place is like a goddamn carnival fun house."

"You've been inside Roanoke a lot?"

His brow furrows. "Umm . . . yeah, with you. Are you having memory problems?"

I lift my leg to scratch the back of my calf with my bare foot. "Not since I left?"

Cooper shrugs. "Maybe a few times with Allegra."

"Were you sleeping with her?" I blurt out, even though I know he wasn't. Even though it shouldn't matter to me what he's been doing since I've been gone.

Cooper's head snaps back a little. "Jesus, Lane," he says, "no." He reaches out, slow, and runs the backs of his fingers down my cheek. "No," he repeats, softer this time.

"Okay," I say. "Sorry." I stumble away from him, turn to the house. "I'll grab the beers and meet you on the screened porch." Inside, I lean against the kitchen counter and tell myself to get it together, press one of the bottles against my cheek to ease the fire burning there.

When I step out onto the screened porch, he's sitting on the old wicker couch, the pink patterned fabric faded now to virtual colorlessness. I hand him a beer, sit down next to him. One of the cats has caught a vole and is playing with it in the dusty barn doorway, letting it almost get away before hooking it again with razor claws.

"Tommy told me you're divorced," Cooper says.

I stare at him until he turns and meets my eyes. "Yep. Why you care?"

He takes a pull from his beer. "Making conversation." He waits a beat until the air turns charged and electric around us, like the heated moment before a lightning strike. "Was it true love?"

"No."

"No?" Cooper laughs. "I almost feel sorry for the poor bastard. He probably didn't know what hit him. God knows, I sure didn't."

"Stop it," I say. "Let's not do this."

Cooper slams his beer bottle down on the old wooden table, and suds spill out of the neck. "What should I do then, Lane? Please, tell me. You waltz back in here and spin me sideways, just like you did all those years ago. What the fuck am I supposed to do? Pretend like nothing happened? Pretend it's all okay?" He drags a hand through his hair, his jaw clenched and his eyes burning.

"I spin you sideways?" I ask. Because for everything Cooper and I ever did together, talking about how we made each other feel was never one of them.

He has his elbows balanced on his knees, his head hanging down, and he turns to look at me, a wry smile on his face, like he can't believe that's the one thing I picked out of everything he said. "Of course you did. Of course you do." He pauses. "How can you not know that?"

My lip trembles when I try to speak. I have to suck in a breath to get the words out. "I don't know a lot of things, I guess."

He holds out his hand, dirty with grease from my car, tan from the sun, still familiar after all these years. I take it, and he pulls me to him. I go willingly, eagerly, like I've been waiting for this moment all along. He tastes exactly the way he did as a boy: cigarettes and mint toothpaste, the sharp bite of alcohol on his tongue. I raise one hand and run it through his gilded hair, down the side of his face. The rough scratch of his stubble tingles against my fingers. Selfishly, I hope there's some part of him, no matter how small, that still belongs to me.

I stand in front of him, and he watches while I undress. There's no point in feeling embarrassed or ashamed. Cooper has already seen my body in every way it can be seen. When I'm naked, I go to him and straddle his lap with shaking legs. His T-shirt is pushed up, and my inner thighs flame when they meet his bare skin. He reaches forward with one hand and runs his fingers up my rib cage, as if he's counting each delicate bone. His hand continues its journey, and my heartbeat stumbles drunkenly when he cups my breast in his palm. With his other hand he traces up my neck to cradle my face, his thumb passing once across my bottom lip. "Still so beautiful," he whispers, his voice rough and dark. It doesn't sound like a compliment. He kisses me again, and we move against each other, our bodies finding the rhythm effortlessly, as if they've never been apart. I am not surprised. This has always been easy between us. It's everything else that's so damn hard.

Then

"The sun is different here."

"Huh?" Allegra sounded like she was more than half-asleep, her voice slurred and heat-soft.

"The sun. It's like heavier or something. It has weight." Even as I spoke, I could feel the sun pushing between my shoulder blades like a slab of brick, oozing down my spine and slipping over my sides like a molten blanket.

"Are you drunk?" Allegra asked, peering at me over the top of her sunglasses. "Because you sound drunk."

I didn't bother answering her question. She'd been with me when we checked the fridge for beer and found it empty. I didn't know if Gran had gotten wise to us or Sharon was due for a trip to the grocery.

"Maybe you have a point," Allegra said. "Because I think I'm melting." She fanned herself with one hand.

"That only makes you hotter."

"Whatever." She flopped over onto her back, heedless of her undone bikini top. Her breasts were paler than the rest of her, and I threw the sunscreen in her direction.

"Might want to put some on."

"I'll roll back over in a minute."

We were stretched out on towels on the flat roof of the screened porch, a vantage reached by clambering through a guest room window. The red bikini I'd ordered after our trip to the swimming hole had arrived today, and Allegra had insisted we christen it immediately. Below us the door to the screened porch opened, and we heard Sharon's voice calling the dogs to come eat some scraps she'd probably tossed out on the ground.

"Think Sharon would bring us a couple of sodas?" I asked, once the door had closed again. "Heavy on the ice?" Allegra and I snickered under our breath. The idea of Sharon doing anything for us beyond the bare minimum was always cause for amusement.

"She would if Gran told her to," Allegra said. "I swear, Sharon would eat Gran's snatch if she pointed her south."

I hooted out a laugh. "Oh my God, that may be the most disgusting thing you've ever said."

Allegra's mouth twisted in a wicked grin. "Disgusting but true."

I propped myself up on my elbows, looked at Allegra, who was still stretched out in all her half-naked glory. "What's the deal with Sharon anyway?" I asked. "Why's she so attached to Gran?"

Allegra rolled to the side so she could see me. "She worked for Gran's family back in Boston. When Gran married Granddad, Sharon came along. Granddad told me Gran's family had been about to fire Sharon, which is why she jumped at the chance to come here."

"Long way to come for a job."

Allegra pursed her lips. "Well, it's not like people in Boston were gonna be standing in line to hire her. She can't cook. She's ugly as hell. And she's a bitch."

"So why does Gran keep her around?"

Allegra shifted back to her original position, boobs pointing to the sky. "I think she likes having a reminder of Boston. Sharon kept her from getting too homesick when she first moved here. And she's got Sharon wrapped around her little finger, like I said. Gran likes being the boss of something, because she sure as hell isn't the boss of Roanoke."

"Hey there now!" Charlie's voice called, and I startled, ducking down to make sure he couldn't see my bare chest. "Put some clothes on, Lane! Cover up!"

I lifted my head to see over the edge of the porch. Charlie stood below, eyes shaded with his raised hand. "We're sunbathing," I called down. "I'm on my stomach. Nobody can see us!"

"Well, I saw you!" Charlie yelled back. "Put on your swimsuit, for God's sake."

A sudden fit of giggles hit me. I turned my head and tried to smother them with my hand. "Allegra's got her top off, too," I managed. "How come you're not yelling at her?"

As I spoke, Allegra sat up, giving Charlie a full view. "Yeah, Charlie," she said in a singsong voice, "how come you don't care if I'm flashing my boobies?"

Charlie lowered his head, flapped a hand in our direction. "Put something on, Lane," he said, walking away. His voice sounded sad in a way that made no sense to me.

"What was that about?" I asked.

Allegra kept her gaze on Charlie's retreating back. "He's probably trying to protect you, save your immortal soul."

"What about you?" I laughed, pointing at her nakedness.

She still wasn't looking at me. "Oh, I'm not the one he's worried about. He already knows it's too late for me."

The sound of crying woke me, and at first I forgot where I was, thought for a split second I was back in our New York City apartment and my mother was having one of her bad spells. They got more frequent as I grew, so that by the year my mother died her life consisted of one long sob. But I smelled the hot night air, thick with prairie grass and remembered . . . Roanoke. I rolled onto my back and lay still, listening.

It came again a few seconds later, a faint whimpering, followed by the sound of muffled voices. I climbed out of bed and opened my door a crack, peering into the dimly lit hall. The voices were coming from the far end of the long hallway, my grandparents' room, and the crying from up above . . . Allegra.

I slid out of my room and down the hall, snuck into the alcove leading to the turret. I raced up the stairs, my heart pounding. Allegra's door was closed, a thin strip of light showing underneath.

"Allegra?" I called. "It's me. Are you okay?"

I put my hand on the cut-glass knob, and it twisted beneath my fingers. The door jerked open. Sharon stood there, blocking my view into the room. "What are you doing?" she asked me.

"I heard crying."

Sharon tutted, shifted the basin she was holding to her hip, but not before I saw the handful of stained washcloths, smelled the unmistakable twang of blood. "A bad stomachache is all. Maybe a touch of fever. Nothing you need to be rushing up here for."

"Can I see her?"

Sharon's free hand reached behind her for the doorknob, pulling the door up against her back. "Probably best to let her rest, come back in the morning."

"Lane?" Allegra's voice called, reedy and weak. "Is that Lane?"

Sharon turned her head. "You heard what your gran said. You need to rest."

"I want to see Lane," Allegra said, a hint of her usual petulance sneaking into her voice.

Sharon sighed heavily and waved me into the room. "Go on," she said, "but don't stay long."

"I won't," I promised.

The room was dark except for a lamp glowing on Allegra's dresser. She was sitting up in bed, wearing a white nightgown not much paler than her skin. The purple shadows under her eyes were as deep and dark as bruises. I didn't understand how she could look so ill when I'd seen her after lunch and she'd been fine. A sheen of sweat glistened on her forehead, and the smile she gave me was pained, like it cost her something to move her lips upward. She patted a spot on the bed next to her, and I sat down. I noticed her other arm remained wrapped around her stomach, as if she was trying to keep her organs from spilling out.

"Are you okay? What happened?"

"Just sick," she said, her voice quiet. Her eyelids were puffy from recent tears. The smell of blood was stronger here, close to her, and I had a sudden image of the bed soaked red underneath her lavender bedspread.

"Sharon said it was a stomachache?"

Allegra nodded, her arms tightening on her middle. Heat pulsed off her, but when I laid my hand gently on her forehead, her skin was clammy and cold. "Did they give you medicine or something?"

"Yeah. Something for the pain." Her glassy eyes met mine, slid away. A tear trailed down her cheek, dripped off her face onto her silk bedspread, where it left a dark stain.

"Are you okay, Allegra?" I asked again. Part of me was scared for her, wanted to stay and hold her hand. The rest of me wanted to flee, scramble back to my room and pretend I'd never woken up. I'd spent the early years of my childhood attempting to comfort someone; I already knew how futile it was.

"I'm sad," she whispered. "Are you ever really, really sad?"

"Sometimes," I said. "Usually I'm more mad than sad," which got a half smile from her. "My mom was sad a lot, though." I remembered what I used to do when I was little and my mom would huddle in bed, weeping until her pillow was soaked through, back when I still thought I might be able to do something to help her. Back when I longed to ease her pain, instead of inflicting more of it. "Lie down," I urged, "all the way."

Allegra slid down in the bed, her face pinching up. "Hurts," she said and gripped my hand so hard my bones screamed.

"Do you want to stay on your back?"

"No." Allegra rolled over onto her side, facing away from me, curled her knees up into her chest. She looked very small under the bedding.

"It's so hot in here." I tugged on the bedspread. "Do you want me to take this off?"

"No!" Allegra fisted the material in her palm.

"Okay," I said, as I stretched out beside her. I ran my fingers through her hair. Starting at her scalp and working my way down. This never made my mother stop crying, but sometimes she'd fall asleep right in the middle of weeping.

I shifted up on one elbow so I could watch Allegra's face. Her eyelashes fluttered as her eyelids drifted downward. "Feels nice," she whispered.

I brushed her hair with my fingers until her breathing evened out and her face relaxed. Her bed still smelled of blood. "What happened, Allegra?" I whispered, not expecting an answer. "Did someone hurt you?"

The lavender lace curtains fluttered in the open window. Barely any relief against the stifling heat.

"We're Roanoke girls, Lane," Allegra said softly, surprising me. I thought she'd slipped over into sleep. "Being hurt comes with the territory."

Although Allegra was still pale and moving slow three days later, she insisted we go into town for the Fourth of July parade and fireworks.

"Are you sure?" I asked her, sitting cross-legged on her bed while she twisted her hair up on her head, slipped into a red and white tank top over an electric-blue bra. "You don't look so great."

Allegra rolled her eyes. "I'm *fine*. How many fucking times do I have to say it?" She grabbed a lipstick from the clutter on top of her vanity and smoothed it over her lips, smacking them together to set the fire-engine-red color. "Besides, Fourth of July is about as exciting as Osage Flats ever gets, so there's no way we're missing it. Stop worrying. It was only the flu."

I caught her gaze in the mirror. "It wasn't the flu. You don't bleed when you have the flu."

Her hands stopped moving, and her eyes dropped away. "I wasn't *bleeding*. I think the heat's made you delusional."

But I knew I wasn't. I'd seen those bloody washcloths. And I could still smell the faint scent of blood in her room, like a pale red cloud enveloping us.

"You said Roanoke girls get hurt," I reminded her. "What did you mean?"

Allegra slid silver hoops through her ears. "I didn't mean anything. I was being stupid." She raised her eyebrows at me. "Like this whole conversation."

"Did someone hurt you?" I persisted. "Was it Gran? Or Granddad?" I couldn't imagine it, but I was a city girl. One raised on stories of kidnappings, molestation, children locked in basement cages. All the vile details just the horrific background music to so many lives. I knew the unimaginable happened every day.

Allegra's mouth dropped open. "What are you even asking me? *Granddad*? Are you *insane*? He would never hurt me. Or you. He's the only person who actually loves us!"

"Right," I said. "I know. But sometimes people who love us can still hurt us." I didn't fault Allegra for her exaggerated eye roll. The words sounded beyond trite even as they left my mouth, like I was auditioning for some particularly shitty public service announcement.

Allegra walked over and rapped with her knuckles against the side of my head. "Hello? Is my cousin Lane still in there? Or has she been body-snatched by a middle-aged guidance counselor who wants to lecture me about stranger danger?"

I jerked my head away, laughing. "Shut up, Allegra."

She beamed at me, threw her arms wide. "You're back! Now, come on, let's get out of here."

Since both Tommy and Cooper had to work until evening, Charlie agreed to drop us off for the parade. The ride into town seemed to take forever, me wedged between Charlie and Allegra on the bench seat of his pickup, Charlie spitting out of the window and Allegra blowing out disgusted breaths every time. No one talked. Charlie pulled to a stop near Main Street and leaned his head around me to look at Allegra, who kept her gaze pasted firmly outside the passenger window. "You feeling okay?" he asked. "Maybe you ought to rest up a little more."

Allegra wrenched the door open and hopped down, stalked off without answering.

"Thanks for the ride, Charlie," I said, sliding across the seat toward the door. "I'll keep an eye on her."

Charlie only nodded at me. I climbed out and gave him a quick wave as he drove away. I caught up to Allegra about halfway down Main, in front of the five-and-dime. "We can sit over there," Allegra said, pointing to an empty spot on the curb. "I'll be right back."

I sank down onto the curb, already wishing for some relief from the heat. Both sides of Main were lined with people sitting in lawn chairs or perched along the curb. A few kids carried red, white, and blue pinwheels that cast off blinding sparks when they caught the sun. Everyone looked sweaty and bored, the blazing temperature subduing even their voices.

Allegra returned a few minutes later with two cold cans of soda and a handful of red and blue plastic necklaces. "Here," she said, handing them to me. "Put these on. That white sundress is too damn boring."

I put the necklaces on as instructed and took my can of soda. Allegra had already opened hers and was gulping it down, but I ran the icy can along my forehead and neck, more interested in cooling my skin than in taking a drink. "When does this thing start?" I asked.

"They're coming now," Allegra said, motioning to the far end of Main.

I leaned forward to get a look and couldn't help the laugh that burst out of me. I hadn't expected the Macy's Thanksgiving Day Parade, but this was so pathetic I wondered why they even bothered.

"I know, right?" Allegra said. "Lame. But this is about as good as it gets here. Sometimes Granddad leads the parade, but he's sitting this year out."

A ragtag line of kids on bikes and trikes led the parade instead, small flags fluttering from their handlebars. Behind them were a few lazily decorated pickup trucks. As they passed, a couple of people hooted and hollered, but most only waved halfheartedly in the heat, as if lifting their hands took too much out of them. At our end of Main, the parade vehicles turned left and disappeared. The whole thing took less than ten minutes.

"Now what?" I glanced at my phone. "We still have like two hours before Tommy and Cooper meet us at the park."

Allegra didn't answer, and I looked over at her. Sweat ran off her face in rivulets, her skin pale. "Maybe we should call Charlie and ask him to come back and pick us up?" I said.

"No." Allegra shook her head without opening her eyes. "I just need to get out of the sun."

"I guess we could walk down to The Eat?"

"Let's go to the park," Allegra said. "I can sit under one of the trees."

We walked slowly, Allegra holding on to my arm like an old lady needing support. The park was already starting to fill up with people anxious to stake out ground for the fireworks display later, but we found a patch of grass under one of the big oaks. Allegra lay down, crossing both hands over her stomach. I could see the veins on her hands, pulsing purple beneath her skin. I sat next to her, my back against the trunk of the tree. We passed two hours this way—Allegra sleeping while I sipped my soda and watched small children sail down the slides. Not one of them smacked their heads, I noticed.

I was dozing off myself, boredom and the heat conspiring against me, when I heard Tommy's voice calling our names. I opened my eyes and saw him crossing the park toward us, waving with one arm, a huge smile breaking across his face. Cooper trailed behind him, not smiling, eyes staring only at me. We'd had sex half a dozen times now, and seeing him brought a rush of heat to my belly, my body waking up and taking notice, waiting for the moment his hands would touch me again.

"Hi, Lane," Tommy said. He glanced down at Allegra, whose eyes were slowly opening. "Happy Fourth, sleepyhead," he said with another grin, sitting down beside her. Allegra smiled up at him, rolled to the side, and put her head in his lap.

"Hey," Cooper said. He lowered himself next to me, gave me a half smile, smoothed the sweaty hair off my neck.

"Hey, yourself." Already I was wound taut, needing more from him than his fingertips on my neck. As if he could read my thoughts, Cooper winked at me, gripped the hem of my dress in his hand. "Nice dress," he said, one of his long fingers slipping underneath to stroke my thigh.

"Thanks," I said. If he'd tried to lay me down in the grass, right there in front of God and half of Osage Flats, I wouldn't have protested. That's how far gone I was.

"You ready for our version of Fourth of July?" he asked me, his finger still sweeping along my leg.

"What's your version?"

"Same as all small towns. The flag, fistfights, and fireworks."

"No fighting," Allegra said. "Last year you two assholes ruined the whole night."

"I didn't ruin shit," Cooper said. "Prick had it coming to him."

"What was the fight about?" I asked, when all I cared about was his finger on my leg.

"Nothing, really." Cooper's eyes swept up my body to my face. "Sometimes I need to hit something." I remembered what he'd told me about beating his father, about all the hits he'd taken himself as a kid. Maybe that wasn't something you could walk away from. All those punches from his father had left their mark on the inside, too, imprinted him with the need to hit back. It made me wonder what awful gifts my mother had passed on to me.

Allegra rolled her head and looked at me. "Keep him occupied. He always picks fights at these things. I think the fireworks make him crazy."

"I'll try," I said as Cooper's finger slid along my inner thigh before he lifted his hand away.

Tommy'd brought sandwiches from home, and we ate as the park filled up with people. "His mommy made them for us," Cooper teased, ducking when Tommy tried to slap his head. Cooper's contribution to our little dinner picnic was a bottle of tequila we took turns passing around.

"This stuff is disgusting," I told him.

"Not stopping you, though, is it?" he said with a laugh.

By the time the fireworks started it was full dark, every available space on the grass taken. Allegra had perked up a little once the sun went down and the alcohol hit. She sat next to Tommy, her head on his shoulder, her hand nestled in his. I wasn't sure if he knew she'd been "sick," but he seemed even more careful with her than usual, treating her like she was a sheet of glass.

"You guys want to move up here?" Tommy asked us, glancing at where we were still leaning against the tree. "Are you going to be able to see from under there?"

"Yeah," Cooper said. "We can see fine." We actually couldn't, but I didn't care. I could feel the restless energy rolling off Cooper, my own body recognizing it and responding in kind.

I wasn't expecting much from the fireworks after the crappy parade, but apparently Osage Flats spent its money on explosives. I leaned forward, craning my neck to see through the thick green leaves as white and blue starbursts lit up the sky. Cooper kissed the back of my neck, and I shivered. "Come on," he whispered, grabbed my hand in his.

I didn't ask questions, just stood up and followed him. We weaved through the bodies sitting on the ground until they thinned out and finally we were alone. Cooper kept walking, guiding me around to the far side of the carousel.

"There's a hole in the fence," he said, pointing out a portion of loose chain link.

"You want to ride the carousel?" I asked, laughing.

"No." His voice was low and quiet, and all my laughter dried up in my throat.

We snuck through the chain link, stepped up onto the carousel. I turned to face him, and he pushed me back against one of the horses. He kissed me, rough and raw, hands already pulling at my dress, lifting it up to my hips. I thought he would fuck me right then, but he dropped to his knees, shoved my legs apart.

"What are you doing?" I whispered. I was pretty sure I knew, but so far we hadn't done anything like this. I could barely breathe, my hands twisted in his hair.

"Shhh," he said, pushing my underwear aside. "Let me . . ." His slick mouth pressed against me, and I stopped asking questions, my back bowed over the horse. I came fast and hard, biting the fleshy pad of my own palm to keep from crying out. Cooper didn't give me any time to recover, turned me around and took me from behind, one hand on my hip, the other tangled in my hair.

When we were done he didn't pull out or away, just rested his forehead on my sweaty shoulder. I reached back and ran my fingers through his hair. The night sky lit up red. "Would it be stupid if I said something about us making our own fireworks?" Cooper asked, his voice hoarse.

I smiled. "Totally stupid. A comment like that gets out, it could ruin your reputation."

Cooper nipped at my neck with his teeth, whispered, "Smart-ass," against my skin. He wrapped his arms tighter around my waist, and we watched the sky catch fire.

Later that night, I was sitting on my bedroom floor painting my toe-nails when Allegra came in. "We waited for you after the fireworks," she said, leaning against my closed door. She was already dressed for bed in some ridiculous baby-doll nightgown that showed half her underwear.

I looked back down at my toes. "We couldn't find you in the crowd."

"You got a ride home from Cooper?"

"Yeah," I said, using a fingernail to catch a smudge.

Allegra walked over and dropped onto her knees next to me, sat back on her heels. Her face was pale, except for two bright red splotches on her cheeks. Her eyes glistened like she was on the verge of tears. That manic energy I recognized so well buzzed around her. Allegra grabbed my hand, digging into the tendons. "I saw you and Cooper," she said, voice low and frantic. "Coming from the carousel."

I wrenched my hand away. "So what?"

"Are you fucking him?"

A laugh tumbled out of me. "Seriously?"

Allegra nodded, her head snapping up and down like one of those bobblehead dolls.

"Why are you freaking out?" I asked, jamming the nail polish lid back on the bottle. "It's not like Tommy and you aren't screwing all over town."

The blush on Allegra's cheeks darkened. I swear she looked on the verge of hyperventilating. "I've never had sex with Tommy," she said, like even the suggestion was completely crazy, as if I'd claimed aliens were landing on the lawn.

I stared at her. "But . . . but you're always talking about it . . . sex . . . and stuff." My words stuttered out of me, my brain not able to reconcile what she was telling me with what I thought was fact.

Allegra flapped both hands in the air like wind-whipped flags. "You can't go around fucking Cooper!"

"Why the hell not? Are you suddenly the sex police?"

She leaned forward and cupped my cheeks in her hands. "It's supposed to be special, Lane. It should mean something."

I jerked my head back. "Says who?"

Allegra sighed like I was a stupid kid, and she was an adult with all the answers. And now actual tears were glistening on her lashes. Her hands had dropped to her thighs, laying there palm up, like she was pleading with me. "*Everyone* says, Lane. It does mean something, something important."

"Like what?" I asked, voice hard. Deep down I hoped maybe she could tell me, could explain the painful heat in my chest when I thought of Cooper. Could tell me how to make it stop.

"Like you're special," Allegra said, voice soft as feathers. "Like you're the most special girl in the world and he can't live without you." She reached over and took my hand in hers, lifted it to her mouth and kissed my knuckles. "It's supposed to mean that you're his favorite."

Now

Cooper leaves sometime after midnight, as the full moon streaks our bodies in cool white light, our legs tangled on the too-short wicker couch, my body lulled by the steady thump of his heart under my cheek. After he's gone, I stumble upstairs and fall across my bed, naked and aching.

Morning comes before I'm ready. My sleep for once was deep and dreamless, and I'm not anxious to leave the oblivion behind. But the sun is too bright against my eyelids, sweat gathers behind my knees and trickles sluggishly along my hairline. When I roll over, the scent of sex leaks off my skin, thick and heavy, like fresh earth overturned. I'm in no hurry to wash it away.

When I wander downstairs, breakfast is long over, so I make a pot of coffee, the caffeine worth the additional heat as I drink. In hopes of catching even a whisper of a breeze, I take my mug out onto the screened porch, where our beer bottles from last night stand guard. I swallow a smile and go back inside to pick up the phone.

"Hey," I say, when he answers. My voice comes out low and throaty. I sound like I smell.

"Hey, yourself."

"I forgot to pay you for fixing my car."

Cooper laughs. "I had other things on my mind."

My body thrums. "Yeah, I remember."

"It's all right to call me," he says, when neither one of us hurries to fill the pause. "You don't need an excuse."

"Okay," I say, but I'm uncomfortable suddenly, my skin itchy and too tight over my bones.

I hear the sound of a cigarette lighter, the rush of air into Cooper's lungs. "Want to meet up tonight for dinner?" I don't respond, and he exhales. I picture the smoke floating away from him, tangling in the humid air. "Chinese okay?" He sounds as awkward as I feel.

"Osage Flats has a Chinese restaurant?"

"In the loosest sense of the term. I think lo mein is about as exotic as they get. And even that's only mediocre."

"Oh."

Cooper sighs. "God, we really suck at this, don't we?"

"The worst," I agree.

"Does six o'clock work? I'll come pick you up."

"Cooper . . . this isn't a date, right?"

He hesitates before answering. "It's whatever we want it to be, Lane. How about two old friends having dinner?"

"Yeah, I can do that," I say. Although I'm not sure I can.

"If it makes it easier, think of it as sustenance before the main attraction."

And that goes a long way toward making it better. I'm able to laugh, at least. The panicky feeling isn't gone, but it's faded to something manageable—the snarling monster back in its cage.

Cooper is late. I'd hurried through a shower before spending longer than I wanted to admit picking something to wear. I went back and forth between shorts and sundress, feeling like a fool as I stared at my reflection in the full-length mirror behind my bedroom door. What did it matter? It wasn't a date. And whatever I wore wouldn't be on my body for long anyway.

When Cooper still hasn't arrived by six fifteen, I go outside and sit on the porch swing to wait. The cicadas who live in the oak trees at the front of the house are singing their full-bodied song, loud enough to almost drown out the sound of Cooper's truck rumbling down the drive. I get up to meet him, smoothing my hair back behind my ears as he pulls to a stop.

"Wow," Cooper says when he's climbed the porch steps, his gaze lingering on me. "A dress. Should I have brought a corsage?"

"Very funny."

He smiles and crosses to where I stand. His body backs me up against the wall, pinning me in between his outstretched arms. "Hi," he whispers. He dips his head and kisses me, first at the curve of my jaw and then on the mouth.

"I thought you said dinner first," I murmur against his lips.

"What an idiot I am." Cooper sighs. "I've got to learn to keep my priorities straight." But he pushes away from me. "You ready?"

"Yep. I'm dying to see Osage Flats's version of Chinese."

"One bite may change your tune."

Cooper opens the passenger door for me, and I climb in. "Where is this place?"

"On the western edge of town, where the Laundromat used to be."

"Where do you live?" I ask, for the first time realizing I have no idea. In my mind, Cooper still lives in his parents' house, although I know that can't be the case.

"The old Stevenson place. I've been renting it for a few years. I've had to do a ton of work, but it's getting there. Figure I may buy it eventually."

"You didn't want to live in town?"

Cooper laughs. "Nope. I like my privacy."

"So you can howl at the moon?" I smile, remembering the times we lay under the stars in the fields behind Roanoke and Cooper bayed to the night sky.

"Seem to recall making you howl at the moon a few times yourself," he teases, chuckling as my cheeks burn.

Both windows are rolled down, and my hair whips into my face, blinding me. I hold it back with my right hand, elbow balanced on the window frame. "Air-conditioning broken?" I ask.

"You can't smell anything with the windows up." I'd forgotten this particular quirk of Cooper's. He's right, though. I smell a whole world in the hot rush of wind in my face: ripe wheat, a hint of smoke, the faint tang of skunk, the warmth of his skin. We ride without speaking, and Cooper reaches over, covers my left hand with his, his callus-rough thumb rubbing circles on my skin. My breath catches in my throat, and he smiles, never taking his eyes off the road.

"You've got to be kidding me." I laugh when he pulls over to the curb in front of a small gray cinder-block building on the outskirts of town. "China Boy? How'd they come up with that name? Not very politically correct."

"I don't think Osage Flats has gotten a handle on political correctness yet."

The restaurant is practically empty, and Cooper guides me to a booth in the back, fake red leather on the benches and chipped faux wood for the table. The air is heavy with the smell of grease. The decor consists of cheap paper fans and a "kimono" that looks more like a bathrobe. "They do know China and Japan are different countries, right?" I say, sliding into the booth.

"I wouldn't count on it," Cooper says, settling across from me.

"I'll let you do the honors," I tell him, ignoring the finger-stained menu. An older woman with a cloud of dyed blond hair brings us two beers without asking and takes our order with a smile at Cooper and a pat of his cheek.

"Still working your magic with the ladies," I say, and Cooper laughs. I poke his arm with the end of a plastic chopstick. "So, tell me about Kansas City. How'd you end up there?"

"How do these stories always start?" he asks me with raised eyebrows. "It was a woman."

"Aaah. You followed her to Kansas City?" I pretend I'm talking about someone I don't know, pretend it doesn't sting to imagine Cooper with a girl who was more to him than a fun time in bed.

"Basically. I met her at a wedding. Remember Mike Tucker?" When I nod, he continues. "He got married in Kansas City and I went to the wedding. She was a bridesmaid."

"This bridesmaid have a name?"

"Kim. Kimberly." It doesn't seem to pain him to talk about her, although I doubt Cooper would show me if it did. "Anyway, there was tequila involved, and after a wild weekend we came up with this half-baked plan that I'd move up there and start my own business."

"What happened?"

"Oh, it was fine for a few months. Then things started to settle down into real life. She was a nurse, worked long hours. Most of the time we barely saw each other. I couldn't manage to fit into life there, kept dragging my feet about getting a business loan, moving into her place. She figured out she'd been slumming about the same time I was ready to come back home."

He says the last part without any trace of self-pity, and I do us both a favor by not arguing with his assessment. I know from personal experience it's probably the truth, remember how Jeff always tried to steer the conversation away from my past at parties, never wanting to admit he'd married a runaway with a GED and a tenth-grade education. The things that attracted him to me in the first place—my youth, my lack of pretension, my blank-slate life he hoped to rewrite—became just more embarrassments by the end.

When the food comes, we dig in to limp noodles swimming in

an overly salty sauce, chunks of meat that might be chicken, might be something else. I'm thinking maybe Sharon could get a part-time job in the kitchen.

"You're right," I say, "this is terrible."

"Keep eating." Cooper eyes my plate. "Sustenance, remember?" His smile is knowing and filled with sex.

I roll my eyes at him, trying to ignore the surge of heat in my belly. He's always been able to do this to me—one word, one look is all it's ever taken. I'm probably the surest thing he's ever found. I let my gaze roam around the restaurant, and when it returns to our table Cooper is watching me, his beer bottle hovering halfway to his mouth.

"What?" I ask.

"Nothing." He gives his head a slight shake. "Just never thought I'd see you again."

"Yeah, me neither." I used to think about him, though, sometimes, on nights I couldn't sleep, when I felt lonely and tired of living. Remembered that somehow his touch pulled me apart and put me back together at the same time. Remembered and tried to forget again.

Cooper picks up a chunk of chicken on his fork, sets it back down without eating it. "Allegra used to talk about you, whenever I saw her. She always wondered what you were doing, where you'd gone. Once she knew you were in California, she thought maybe she'd see you someday on the cover of a magazine or in a movie."

I snort out a laugh. "A guy offered me a thousand bucks to make a porno in his garage once. That's as close as I ever came to the movie-star life."

"You take him up on it?" Cooper asks with a grin.

"Nope. I do have some standards."

Cooper's face turns serious again. "I think Allegra always held on to this sad little fantasy that you'd come back and live with her at Roanoke forever."

My throat burns, and I jab my fingernails into my bare thigh, concentrating on the pain in my leg instead of the one in my heart. "Tommy came out to Roanoke the other day. About Allegra. He said she may have been pregnant."

Cooper takes a long draw from his beer. "Tommy's?" he asks finally.

"I don't know," I say, remembering the way Tommy refused to look at me as he drove away. Loyal-to-a-fault Tommy. What would he do if caught between two competing loyalties? "Maybe. But I always thought marriage meant something to Tommy, more than to most people, at least."

"Yeah, it does," Cooper says. "But last time I checked being married didn't mean your dick stopped working. Look, Sarah's a nice woman, but if I had to wake up next to her every morning for the rest of my life, I'd blow my brains out. I think if Allegra wanted to keep her hooks in Tommy, it would've been an easy job."

"Her *hooks* in him?"

"Simmer down." Cooper taps his fork against the back of my hand. "You know what I'm saying. Allegra liked Tommy under her thumb." He grinds his thumb into the tabletop in demonstration.

"Yeah, okay," I concede. "I know what you're saying."

"Besides Tommy, any other candidates for the father?" As Cooper speaks his eyes never leave my face. Not for the first time, I wonder how much he knows. He's always been observant, his gaze taking in more than people are willing to give away. And he grew up in darkness, knows how it hides in plain sight. Unlike most people, Cooper isn't afraid of looking into the shadows.

"Your guess is as good as mine." I spin a chopstick across the cracked tabletop, and Cooper reaches over and covers my hand with his, stopping the movement. "Tommy thinks she might have left when she found out about the baby. Took off."

"But you don't?"

"No." Now it's my turn to gulp some beer. "If she is pregnant, I'm pretty sure it's not the first time. That summer ...." I pause.

"Yeah?"

"I think she had a miscarriage right before the Fourth of July. She wouldn't ever admit it, but there was blood. And her story was ridiculous." I don't tell him about the morning a few days after the Fourth, when I found ʙᴀʙʏ gouged into Allegra's floor, the letters a tiny scrawl, not quite fully formed. Just like what Allegra had lost. *Baby.*

"Jesus." Cooper sighs.

"Yeah." I push my plate away. Cooper's hand is still on top of mine, his thumb gliding over my skin. "Putting aside the fact Roanoke was the only home she ever had, it doesn't make sense for her to leave. If she didn't run when she was fifteen and scared, why would she run now, when she's a grown woman?" I take a deep breath. "Maybe she killed herself," I say to see how the words sound, testing if I can stand to hear them.

"That's what I thought at first," Cooper says. "But where's her body? And Allegra always struck me as someone who'd leave a note. Make sure everyone knew exactly why she did it. Hell, she'd probably hire a skywriter to give us all one last fuck-you."

I let out a watery laugh. "Do you think we'll ever find out what actually happened to her?"

Cooper isn't the type to offer false comfort, to make promises that can't be kept. He squeezes my hand until my eyes meet his. "I don't know," he says. "But I do know if she comes back, she'll be so happy to see you. She told me once she thought her whole life might've been different if you'd stayed."

"That doesn't exactly make me feel better. What did you tell her?"

Cooper lets go of my hand, drains the last of his beer, and picks up the bill from the edge of the table without looking at me. "I told her I thought my life might've turned out different, too."

Like the old days, Cooper and I end the evening in his truck. He offers his house, but I pretend I'm too impatient, instead of scared of what walking through his front door might mean. After, he drops me off with a smile and the brush of his fingers down my cheek.

Roanoke is dark and silent, and I drift, restless without knowing why. There's a faint light coming from the hidden hallway off the kitchen, and I realize I haven't walked down it since I've been back. As if it's beckoning me, a dim ceiling light glows above the frame housing the photographs of the Roanoke girls. I stand in front of the frame and study their beautiful faces.

"Where did you go, Allegra?" I ask her photograph. "What happened to you?" I run my fingers over her teenage face, wondering how much it's changed in the years I've been gone. Even in black and white, it's impossible to miss the spark of mischief in her eyes. The still-blank spot next to her picture mocks me, and I can't tell if what I feel is relief or regret at its emptiness. I cover the space with my palm.

"Allegra tried to put a photograph of you there," Gran says from the end of the hallway, startling me into taking a small, stumbling step backward. "But the only ones she had were in color. I told her it would ruin the composition." Gran is wearing a string of fat pearls, and she slides them through her fingers as she walks, her pale pink nails clacking against each jewel. She stops when she's next to me, close enough to smell the subtle hint of her perfume.

I look at Gran, but her gaze remains on the photographs. "Tommy told us Allegra tried to call you, right before she disappeared." She turns her head slowly, runs her eyes over my face.

"Yes," I say, swallowing hard. "But I didn't call her back."

"That must be difficult. Knowing she wanted to talk and you weren't able to make time to get in touch." Gran's nails continue to glide over the pearls. *Clack, clack, clack.*

Her words punch into my chest like spikes. I stare at her, aware for the first time of exactly what her calm blue gaze conceals. I have no idea how it took me this long. "You hate me," I say. "You've always hated me." I wish I didn't sound so sad.

Gran drops her pearls. "Oh, Lane." Her smile is full of sympathy, the most maternal she's ever looked. "I hate *all* of you."

The hall feels too small suddenly, the walls closing in so that I can barely breathe. Beside me, the Roanoke girls wait and watch. "Did you hurt her?" I whisper. "Did you hurt Allegra?"

Gran shakes her head with a wince, like my question has disappointed her. "I've lived in this house more than half my life. Watched him fall in love with you girls over and over again. I know how to *endure*." Gran flutters her hand through the air before it settles back on her pearls. "And I know how to deal with Allegra. She's no threat to me."

"I don't understand," I say, "how you could let it happen. They were your daughters. Your granddaughter."

But Gran is already turning away. "This conversation is tiresome, Lane. Next time, please let Sharon know if you're not planning to join us for dinner."

Once Gran is gone, I lean back against the wall. My stomach rolls, heavy with oily Chinese food, and I fold my hands between my thighs to stop their shaking. Charlie is right—this place is no good for me. Already Roanoke is tunneling into me, working its dirty fingers under my skin. Guilt may have brought me back, but the need to know what happened to Allegra has kept me here. Her life is small, limited to this house and a handful of people—Granddad, Gran, Sharon, Charlie, Tommy, Cooper. But those people know pieces of her, not all of her. I'm the only one who has seen the whole picture that makes up her life. Only I can pry out the truths from all the various players. I don't know if I'm strong or determined enough to do what needs to be done. But I have to try. *You're the only one I can talk to about this.* It's what Allegra wanted.

The next day, I'm waiting outside the police station when Tommy emerges into the early evening heat. His steps falter only a little when he sees me perched on the trunk of my car.

"Hey," I say, "thought maybe you'd wanna go for a ride? Show me the old sites."

Tommy glances down at his watch. "Sure, I've got some time. Your car or mine?"

I give my car a dubious glance over my shoulder. "How about yours? Cooper's got mine running again, but it's still a piece of shit." I hop off the trunk. "Like pretty much everything else I own."

Tommy smiles, points me toward a blue sedan at the back of the tiny police lot. "Let it air out for a minute," he says, once the doors are open. The heat of the day barrels out of the interior, smacking into my body like a wall, and I do as he says, waiting until he's got the air-conditioning running high before I climb inside. The second my back hits the seat, I start to sweat. "Jesus," I say, "I forgot how hot it is here."

"And it's not even August yet." Tommy unbuttons his uniform at the neck, slips on a pair of mirrored shades.

I smirk at him. "Been shopping at Cops-R-Us?"

"Roger that," Tommy says, deadpan. "Where to?"

"Wherever." I lean forward and unglue my sweaty shirt from my back, for all the good it'll do.

"How about out to the old silo, loop around?"

"Fine by me." There are dozens of grain silos dotting the outskirts of Osage Flats, but I know exactly the one Tommy's talking about. It was abandoned years ago, its roof caved in and stone exterior slowly crumbling to dust. An eerie sentinel on the prairie, used mainly as a teenage party location the summer I lived here.

We drive in silence for a few minutes, through the deserted heart of town, out onto County Road 7. The only sound is the steady *whup-whup* of tire on asphalt. Tommy glances over at me, then back at the road. "Remember the last time you and I were in a car together?" His fingers drum a restless rhythm on the steering wheel.

"Let's not go there," I say, turning to look out the window, watch crops bathed in pre-sunset gold roll by.

"I'm guessing you haven't reconsidered talking to Cooper, then?"

"Nope."

Tommy turns onto the gravel road leading to the silo. He slows to barely a crawl, making allowance for the potholes and stands of tall weeds growing down the center of the road. "I still think you should be honest with him, Lane. It'd be good for both of you."

"Honesty is the best policy?" I brace one hand against the door as we hit a hidden dip in the road. "That the motto you live by, Tommy?"

"Try to," he says, and I don't miss the way his hands tighten on the wheel. He knows what's coming, has probably known from the second he saw me outside the police station. I have to give him credit for not trying to avoid it.

I shift, jackknifing one leg up onto the seat as I turn my body toward his. "Then why didn't you tell me you were fucking Allegra?"

Tommy pulls up in front of the silo and puts the car in park, turns off the engine. He reaches down, and the windows open with a whir. Hot evening air floods in, tangling my hair across my face. Tommy stares straight ahead, then lowers his forehead to rest on the steering wheel. I look out at the crumbling silo. The ground at its base is littered with beer cans, crumpled fast-food bags, probably a generous sprinkling of used condoms, too, if memory is anything to go by. It all looks virtually the same as the last time I was here, more than a decade ago. Cooper and I had sex in his truck in almost this exact spot. I still remember the sound the bench seat made as its springs creaked under my knees, the feel of Cooper's fingers scraping along my spine. Tonight the wind whistles through the gaping holes in the silo, rustles the tall wheat on either side of the car so that it sounds like something is slinking toward us, hidden in the grain.

"It was one time," Tommy says, breaking the silence. His voice is hoarse and low as if he's crying, but when he raises his head to look at me, his eyes are dry. "It only happened once."

"Is this where you say it didn't mean anything?" I ask with raised eyebrows.

Tommy shakes his head. "It meant something. At least to me. As for Allegra . . . I wouldn't venture a guess." It's the first time I've ever heard him say her name like the taste of it is bitter in his mouth.

"How did it happen?"

Tommy shuts his eyes and leans his head back, against the headrest this time. "It was a couple months ago. I was having dinner at The Eat. Sarah was in Wichita for the weekend at a bridal shower. And Allegra came in. Sat right down at my table like it hadn't been more than a year since we'd talked. She was sweet, funny, laughing. Kept touching my arm. You know how she could be when she felt like it."

I nod even though he can't see me. That was always the trick with Allegra—her moods were erratic and her goodwill was only ever offered on her terms.

"She asked me to drive her home. Said your gran had been uptown with her but had gone back to Roanoke earlier and Allegra didn't want to call Charlie for a ride. And it just happened, Lane." He turns his face toward mine and opens his eyes without lifting his head from the headrest. "The thing I'd been wanting my whole goddamn life. She finally let me touch her all the way. She finally said yes." He sighs out a shaky breath. "I didn't even think about Sarah. My own wife didn't cross my mind."

"Why that night?" I ask. "After all these years?" But I think I already know the answer, picture Cooper's thumb grinding into that tabletop. In Allegra's mind, Tommy was supposed to be hers. Her backup, her just-in-case. She wanted to prove to him that he could try to walk away, but he wasn't going to make it far. But it's possible I'm being unfair, maybe she actually loved him and only realized it once she lost him. Or maybe she was simply being Allegra, who never learned how to be anything less than the favorite.

Tommy laughs, but it's not a sound I've ever heard from him

before. It's coarse and jagged and makes my heart jump against my ribs. "I have no fucking idea. She could have had me a thousand times. But she waited until I got married. She waited until I said vows to someone else." He lurches forward, startling me. "Who does that?" he demands. He slams his hands against the steering wheel hard enough to shake the car.

I've never seen Tommy like this—angry, unpredictable—but it shouldn't surprise me. I've learned by now that life picks away at all of us, backs us into corners we never anticipated. Turns us into people we never thought we'd become.

"What did Sarah say?"

Tommy swivels his head in my direction so fast it's a wonder he doesn't give himself whiplash. "Sarah doesn't know."

"Tommy . . . come on."

"What? I sure as hell didn't tell her. No one knew but Allegra and me."

Sarah may be naïve, but she's not stupid. If she doesn't know, it's only because she doesn't want to. Willfully blind to what's right under her nose.

"Why didn't you say something earlier?" I ask. "You think I give a shit that you cheated on Sarah?"

"*I* give a shit, Lane!" Tommy exclaims, pounding the steering wheel again. "I'm not that guy. I don't want to be that guy."

"Looks like you are, though."

Tommy shakes his head, covers both eyes with his palms. "Goddammit, Lane, do you ever ease up, even for a minute? I mean . . . Jesus Christ."

"Hey, if you were hoping for hand-holding, you picked the wrong person to confide in." I nudge his shoulder until he lowers his arms and looks at me. "But I'm not judging you, Tommy. God knows, I'm not in any position to do that."

He blows out a breath and points to the glove compartment. "Can you pass me the cigarettes? Should be a lighter in there, too."

"Since when do you smoke?" I ask, rooting around until I come up with a crumpled pack of Marlboros and a scuffed plastic lighter. Today must be my day to learn new things about Tommy.

"Since never, really," he says, lighting a cigarette. "Cooper left those there, and every once in a while, on really shitty days, I get the urge." He takes a drag, holds the smoke so long I wonder if he's inhaled it, before twisting his head to blow it out the window.

"You must not have too many shitty days, if you still haven't finished the pack."

Tommy smiles, sad and small. "More than you'd think."

I give him a minute, let him calm himself with nicotine and oral fixation before I keep prying. It occurs to me that some part of Tommy must want, *need,* to talk about this. He could easily shut me down otherwise. He's the cop, after all.

"So, then what?" I ask, after he's taken a couple of puffs. "With Allegra."

"Then . . . nothing." Tommy's voice breaks a little, and he clears his throat. "I called her two, three times a day for weeks. Left messages, begged to see her. I was a zombie at work, barely better at home. I was ready to uproot my entire life for her, let the whole town know I was a cheating, lying bastard if it meant I could finally have her. I was willing to give up everything. And she wouldn't even answer my calls. Couldn't be bothered to pick up the phone."

Tommy sounds sincere, but my internal bullshit alarm is pinging. It matters to Tommy what people think of him. It always has. He likes being seen as the good guy. And I don't think that would change just because he managed to get into Allegra's pants. "Did you try and go see her?" I ask.

Tommy laughs again, that sharp bark I still don't recognize. "Try? You have no idea. I practically lived on the road outside Roanoke for a solid week, but she never left the house. Eventually I came knocking, and your granddad said she wasn't interested in seeing me. Sent me away like a little kid, like a beat dog with my tail between my legs." A muscle jumps in his jaw, his fingers twitch on his leg. "I can't remember ever being that angry. Goddamn *pissed*. She waited until I was married, until I'd moved on. And *then* she fucked me. And afterward, she wanted to pretend like it'd never happened. I swear to God . . . I could have killed her."

I suck in a swift, startled breath, and Tommy's gaze flies to mine, his hands already coming up to reach for me. "No, Lane, no," he says, the words practically tripping over themselves they're in such a hurry to leave his mouth. "That's not what I meant. I wouldn't—" A long cylinder of ash tumbles from his cigarette and lands on my bare leg. I flinch, brushing it off, Tommy's hands getting in the way of my own. "Shit, I'm sorry. Are you okay?"

"Yeah, I'm fine. It's fine." I wet my thumb and concentrate on rubbing the ash mark off my skin so I don't have to meet his gaze. Good, sweet Tommy is only a memory now. Replaced with flawed and human Tommy, who is probably capable of almost anything, like all the rest of us.

Tommy stubs out his cigarette on the side-view mirror, tosses it out the window. "This is such a fucked-up mess." The coming night bathes his face in shadows. The smell of smoke wafts toward me on his breath. "My life. Allegra gone." He pauses. "What if she really is pregnant? What if it's mine?" He looks at me with weary, defeated eyes. "How did it all get so fucked up?"

It's not the kind of question that can ever have a good answer, so I don't even bother to try.

Camilla

(b. 1971, d. 2004)

There was a war inside her head, and she wished it would stop. Every day a raging battle, an endless, exhausting tug-of-war. She knew it was wrong, what they were doing. She *knew* it, no matter what he said. Carried the evidence in her hollowed-out cheekbones and bitten-to-the-quick fingernails. But she loved him. Not an easy butterflies and sunshine kind of love. Not a fairy tale. A dark, twisting horror show of love. Love that spread through her like poison, coiled like inky tentacles that slowly squeezed out all the light.

Sometimes she went into town and had sex with whomever showed the slightest interest. And let's face it, she was a beautiful girl. There was plenty of interest. Other nights it was alcohol, pills in a plastic baggie, white powder snorted from the back of someone's dirty hand. She hoped that maybe if a stranger fucked her hard enough, if she emptied her guts until it felt like her stomach was going to rip out through her throat, she'd be able to rid herself of him. Of the never-ending *need* that lived inside of her like a sticky vine, refusing to surrender.

She wished she was more like Eleanor, who didn't seem to feel anything at all, looked at the world with hard eyes, gaze always trained on some distant horizon. Eleanor was going to run, Camilla was sure of it, even though Eleanor didn't talk to her anymore. Didn't talk to any of them, really. Bided her time. Eleanor went into their father's study and closed the door when he called for her, stole money from Sharon's grocery cash, and waited for her moment.

Camilla tried to imagine a life away from Roanoke. A life without his face, without his hands on her body, without his voice saying her name. The thought made it hard for her to breathe. It felt like freedom. It felt like death.

Lately, every time he touched her, she pictured her organs turning black and rotten, even as she keened with pleasure. Whatever sickness they both had was working its way through her skin, deep into bone and tissue. Her love was knotted with so much darkness. She'd never be able to separate all the tangled strands. Would never be able to love someone without hating them, too.

Then

In New York you could hardly see the stars, which I never thought about one way or the other when I lived there. Our apartment wasn't exactly the penthouse, so I wouldn't have been doing a lot of stargazing, even if there had been something to see. In books, people always said lying underneath the stars made them feel small. But stretched out on a blanket in the bed of Cooper's truck, the net-of-pearls stars didn't have that effect on me. Lying there, looking up at the inky black shot through with pinpricks of brilliant light, I felt my whole body expand like I was as big as the entire universe.

"I never saw the stars before," I said. "Not really."

Cooper shifted next to me, his naked leg rubbing against mine. "Too many lights?"

"Yeah." The warm night air pressed down on me like a sticky hand. A bead of sweat slithered along my neck. I turned my head and looked at him. "You know, you're the only person here who never asks me about New York. Everyone else is always asking a million stupid questions, but you never do."

Without using his hands, Cooper moved the toothpick he had clasped between his teeth from one side of his mouth to the other and back again. "Figured it was the same bullshit, different scenery." He tilted his head to look at me. "Right?"

I smiled. "Yeah, pretty much." I shifted onto my side, kissed his bare shoulder and the curve of his collarbone. He smelled like smoke and summer. Out here in the fallow land behind Roanoke, we didn't have to worry about putting our clothes back on after or how loud I moaned when he fucked me. The heat and scratchy blanket beneath us felt like a small price to pay for the privacy. I ran my fingers over a scar at the top of his arm, asking a question with my fingertips.

"Belt buckle," he said. "Same as the ones on my back."

"What made him so angry, so mean? Was his dad like that, too?"

Cooper pulled the toothpick from his mouth and tossed it over the side of the truck. "Don't know. Don't care. Whatever it was, it's not an excuse. I think maybe he was born pissed." He ran a hand through his hair, eyes on the stars. "The thing I can never wrap my mind around is how my mom ended up with him. You don't look at her and think she's the type to put up with that shit."

Cooper was right. The first, and only, time I'd met his mom, she'd surprised me. I'd expected someone mousy and meek, the kind of woman who would startle in a strong breeze. But Mrs. Sullivan looked like hardy farm stock, tall with broad hips and a no-nonsense smile. She looked at the world out of Cooper's golden eyes. Her handshake was strong and firm. It was hard to imagine her cowering in a corner, but I knew that was where she'd spent a good portion of her married life.

"When I was a kid, all I wanted to do was protect her, keep her from getting hit. But once I got older and realized she wasn't as quick to shield us when he got going . . . it made me hate her sometimes. There were times I let my dad throw a few good punches before I'd step in to protect her." Cooper's voice was matter-of-fact, but I knew him well enough now to hear the shame underneath.

"I hated my mom, too," I told him. "And not some of the time. I hated her every second of every day."

"Why?"

I shrugged. "Because she wouldn't let me love her instead."

We were both silent for a minute, and the sky was so vast, the stars so bright, it was almost possible to believe you could hear them burning.

"Remember how I told you I beat up my dad?" Cooper asked. "That night on your screened porch?"

"Yeah?"

"The first thing he did once he regained consciousness was laugh. He laughed so hard, blood pouring out of his nose. Said I was going to turn out exactly like him." Cooper reached over and hauled me on top of him, our hard and soft spots fitting together like puzzle pieces. I propped myself up on his chest so I could see his face.

"You think you're going to?" I asked. "Turn out like him?" No one had to explain to me the power our childhoods had over us, even when we fought like hell against them. I wasn't stupid enough to think Cooper could snap his fingers and become a different man than the one his father was trying to mold him into. I wondered if a boy bred and raised by a man with hungry fists and an appetite for pain could ever escape the violence in his blood.

Cooper's body tensed beneath mine, his heart beating against my rib cage. "I hope not," he said finally. "But that bastard's with me all the time, whispering shit inside my head."

I nodded, understood exactly what he was talking about. I could still hear my mother's voice, her wails, her fears, echoing in my own skull. Cooper's arms tightened around me, and he hitched my body up, my breasts sliding over his chest. "I try not to give in to it, though. That urge to pound someone. Because whenever I do, it feels worse than all the times he beat me. Like I'm turning into him, exactly like he said I would. I tell myself every day I go without doing it makes it easier. Makes me less like him."

"Does that work?"

Cooper tipped his face up toward the sky. "Hell if I know. But it's all I can think of to do."

I traced a figure eight onto Cooper's chest, his skin pebbling under my touch. "Sometimes I'd tell my mom to go ahead and kill herself. I knew she wanted to, so I'd egg her on. I never thought she'd have the guts to actually do it. She had nightmares a lot, too. And I stopped waking her up, bringing her cold washcloths, and helping go back to sleep. I let her scream and cry. By the end, I didn't care anymore."

I raised my eyes and found Cooper's. He smoothed my hair back, tucked it behind my ear. He didn't tell me it was okay, or he was sure I hadn't meant it. He knew it wasn't okay, that it never would be.

"That's it?" he said instead, voice quiet. "That's the worst you got?"

It wasn't. But there were some things I could never say aloud, not even to Cooper, a boy as damaged as I was. How sometimes when I whispered those awful words to my mother the veins in her neck stood out so far from her skin I thought they might explode. How her fingernails would leave red welts down the side of her face. On the nights my words cut deepest, sliced quick and deadly as scalpels, her eyes practically bulged from her face, and I was filled with a rotten, hellish joy because at least she was looking at me. At least she finally, *finally,* saw me. "Stop it," she screamed sometimes, staring at me from between the bars of her fingers. "Stop it, you evil little bitch! Stop it! *Stop it!*"

To me, it might as well have been a love song.

Allegra had locked herself in her room, talking on the phone, which is how I ended up perched on a wooden ice cream freezer while Granddad turned the crank. We were outside, the overhang of the screened porch roof protecting us from the afternoon sun, but sweat still rolled off Granddad's face as he worked. He took a quick break to wipe his forehead and noticed Charlie, who watched us from the barn doorway.

"I'd like to have that hole in the stall fixed today," my granddad called, a hint of steel in his tone. He kept his gaze on Charlie until he moved inside the barn, then turned his attention back to me. "Careful now," he said. "Make sure you keep the blanket underneath you. Otherwise your legs are gonna stick to the metal."

I shifted, the cold seeping into my skin through the thin blanket he'd draped over the top of the barrel. "Why don't you just buy ice cream?" I asked.

It seemed like a reasonable question, but Granddad looked at me like I'd lost my mind. "Wait until you taste this, girl, and you'll never ask that question again."

"What flavor is it?"

"My daddy's creation," Granddad said. "Pineapple, peach, and banana." He glanced at me and laughed. "Don't go making that face."

"I don't like fruit-flavored ice cream."

"You'll like this. Trust me."

The screen door banged open behind us, and Allegra stepped out, her cell phone clenched in her hand. "Who were you talking to?" I asked.

Allegra rolled her eyes and huffed out a dramatic breath. "Kate. She's all worked up over Cooper."

Hearing his name was like a hot poker in my stomach, but I tried to sound unconcerned. "Why? What's up with her and Cooper?"

"Nothing," Allegra said. "That's the problem." She jabbed me in the shoulder. "And don't gloat."

"I'm not gloating," I said, but I couldn't keep the grin off my face. "What did you tell her?"

Allegra folded her arms and stared at me. "I told her she could do a lot better than Cooper Sullivan. Boys his age only want one thing. They don't care about your mind. Or your heart."

I laughed, until I realized Allegra wasn't joining in, her face serious.

"You don't think that's true?" my granddad asked, and I swung my head in his direction.

"I don't know," I mumbled, thinking of the way Cooper touched me. All the time, like he couldn't get enough. But I was just as bad, practically stripping him naked as soon as he was within reach.

Granddad smiled at me, put one hand on my bare thigh. "Ain't nothing wrong with it, Lane. It's the way boys that age are made. All hormones. They can't help themselves."

"But we're special," Allegra cut in. "We deserve someone who'll treat us better. Who won't break our hearts."

"That's right," Granddad said, smiling at Allegra now. "Boys like Cooper don't understand what a gift you girls are. What a prize." He squeezed my thigh gently as he spoke. "Remember what I'm telling you, Laney-girl. And if that Sullivan boy ever hurts you, I got no problem kicking his ass."

"Cooper's kicked an ass or two in his time, too," I said, irritated for no good reason.

Granddad blew out a slow breath between pursed lips. "I've been throwing punches since before that boy was born. And let me tell you, he hurts one of my girls, he's going to be a sorry son of a bitch."

"You can't go around beating up boys every time they do something Allegra or I don't like!"

"The hell I can't."

"This is stupid," I said, throwing up my hands. "Cooper didn't even do anything to me."

"And I'm trying to keep it that way," Granddad said, voice serious. After a lifetime of relying only on myself, believing in someone else felt nearly impossible. But the look in his eyes, as if I were the most precious thing he'd ever seen, made me want to try, to give in a little and trust that maybe he wouldn't let me down.

"Okay," I said quietly, and Granddad smiled, his gaze pinned on me. Warmth flooded my body even as cold from the ice cream freezer settled into my skin.

"What are you doing?" Allegra demanded. I'd almost forgotten she was there. She jabbed me in the shoulder again to get my attention. Harder this time.

"She's helping me make ice cream," Granddad said, voice mild.

"That's my job!"

"You were busy, so I asked Lane."

"Well, I'm here now," Allegra said. "Get up."

I started to move, but Granddad's hold on my thigh tightened, his pinkie slipping under the edge of my jean shorts. "Nope," he said, looking up at Allegra. "You can help next time. This time is Lane's turn."

Allegra stood there for a minute, her gaze shifting between Granddad and me. Her mouth pulled into a scowl, but I could see the flare of hurt in her eyes. "Fine," she said. "I didn't want to help with your stupid fucking ice cream anyway." She stormed into the house, slamming the screen door behind her.

Granddad went back to churning the ice cream like nothing had happened, still using one hand on my thigh for leverage. "She's going to hate me now," I said with a sigh.

Granddad laughed. "She will, but not for long. Allegra has moods. But they never last. Can't take 'em personally. Gotta ride 'em out."

I thought of the way Allegra sometimes looked at me after Granddad and I had been working in the barn or when Gran offered to braid my hair. "I think there's times she wishes I hadn't come to live here."

"No," Granddad said. "That's not true. Never seen her so excited as when we found out you were coming to stay. Girl near about worked herself into a fit waiting for you." He stopped cranking and took his hand off my leg, sat back on his heels. "But Allegra's been the center of the universe her whole life. Sharing the spotlight doesn't come natural to her, but she'll learn." He stood and held out his hand for mine. "Now get on up from there. You're in for a treat."

I hopped off the freezer and watched as Granddad lifted the metal tube from its bed of crushed ice and rock salt. He winked at me as he twisted the lid off, motioned for me to dig in.

I laughed. "I don't have a spoon."

"Hell, girl, you don't need a spoon. Not for the first bite." He dipped his index finger into the ice cream and lifted a giant glob to my mouth. I hesitated only a second before licking the ice cream off his finger. It was delicious, just as he'd promised. Rich and freezing cold, the flavors bursting on my tongue. It tasted nothing like ice cream from a grocery store carton.

"See?" Granddad said, eyes gleaming. "What did I tell you?" He grabbed a lock of my hair between his thumb and forefinger, gave it a gentle pull. It had become his signature move with me, tugging on a loose piece of my hair or the end of my ponytail. With Allegra it was smoothing her eyebrow with his index finger. Funny how such a simple gesture had the power to make me feel so special. I wondered sometimes if he'd done something similar with my mother, but so far I hadn't asked. I didn't want to know if it was the same. I wanted a ritual that belonged to only me.

I'd been collapsed on Cooper's body for at least ten minutes, our naked, sweaty skin stuck together, but I didn't want to move. I liked the feel of his hand sweeping up and down the length of my spine, the smell of his skin under my nose. "Am I getting heavy?" I whispered.

"Nope," he whispered back, nuzzling the side of my neck and making me smile.

We were in his bedroom, the first time we'd had sex in an actual bed. His dad was working all day at the garage, and Holly and his mom had gone to Parsons to do a little shopping. I rolled off him, sighing when cooler air hit my overheated chest and stomach.

"I may not be heavy, but we're about to drown in sweat." I turned onto my side and propped my head up with one hand to look at him. Occasionally I wondered if staring at him would ever get old. "What would we do if your dad came home early?" I asked with a grin.

Cooper's eyes traveled down the length of me before meandering back up. "Getting dressed might be step number one." He rolled toward me, ducked his head, and dropped an openmouthed kiss on my breast.

"Cooper . . ." I breathed. "We were supposed to meet Tommy and Allegra at the pool an hour ago."

"So?" His mouth moved lower. "You really want to spend all afternoon at the pool?"

I didn't. I hated the pool. I preferred the swimming hole any day of the week. The town pool was small and always crowded, bodies stuffed into the marginally clean water and smashed together on the concrete, wet towels overlapping. So many people you couldn't cool off, even in the water, and the whole place stunk of rank sweat and a lethal dose of chlorine. I'd only been twice, but both times it had closed early after some kid puked in the water. I didn't think Allegra liked it, either, but she'd ordered a new bikini and wanted to show it off to as many admirers as possible.

"Not really," I admitted. "I swear, last week I saw Mike Tucker and some girl fucking in the deep end. Little kids swimming right next to them."

Cooper snorted, his mouth still drifting steadily downward. "That explains what I saw floating in the water. Mike's spooge."

"Oh, gross." I laughed. "Now it's official, I'm never getting in that pool again."

Cooper wedged himself between my thighs, rested his head on my stomach. "We can go, if you really want to. Allegra'll probably flip her shit if we don't show up at all."

I raked my hand through his hair. "I don't care. Screw her." Allegra was still mad at me for helping Granddad make the ice cream, so I wasn't too worried about pleasing her. And I liked being alone with Cooper, the two of us tangled in his soft sheets.

"Yeah?" He shifted his head and pressed his chin into my belly button.

"Yeah," I said, squirming. "Let's stay here."

Cooper grunted his agreement and settled his head back on my stomach. My gaze drifted around the room, drinking it in. I hadn't gotten much of a look earlier, when Cooper had crowded me through the doorway, pushed me back onto his bed. From what I'd seen, his small, shabby house had been about what I'd expected, but his room surprised me. It was uncluttered and mature in a way I couldn't quite put my finger on, no posters of half-naked girls or muscle cars, no piles of dirty clothes or empty beer cans. Just a single black-and-white print of a forest above his double bed, clean white blinds, and a scuffed red toolbox against the wall. Out of the corner of my eye, I saw Cooper following my gaze.

"Can't leave it in the truck," he said. "Dumb asses try and steal tools."

I nodded. "Do you want to be a mechanic? Like your dad?"

Cooper looked up from where he was drawing circles around my belly button with his index finger. "Not really," he said. "But I'm good at it. It's steady work. Everybody's car craps out from time to time, right? What the hell else am I going to do?"

For the first time it occurred to me maybe Cooper wasn't as okay with following in his father's footsteps as he always seemed to be. Maybe Allegra's constant digs about taking over the garage were hitting a tender spot, exactly as she intended.

I ran my hands up his arms to his shoulders, shifting my body lower. "Right," I said. "But that doesn't mean you have—"

Cooper was shaking his head before I even finished my sentence. "Not everybody has the choices you have, Lane. Not all of us are Roanokes." His voice wasn't bitter or bored, the way it was when he talked to Allegra about this subject, only resigned.

"But maybe you could go to junior college or something?" I said, knowing how stupid and pointless it sounded from the look on his face. Before my mother died and I'd come to Roanoke, my chances of doing anything after high school beyond some shit job had been exactly like Cooper's. I knew well the painful futility of reaching for more than you were ever likely to get, how much easier it was to simply accept the limits of your world.

"That's for Holly," Cooper said. "College. She's got four more years and then she's getting out of here. I'm already saving so she can go."

"You're doing that for her?" I asked. Cooper, who smoked and drank too much, who picked fights and acted like he didn't give a shit about anything, giving his future away to his little sister. Something inside my chest cracked open.

Cooper nodded, crawled up my body. "Now stop talking. We're wasting a perfectly good bed."

He slid into me without preamble, and I arched my back, hissing a breath through my teeth.

"Too much?" he asked, even as his hips snapped forward.

I shook my head, tightened my arms around him. He stared down at me, and suddenly it *was* too much. I felt the urge to lash out, claw and bite, desperate to escape. Fear pounded through me, nipping right on the heels of pleasure. I closed my eyes and turned my face away.

Now

I'm heading into town to see about catching Cooper for a late lunch when Sharon calls to me from the screened porch. She's standing on the back step, holding out something in her hand.

"Yeah?" I ask.

"If you're going into town, can you drop these off?" She shakes the object in her hand but doesn't move from the step. Waiting for me to come to her. Typical.

"What am I dropping off?"

Sharon sighs. "Sunglasses. That wife of Tommy's left them on the front porch when she visited Allegra. I've been meaning to give them back but keep forgetting."

My steps falter to a stop. "What? When was Sarah out here?"

"Oh, for heaven's sake." Sharon marches across the dusty back-yard and slaps the sunglasses into my hand. Tacky white and cheap, probably purchased from the revolving rack at the five-and-dime. "It was a few days before Allegra went missing, I'd guess."

"What did she want?"

"I have no earthly idea. She didn't stay long and never came in-side the house, as far as I know." Sharon cocks her head at me. "You taking them or not?"

"Yeah," I say, voice slow like I'm just waking up. "I'll give them to her."

Tommy's front door is adorned with exactly the kind of wreath I'd expect. Fake flowers ringing a jaunty hand-painted wooden Welcome sign. Judging from the way Sarah's face falls when she sees me, she's forgotten the message on her own front door.

"Oh, hi, Lane," she says, glancing behind her as if the empty house will save her from having to invite me in. "What are you doing here?"

"Thought I'd stop by." I give her my friendliest smile. "It gets a little lonely out at Roanoke." I pull open the screen door without waiting for her to ask, and Sarah's too polite to do anything but stand back, gesture me into her home.

The front door leads directly into the small living room. Lots of knickknacks, cheap throw pillows, walls overstuffed with sterile, mass-produced "art." Vacuum marks crisscross the beige carpet, not a speck of dust in sight. The air reeks of potpourri overlaid with the smell of roasting meat, and late afternoon sunlight beams in through gleaming windows. The entire scene smacks of trying too hard. I'm guessing Sarah's the type of woman who would rather die than let Tommy catch sight of a used tampon in the trash, who runs to brush her teeth when she hears his car in the drive, changes her outfit an hour before he's due home. She must be so tired. The saddest part is, if she really knew Tommy, she'd know he doesn't care about any of this. Allegra is a mess, in every sense of the word, and Tommy adores her. Sarah probably thinks being perfect is the only way she can compete. And it will never be enough.

"Can I get you something to drink?" she asks. "Lemonade? A soda?" She's wearing the hideous floral print dress she found the day we were both at the secondhand shop, and it doesn't fit quite right, too loose in the boobs, too tight in the butt—a lethal combination. She yanks at it with one hand as she walks.

"Lemonade's fine," I say, following her into the kitchen. There's a pie cooling on the counter next to a steaming Crock-Pot. Tommy's going to get fat if he's not careful. Sarah pulls a pink glass tumbler from the shelf, reaches into the fridge for a pitcher of lemonade.

"Oh yeah," I say, when her back is turned. "I have your sunglasses, too. The ones you left out at Roanoke."

Sarah's entire body stiffens, but I have to hand it to her, she keeps on pouring the lemonade without spilling a drop. When she passes me my glass, I hold out the sunglasses. "Thanks," she says, without meeting my eyes. "I've been looking for those." She takes them from me and places them carefully on the counter.

"When did you find out Tommy and Allegra were screwing?" I ask. "Right before she disappeared?" I take a sip of lemonade and tilt the glass in Sarah's direction. "Good stuff."

A bright pink blush climbs up Sarah's neck into her cheeks. She rubs both hands down the sides of her dress like she's trying to dry her palms. "He told you?" She releases a sad little laugh. "He hasn't even told me."

"He doesn't think you know."

"Of course I know." Sarah sags back against the counter. "How could I *not* know? He barely looked at me for an entire month. Didn't eat. Stayed up all hours. He kept his phone with him even when he went into the bathroom." She shakes her head. "I'm not stupid."

"That's what I told him." I set my glass down on the tiny kitchen table. "So why did you talk to Allegra about it instead of talking to Tommy?"

Sarah looks away. "I thought maybe I could convince her to let him go."

"Could you?" I ask, but it's only a formality. It wouldn't have mattered if Allegra didn't want Tommy, she never would have given him up on Sarah's say-so.

"No." Sarah crosses her arms over her stomach, swings her eyes back to me. "I thought she would be angry, but she wasn't. It was like she was talking to the mailman or, I don't know, some salesperson. She didn't even care that she was ruining my life, my marriage. She acted like none of it mattered. Especially not me. It sounds crazy, but I think it would've been better if she'd been furious."

"Allegra could be selfish," I acknowledge, and Sarah's face opens up, thinking maybe she's found an ally. "But no matter what Allegra did, no matter how she acted, I'll never take your side over hers," I continue, shutting her down fast. I know I should feel sorry for Sarah. She's the only truly injured party here. But my allegiance lies with Allegra and it always will.

"I know that," Sarah says, a trace of anger in her tone. "No matter what, Allegra always wins."

"When you were out at Roanoke, did she tell you about the baby?" I ask, and Sarah's whole face caves in, which is answer enough. "Did she say if it was Tommy's?"

"No. But she said if she wanted Tommy, she could have him. All she had to do was snap her fingers and he'd come running." It's not a flattering picture of Tommy, but I can't argue with the truth of it. "I reminded her Tommy was married now," Sarah continues. "And Allegra laughed. That's when she told me she was pregnant. She said . . ." Sarah's voice falters and two fat tears slide down her cheeks. She doesn't bother to wipe them away.

"She said what?"

Sarah steeples her hands over her nose, takes a deep breath. "She said she could give Tommy something I couldn't. She could make him a father."

Ah, Allegra. Going right for the jugular. "And you never told Tommy you went to see her?"

"No."

"Why not?"

"I thought if I confronted him, it would force his hand. And we both know who he'd choose, wedding ring or no wedding ring. I hoped if I ignored it, Allegra would lose interest again, and Tommy would come to his senses."

"Wow," I say, "sounds like a recipe for an *awesome* marriage."

"What would you know about it?" Sarah snaps with more fight than I've seen from her so far. "Aren't you divorced already?" Her own boldness seems to shock her, her eyes opening wide and her hands back to rubbing furiously against her dress.

"Yep. And I would say it looks like you'll be joining me there soon, except things have worked out pretty well for you."

Her hands stop moving. "What do you mean?"

"You know what I mean, Sarah. Don't play dumb. You already said you aren't stupid. Allegra's gone, along with the baby that might have wrecked everything for you. You've got Tommy all to yourself now."

"No, I don't," Sarah says. "It doesn't matter if they never find Allegra. I'm always going to be second best in his mind."

When I first met Sarah, I might have said there was no way she'd ever hurt Allegra. She didn't have the guts or the fire. But Tommy, this house, her vision of herself as the perfect wife—they're her whole world. And most people will do whatever it takes to protect their entire world. "That's probably true," I tell her, "but it's also a lot easier to live with being second best when first choice is never coming back."

My forced glibness must get to her because Sarah's hands ball into fists at her sides. "Girls like you and Allegra have it easy," she says, words trembling on her lips. "You don't understand what it's like for the rest of us. How we have to work for every little thing, for every scrap of attention. And you smash into the world. Take things that don't belong to you. Knock people over like we don't even matter, like you're so special." Sarah is breathless now, giving voice to her grievances sucking the air from her lungs. "Allegra always got whatever she wanted, but she didn't get Tommy. Not this time."

The smell of meat from the Crock-Pot is suddenly overwhelming, making my stomach heave, heat pooling in the back of my throat. "You don't know what the fuck you're talking about," I say, vicious and razor-edged. I have to resist the urge to slap her, send her frizzy head flying into the cabinet behind her. To Sarah, Allegra is simply a bitch. A spoiled man-stealer. But not one single second of Allegra's life was easy. I know the agony she lived with every day. And I understand how sometimes you have to pass the pain around in order to survive it. No matter the wrongs Allegra committed, Sarah doesn't get to judge her. Not when she wouldn't have lasted one day in Allegra's shoes.

I brush past Sarah, out of the kitchen and to the front door before I do or say something I can't take back. She follows behind me, hovering over my shoulder. "Are you going to tell Tommy?" she has the nerve to ask. "That I know? That I talked to Allegra? Please don't," she pleads. "I can't lose him, Lane. He's all I've ever wanted."

I stop and look back at her. "Hard to lose something you never really had," I say, just to watch her flinch.

After our one failed attempt at a family dinner, there have been no more formal summonses for me to appear in the dining room. As far as I know, Sharon is still making her dubious creations, but I either forage from the kitchen after dinner or, more often than not, meet Cooper in town. Tonight, though, Cooper has to work late, and I'm rummaging through the fridge, not willing to choke down Sharon's leftover tuna casserole if I can help it. I throw together a quick sandwich and take it out on the front porch, my footsteps slowing when I see my granddad has already claimed the porch swing. I didn't expect him. The porch swing is usually where Gran roosts on warm summer nights, and never until later.

"There's room," he says, looking up at me with a smile.

I'm dismayed by how much my body wants to keep moving in his direction, sit beside him, and rest my head on his shoulder. "I'm okay over here," I tell him, dropping down to sit with my back against the porch pillar. The June bugs are already out in force, throwing themselves against the window screens with a sound like popping corn. I wave a few away from my head, their hard shells bouncing off my fingers.

"Sharon made plenty of dinner earlier. You could have had a real meal with us."

"I wasn't in the mood for something hot." And not in the mood to sit around the table staring at my grandparents and Allegra's empty chair. "A sandwich is fine."

"You've been eating in town a lot," Granddad says.

I take a bite of my sandwich. "Yep."

"With Cooper Sullivan?"

"Yep."

The sun is sinking in the evening sky, and I hear Charlie around back calling for the dogs, who bark joyfully in response. Granddad leans back in the porch swing. He's got a beer bottle balanced on his knee. "Not surprised, you know," he says with a little smile. "About you and Cooper starting up again."

"We're not starting up again."

Granddad cocks his eyebrows at me. "Boy never did get over you." He pauses. "You sure left a string of broken hearts when you went away."

I put my sandwich down, no longer hungry. "Stop it." My voice is harsh, ugly, but my granddad doesn't drop his eyes and the expression on his face doesn't change.

"Cooper. Allegra." He takes a quick swig of beer. "Me."

I bark out a laugh. "How come nobody's concerned with my broken heart?"

"Was your heart broken?" he asks, voice quiet.

My throat burns, and I'm glad I set my dinner aside already so I don't choke on a swallow. "You know it was," I say. "It still is."

"I'm sorry," my granddad says. And he sounds like he means it, which only makes it even more unbearable. "I'm so sorry, Laney-girl."

"Don't call me that!" I suck in a deep breath. "You know, I thought I'd escaped this place. The only one who ever did with only minor damage. That's what I comforted myself with when I was scared or lonely, which was most of the time."

Granddad looks like he's about to get up and come over to me, but I stop him with a single glance. "But in the end, none of it mattered, because here I am again and it's like I never left. This place never let go of me. I've carried it all these years. Like a disease. Like a tumor." My voice breaks and I drop my gaze. "It's killing me." I look back at him. "Did it kill Allegra, too?"

Granddad shakes his head, the muscle in his jaw thumping.

I point at him with an unsteady finger. "You shake your head all you like. But I'm going to find out what happened to her. I'm going to find out what you did. I'm going to *know*."

"I didn't touch one hair on her head," Granddad says in that tone of voice that means he's had about enough. "I would never hurt her."

"You hurt her every goddamn day of her life!" I shoot back.

Granddad sighs, rubs his eyes with one hand. "You want to make me a monster? Pretend you hate me, Lane? Go ahead, if that makes it easier for you."

"I *do* hate you!" I say, voice rising.

He drops his hand, lifts his eyes until they stare right into mine. "No, you don't."

I try to hold his gaze, but my eyes slide away first. One of the barn cats sneaks out from underneath the steps, stalking my abandoned sandwich. I pull out a piece of turkey and toss it to him.

"Did you know about the baby?" I ask. The cat snatches the turkey from the ground and disappears back under the porch.

"No. If she was pregnant, she hadn't told me yet."

"What makes you think she was planning to?" I look at him

again. "How do you even know it's yours? It could be Tommy's. Or some random guy's, even. Outside sperm probably have more of a fighting chance, don't you think?"

My granddad doesn't have any visible reaction other than a slight shrug of his shoulders. "Wouldn't have mattered to me. Would have raised it like one of my own."

"What if Allegra didn't want that? What if she wanted Tommy?" I know in my gut this isn't true. Allegra would never have chosen Tommy over Granddad, but I want to push him, see if he cracks.

"You think I killed her to keep her from leaving me, taking the baby, is that it?" My granddad snorts, amused rather than angry. "Are you forgetting your mama took off, once upon a time, and I didn't stop her?"

"That was different. You still had Eleanor. But Allegra was the last Roanoke girl. If she left, that would be the end."

"Your logic is failing you, Lane. If I killed Allegra, I'd be in the same boat as if she left. No more Roanoke girls." He hesitates, tips his beer bottle in my direction. "Except for you."

His words slam into my body, violent as punches, and I struggle for air against the rising tide of my heartbeat. *Except for me.* Why didn't I see it before? One Roanoke girl gone and another fitted seamlessly into her spot. Dread zips along my spine. "So Allegra's missing, and here I am," I manage to say. "I came home like you wanted."

"You came home," my granddad agrees. He smiles, slow and easy. "Right where you belong."

The breeze picks up and carries the faintest hint of his cologne. And in an instant I'm transported back to all those mornings with him in the barn, when we'd work together feeding the animals. Probably the only time in my entire life I felt loved. I bite down hard on my lip to keep from screaming, taste the warm tang of blood on my tongue.

Run Lane. Run.

I spend the early evening hours getting single-mindedly drunk out on the screened porch. Each sip is a mercy, leading me further into oblivion. Every swallow makes it easier to forget. I work my way through a bottle of wine I found in a kitchen cabinet. Follow it with a shot of vodka and a couple of beers for variety. Finish with a heel of stale bread to keep it all down.

So it's fair to say I'm not at my best when I wander through the door of Ronnie Joe's long after dark. It's more crowded than last time. There's an overflow of bodies packed onto the tiny dance floor. They sway in rhythm to a song, heavy on the nasal drawl, warbling from the jukebox in the far corner. The air is thick with smoke and the stench of armpit.

Cooper is seated at the bar, hunched over his drink. His grease-stained fingers hold a cigarette smoked almost down to the filter. I elbow my way through the throng of people near the door and swing up onto the empty stool next to him.

"Hey," he says with a smile when he turns and sees it's me. "What are you doing here?"

I shrug. "Needed to get out." I signal the bartender by pointing at whatever Cooper has in front of him. Whiskey, maybe, straight up. "What's the deal tonight? Isn't it a little crowded for a Tuesday?"

Cooper's eyes roam over my face. "Dollar draws. On Tuesdays."

"Tuesdays are big days around here. Tacos *and* beer. Osage Flats—home of the fat and drunk." I laugh, a sloppy, liquid gurgle. "Sounds like an appropriate slogan."

The bartender brings over my drink, and I start a race to the finish line. The cheap whiskey flames on the way down; I can picture blisters coating the lining of my throat.

"How much have you had?" Cooper asks, eyes back on his own drink.

"Not nearly enough," I say. "But don't worry, I didn't drive. Charlie dropped me off."

Cooper's knee nudges mine underneath the bar as he stubs out his cigarette on the pockmarked bar top. "Think maybe you should slow down?"

"Nope."

He nods at that, spins his half-empty glass between his hands. "Wanna talk about it? We could go back to my place. I've got whiskey there if that's what you need."

I shake my head. I can't stand that he's being kind to me, can't stand the ache spreading through my chest that being near him brings. Can't stand all the things he makes me remember, when I'm trying so hard to forget. It makes me want to hurt him, just because I can.

Something hits me hard in the shoulder, and I stagger forward on the stool, throwing one arm out to catch myself against the bar.

"Oh, whoops, sorry!" The guy behind me steadies me with his hand. I turn to get a better look at him. He's around my age, dressed in jeans and a light green T-shirt, a Kansas City Royals baseball cap on his head. His neck is pinpricked red with razor burn.

"I'm David." His small huddle of friends, all male, watch our interaction with hungry eyes, leering into their beers.

"Lane," I say.

He grins at me. His eyes are glassy, and beer fumes waft off his skin. "Wanna dance?"

"Maybe," I say, as I turn on my barstool, a little lilt in my voice. I glance over at Cooper. He's watching me, waiting to see what I'm going to do.

David shifts his body until he's between Cooper and me, cutting off our eye contact. His fingers dig harder into my arm. "Whadya say? One dance?"

"Okay. One dance." I let him pull me off the barstool and onto the dance floor. I don't look back at Cooper. The jukebox is not playing a slow song, but David drags me into his arms anyway, holds me too close. "God, you're gorgeous," he breathes against my cheek. "Way hotter than any of the other girls around here."

I fix my gaze somewhere over his shoulder. I have to concentrate as we spin in slow circles to keep from getting sick. The mirror behind the bar reflects my flushed face on every pass, my eyes wide and unfocused. Cooper never once looks in my direction.

After a while, it could be five minutes or an hour, my brain isn't keeping track very well, one of David's friends cuts in with a fistful of shot glasses. Tequila, not my drink of choice. But it turns out the old lick, drink, suck routine comes back easily, like riding a bicycle. When I pass over my empty shot glass, David ducks his head and kisses me. His tongue burrows into the back of my mouth, his teeth clanking against mine. Lime and salt burn on my lips. I pull away, but not as fast as I should.

David puts his arm around me, tight and overly familiar. He leans into my ear. "You wanna get out of here?"

I look over his shoulder and see Cooper's empty barstool. I push away from David, stumble over his feet, and crash into a couple still dancing. "Excuse me," I mumble. "Sorry."

I ignore David calling my name and slam out through the door of Ronnie Joe's. It's no cooler outside, but at least the air is clean and clear. The full moon pokes through a tear in the black clouds and illuminates Cooper's back as he disappears across the parking lot. I inhale deeply, the sick swirl of my head fading into the background.

"Hey, wait!" I call. "Where are you going?"

"Home." He doesn't stop or turn around.

I hurry after him, not running—I don't think my stomach can handle it—but quick, fumbling steps. "Don't go. Wait!"

He slows only when he reaches his truck and shifts to greet me with a sigh. "What?"

"Why are you leaving?"

"Because it's late and I have to work tomorrow."

"We could have one more drink."

"You have one more drink and you're gonna pass out on the floor or end up spread-eagle in the backseat of that guy's car." His eyes are like flint. "Thanks, but no thanks. Either way, that's a show I don't need to catch."

"Cooper." I reach out and grab his hand, the skin rough and warm under my fingers.

"Don't you ever get tired of your own bullshit?" he asks, yanking his hand free. "What in the hell do you want from me? You want me to go back in there and beat the shit out of that guy? Pound him the way I used to? Find some girl to fuck so we're even? So you won't have to feel guilty?" Cooper is breathing hard, his hands curled into fists. "You want it to be like old times, is that it?"

I throw myself forward, pressing my body against his, and Cooper chokes out a sound that's not quite a swear. I think there's better than even odds he'll shove me away, but he spins us around instead, slams me back against his truck, his hands touching whatever part of me they can reach. I work a hand free and pull on the driver's door, opening it far enough that Cooper can push it wide with his hip, toss me onto the bench seat, and climb in on top of me.

He raises his head, opens his mouth like he's going to try to say something, and I clamp a hand over his lips. "Please," I whisper, as I lift my hips. I sound like I'm begging, and I hate him for making me do it. My lips find the hollow of his throat. "Please."

He grabs my head in both hands, forcing me to look at him. "Goddamn you, Lane," he says through clenched teeth, but he pulls me closer, his hands already ripping my shorts down over my hips. And if he's rougher than he needs to be, if there's a knife's edge of violence to his touch, who am I to complain? After all, it's no more than I deserve.

Emmeline

(b. 1984, d. 1984)

They buried her in a white casket lined with pink satin. Dark hair curled like silk against her tiny skull. Rosebud mouth. Lids stitched closed over the Roanoke eyes. Fifteen pounds and twenty-seven inches. Six months old.

Emmeline Justine Roanoke

Beloved Daughter
Cherished Sister
Our Beautiful Girl

Then

Now that Allegra was over her "mood" and we were back to talking, she had enlisted me to help find her mother's diary. The few pages she'd found last year had been wedged into a crack between boards in the hayloft, but she'd never come across the rest of the diary. Today we were tearing apart the library looking for it. Allegra had the idea maybe her mother had stashed the diary in among the regular books. Perfect camouflage, according to Allegra.

"Why do you want to find it so much?" I asked, pulling a stack of books off the shelf.

Allegra paused in the act of flipping through pages. "Because I don't know anything about her. Not really. Only stupid stories from Granddad that sound like they're made-up she was so perfect. I mean, duh, clearly she wasn't a saint."

I had to laugh at that. "I don't think any of them were. Or us, either."

"Don't you want to know more about your mom?" Allegra asked. "If you could find out what she really thought or felt, wouldn't you want to know?"

"Not particularly." I set the first stack of books aside and reached for another. The library was cleaned regularly, but still dust had settled and my nose itched. I scrunched up my face to hold in a sneeze. "My mom's brain isn't a place I want to spend quality time."

Allegra's eyes flared, her hands tightening on the book she held. "Well, I'd like to know why my mom was so quick to abandon me. At least yours took you with her."

"She didn't have much choice," I said. "Considering I was inside her."

Allegra rolled her eyes. "You know what I mean."

"Have you ever tried looking for your mom?"

"No." Allegra bit her lip, kept her gaze on the book in her hands.

"Never?" I couldn't believe the lure of the computer hadn't called to her, at least once.

Allegra shrugged. "Okay, yeah, I googled her a couple of times. Nothing ever came up. She obviously doesn't want me to find her." The sadness in her eyes surprised me. Here she was, longing for her mother, and most days I wished my mom had been the one to leave me behind.

"Honestly, Allegra, you might have gotten the better end of the deal. Living with my mom wasn't exactly an advertisement for family."

Allegra got that look on her face, the same one she'd had at the swimming hole, like something was pushing its way out of her, her lips already forming the words I was dying to hear.

"What are you girls doing?" Gran asked from the doorway, and the moment passed, quicker than a snap of my fingers. My chance to know what Allegra was keeping inside whisked away again.

"Looking for my mom's diary," Allegra said without turning around.

"Oh, for heaven's sake," Gran said. "I want all these books put back when you're done. Did you hear me, Allegra?"

"Yeah, whatever," Allegra mumbled.

Gran ventured a little farther into the room, sidestepping our piles of books. "If there's something you want to know about your mother, you can always ask me," she said.

Allegra didn't even look up. "I've tried that before. You never want to talk about her. And all I get from Granddad are stories about how she could commune with the animals and wandered around singing happy songs."

"Like Cinderella?" I asked.

"Exactly," Allegra said, "slutty Cinderella," and we both cracked up.

"That's not true," Gran said.

"Please," Allegra said. "All Granddad does is sugarcoat."

I sat down on the floor and started sorting through the books, looking for one that didn't belong.

"You know," Gran said, stepping around me. "I have no idea where Eleanor's diary is, but I have something else you might find interesting."

"What?" Allegra asked, hopping to her feet.

Gran scanned a row of books, standing on tiptoe to reach the top shelf. She pulled down a wide, thick book, covered in faded black fabric, the pages bunched and uneven. "Here it is." She sat down in one of the armchairs near the fireplace, and Allegra and I stood on either side of her, both of us peering down at the book on her lap.

"What is it?" I asked. The front of the book had no markings or title, and the whole thing looked homemade.

"A hair book," Gran said, lifting the cover gently.

"What the hell is a hair book?" Allegra asked, raising her eyebrows in my direction. I mouthed, "I have no idea," and turned my attention back to the book in Gran's lap.

Gran sighed, gave Allegra a long-suffering look. "A hair book is exactly what it sounds like. A book of hair." Gran opened the book, and there, right on the first page, was a collection of hair. Some of it short and wispy, as though saved from a baby's first haircut, other locks longer and thicker and bound to the page with frayed ribbon.

"This is a Roanoke family heirloom," Gran told us. "Your granddad's grandma started it, and everyone's added to it over the years." Gran flipped to the back of the book. "This is your aunt Penelope's hair." Gran ran her thin fingers over a heavy braid, tied at the end with a dull white ribbon. "We cut it right before she was buried." The hair was dark, like Allegra's and mine, but gilded with a hint of blondish highlights as the sun coming through the library window hit the strands.

"She fell down the stairs, right?" I asked. I wanted to reach down and touch the braid, but I wasn't sure if Gran would allow it. Her fingers on the braid looked possessive, like she might pinch me for getting too close.

"Yeah," Allegra said. "It was the middle of the night. Snapped her neck." She made a harsh clicking sound between her teeth.

"Oh, Allegra," Gran said. "Don't mock. It was horrible. Horrible." She ran the braid between her fingers. "I raised her from the time she was a baby."

"How old was she when she died?" I asked.

"Barely fourteen," Gran said. "Still a little girl. I'll never forget how she looked. Tangled up in her white nightgown." I glanced from the book to Gran's face, searching for tears, but Gran's expression was as placid as ever. She turned the page.

"Now this," she said, tapping a smattering of hair glued to the page, "this is your mother's hair, Allegra. And this"—she pointed to an identical lock next to it—"this is your mother's, Lane. I kept a bit from haircuts they got when they were young." She smiled down at the page. "Camilla raised an absolute fit about it. She hated this book. Thought it was disgusting and creepy."

"It *is* disgusting and creepy," Allegra said, but with a tone of voice that conveyed how much she loved its strangeness.

I couldn't resist the urge any longer, leaned over and ran my finger along my mother's hair, *Camilla, 1981, age 10*, written above it in a careful hand. Both my mother's hair and Eleanor's hair were exactly like Allegra's and mine, down to the coppery undertones nestled in all the dark. I doubted you'd be able to tell our hair from theirs if ours made its way into the book someday.

Gran started to close the book, but Allegra's hand stopped her. Allegra turned the final page even as Gran tried to rise up from the chair. "What's on the last page?" Allegra asked. The book fell back open on Gran's lap, a few wispy tendrils of hair attached to the page with a pale yellow ribbon. *Emmeline, 1984, 6 months.*

"Oh," Allegra breathed out. "The dead baby."

"Did you cut it yourself? Before the funeral?" I asked, and Gran gave me a startled look. Maybe surprised I could be as unfeeling as Allegra when the mood struck me.

"Yes," she said.

"She died in her crib," Allegra said, glancing at me.

"Yeah, you already told me."

"You were the one who found her, right?" Allegra asked, poking Gran in the shoulder. Twisting the knife.

"She looked like she was sleeping," Gran said. "Except her little lips were blue. And she was so cold. I thought if I warmed her up, she'd be all right. Your granddad had to pry her out of my arms. I cursed him something awful. Swore I'd never hold another baby again." Gran took a deep breath and closed the book. She looked up at Allegra. "Of course, you came along and made a liar out of me." Gran still wasn't crying, but there was a slim crack in her facade, like the tiniest fissure in a smooth pane of glass.

Allegra hesitated for a second and then leaned over like she was going to give Gran a hug. Gran made an impatient sound, batted Allegra's arms away as she stood. I already knew Gran wasn't a hugger. Maybe now I knew why. Maybe that final embrace with Emmeline was the last one Gran ever wanted.

When Tommy pulled up to the end of the drive to pick up Allegra and me, Cooper wasn't with him. "He's meeting us at the party," Tommy said with an apologetic smile.

"Why?" Allegra asked.

"Don't know," Tommy said, but the flush on the tops of his ears gave him away.

"Did you know he wasn't coming?" Allegra asked me, as she climbed into the passenger seat and I got in back.

"No," I said. "But it's not a big deal." But inside I had a feeling it was. Ever since the day we'd spent in his bed, things had been different between Cooper and me. Nothing had changed to an outside observer. We still spent time together, still slept together, still gravitated toward each other whenever we were in the same room. But underneath something had shifted, at least for me. Every time I saw his face, I could feel a dark swirl of meanness and fear rising up in me, the emotions so entwined I couldn't distinguish where one ended and the other began. I told myself to stop, but I couldn't seem to find the switch that turned off my own worst impulses. Instead, I avoided conversation, ducked out from beneath Cooper's arm, and never let my eyes meet his when we had sex. I tried to tell myself Cooper didn't notice the difference, but maybe him not coming with Tommy tonight meant he did.

The party we were going to was being held at some guy's farmhouse. His parents were out of town and the whole place was overrun with kids. There was a huge bonfire burning in a pit in his back lawn, and already the ground was littered with crushed beer cans. My eyes were immediately drawn to Cooper, who was leaning back against the deck, a beer in his hand. A girl I didn't recognize was draped along his side.

"Oh my God. I can't believe that *slut* is here!" Allegra said in a voice designed to carry.

"Who?" I asked, looking away from Cooper.

"Becca James," Allegra said. "The one eye-fucking Cooper. They dated a few years ago, before he dumped her *lame ass*," Allegra practically yelled. "She's been trying to get him back ever since."

I glanced over at Cooper and Becca again. Her face was tipped up to his, her body turned toward him. He wasn't touching her, but he wasn't walking away from her, either.

"I'm gonna go get a beer," Allegra announced. "Want one?"

"Sure," I said.

Allegra stalked off with a blistering look at Becca, and Tommy stepped up next to me. "Cooper had a fight with his dad today," he said, voice lowered.

"I thought that was over," I said. "I thought Cooper ended all that."

Tommy's smile was sad. "I don't think it ever really ends, Lane. I mean, his dad doesn't beat him bloody anymore. But they still hate each other. It's always going to be a battle." Tommy laid a hand on my arm. "It might be better to stay away from him tonight. When he gets like this . . . he does things he regrets later."

Allegra sidled up with three beers balanced between her hands, and Tommy and I each took one. I let my mind linger on what Tommy had said. I didn't feel jealousy over Becca or concern about Cooper. What I felt was a weird kind of relief. I knew how to hurt him now. And how to let him hurt me back. The dance was a familiar one. My mother had helped me memorize the steps long ago.

Allegra popped the top of her can, gave Cooper a swift once-over. He still hadn't moved from his spot beside Becca. Allegra turned her attention to me. "Screw him, Lane. Plenty of other guys around here. Wanna meet some?"

"Sure," I said. "Why not?"

"Allegra," Tommy said. "Maybe you shouldn't—"

But Allegra was already waving to a group of guys standing near the bonfire. "You have to meet Nick Samson," Allegra told me. "He'll be a senior this year. He played football with Tommy. He's completely adorable."

I let her drag me toward the bonfire, Tommy choosing not to follow. Nick turned out to be a thick-necked, dark-haired boy with hands like paddles. When he smiled at me, a wad of tobacco peeked out from his bottom lip. Not exactly my idea of adorable. I looked back at Cooper, saw he'd turned his whole body in my direction, Becca finally forgotten. Tommy had one hand on Cooper's chest, like he was holding him in place, and Allegra stood off to the side watching, gaze darting among all the various players. My eyes met Cooper's, and something dark and electric sizzled through the air between us.

Oblivious, Nick leaned over and put a hand on my waist, got right down to business. "Wanna take a walk?" he asked, his voice a low rumble.

"No, she doesn't fucking want to take a walk with you," Cooper said from behind me. Before I could even react, he'd shoved me aside and taken a wild, but hard, swing right at Nick's head.

They fought fast and furious, Nick grunting with exertion while Cooper saved his energy for punching. Nick was bigger but Cooper was angrier, and they might have gone on beating each other all night if Tommy and a couple other guys hadn't pulled them apart. Allegra stood next to me, her whole body vibrating with excitement. "They were fighting over you," she whispered. "That's so cool."

"It's not cool," I said, watching blood drip from Cooper's lips. Nick's school ring had caught him on the teeth, and he leaned over, spat a sliver of ivory into the grass. His hands shook with rage, but his eyes were distant. I wondered if he pictured his father's face when he hit Nick. Or maybe it was my face he longed to punch. I remembered his words about not wanting to turn into his father, about how every day he went without hitting someone took him a step further away from that destiny. Tonight, Cooper may have taken the first swing, but I'd led him right into the ring. I doubted he'd ever forgive me.

I knelt down beside Nick, took his hand and helped him stand. "If you're up for it," I told him, "I'll take a walk with you now."

"Sure," Nick said, his voice stuffy around a probable broken nose.

It didn't slow him down any though. He shook out his knuckles, wiped blood off his cheek with one hand. Now that the fight was over, everyone went right back to drinking like nothing had happened. They were used to swift flashes of violence. Especially from Cooper.

I didn't look at Cooper as Nick and I walked into the darkness. Outside the ring of light, Nick turned to me, pushed me back against a tree. His mouth was too wet. His tongue too meaty. He smelled like stale sweat and beer. I let him touch me, lift my shirt, and shove his hand down my shorts. I let him do what he wanted because I couldn't think of a single reason why I shouldn't.

Now

When I open my eyes, Cooper's already awake next to me. I can tell from his breathing. I've never slept all night in a bed with him, and if I ever pictured it happening, it was not like this. The smell of alcohol is strong, leaking out of my pores onto the soft cotton sheets. Sunlight streams in through the window and colors my naked skin a warm honey yellow. I turn my head to look at him, and my brain protests the movement, sends the room into a fast spin. My stomach somersaults up into my throat.

"Oh, shit," I moan and cover my eyes with one hand.

"You're hurting," Cooper says. It's not a question, and he doesn't sound particularly sympathetic.

"Yeah, I overdid it." My voice is husky and weak.

"Want me to get you some water? Or something for your head?"

"No. Just give me a minute." My whole body throbs, not only my head. "How long have you been up?"

"A while. I'm gonna go make some coffee."

I peek out at him from between my fingers. "Okay. Thanks."

Cooper rolls away from me, his spine stretching underneath his sun-brown skin. Once he's left the room, I force myself to sit up. The pounding in my head increases, and I take a few deep breaths, tell myself I'm not going to be sick. I manage to find my shorts and underwear tangled on the floor, but I don't see my bra or shirt anywhere. For all I know, they're still in Cooper's truck. I grab a faded T-shirt of Cooper's from his dresser and pull it on.

I make my way gingerly down the steep staircase, narrowly avoiding tripping over the black Lab sprawled at the bottom. I squint against the morning sunlight flowing in through uncovered windows. Already I smell coffee brewing. Cooper's house is clean and spare, the colors light. I imagine there's relief in stepping through this front door after a day at the dank garage. He loves this house; it's obvious with one glance. It's there in the polished wood floors and the fresh paint, the framed photographs on the mantel and the easy charm. It's a good room, a good house, and I feel childishly jealous.

I never had any plans to return to Osage Flats, but if I did, I always expected to find Tommy settled. It was no surprise to learn of Sarah. But somehow I never thought Cooper would have a place to call his own. I thought he'd end up more like me, a drifter even if he never set foot outside of Osage Flats, someone content to float from bed to bed, day to day. Seeing this house Cooper has turned into a home makes me feel even more like an impostor in a grownup's body. My life could be an eighteen-year-old's. And Allegra, still living at home, still sleeping in the same bedroom she's had since birth. All the Roanoke girls somehow unable to grow up, stuck in a suspended childhood their entire lives.

I follow the gurgle of brewing coffee into the pale yellow kitchen. The room is small and needs updating, but it feels cozy, the window above the sink giving a view of wheat fields that melt into the horizon. I pull out a chair and sit down at the table, rest my forehead in my hand.

"You might want to invest in curtains," I tell Cooper. "All this sunshine is a killer."

He snorts. "I think the real problem is the forty drinks you had."

"It wasn't forty," I grumble. Cooper puts a mug of coffee down in front of me, and I cradle it between my hands, breathe in the bitter smell. "Your dog almost made me break my neck, by the way."

"That's Punk. He's good people."

I attempt to roll my eyes before thinking better of it, wary of the pounding in my head. Cooper takes his own mug and hops up onto the counter, long legs dangling. "You want something to eat?" he asks. "I can scramble some eggs. Or make some toast."

I shake my head carefully, but even that's a mistake. "No, coffee's good."

"So," he says, after we've both had a few fortifying swallows, "what set you off last night? You came into Ronnie Joe's in pretty bad shape."

"Nothing."

"Nothing?"

"Can we not do this right now?" I ask with a sigh.

"What? You mean talk, like normal people?"

"We've never been normal people, Cooper," I say, which doesn't even net me a hint of a smile.

Cooper sets his mug down on the counter next to his hip. "We're not kids anymore, Lane. It's time to grow the fuck up." He's not quite angry, but he's somewhere in the neighborhood.

"What's that supposed to mean?"

"It means I've tried to make a life for myself, a decent one. It means that I've worked really hard not to turn into my father. To not use the way I grew up as an excuse. I'm not willing to go backward."

I glance over at him. "Yeah? Don't you still work at his garage?"

Cooper's face hardens. His hand clenches on his leg. "Low blow," he says, voice tight.

I shrug, remembering all the nasty, unfair things I said to Jeff near the end. "What did you expect? People don't change, Cooper, not really."

"Yes, they do. If they really want to. And no matter what you think, I'm different than I was at eighteen. I'm not interested in a repeat performance. And last night felt like that's where we were headed." He runs a hand through his hair. "I can't do it again. It hurt too much the first time around."

This is a Cooper I've never met, one I didn't know existed. Part of me didn't truly believe he was capable of being hurt, at least not by someone like me. But age has made him braver, more willing to put all his past grievances on the line. For me, the passing years have had the opposite effect. I'm more scared than I've ever been.

He hops down from the counter and leans over me, his hands on the chair back behind me. "But we could start over," he says. "Couldn't we? I think we had something, Lane, even way back then. Something good hidden underneath all the crap we threw at each other."

I force myself to look up at him, keep my breathing steady. I feel trapped in a way that has nothing to do with his arms bracketing me, holding me in place. "What are you even talking about?" The annoyance in my voice is a relief to me. I wasn't sure what I would give away when I opened my mouth.

"We could start over," he repeats as he traces one finger down my cheek, slides it gently across my bottom lip. I open my mouth, let him slip his finger inside, lick the tip with my tongue. I wait until his eyes go soft and hazy and then bite down. Hard.

"Jesus!" Cooper hisses, yanking his hand free. "What the hell was that for?"

"Don't do that again." My heart hammers so violently I imagine it's about to barrel right out of my chest.

"Don't do *what* again?"

"Don't try and pretend we're something we're not." My breath is coming fast and sharp, stinging in my throat. "It's bullshit and it makes me want to puke."

Cooper backs away, his face a careful blank, eyes empty. It's a look I remember well. "Maybe you're right," he says. "Maybe people don't change. Because God knows, you're still the same heartless bitch you've always been."

Sometimes it's a revelation, even to me, how much more comfortable I am with cruelty than with kindness.

I spend the day sleeping off my hangover in my humid, stuffy bedroom, sheets slick with sweat. Around six Granddad knocks on the door to see if I want to drive into town with them for dinner, but I ignore him until I hear his footsteps retreating down the hall. After Granddad's truck rattles down the drive, I get up and shower, find myself some leftover macaroni in the fridge, and eat it cold while standing against the counter.

Twilight is settling in, lighting up the sky with the reddish glow that means a storm is on the way, when I decide to go into town. Charlie is out in the barn feeding the cats and gives me a wave as I drive past.

"Still here?" he calls, and I stop, lean over to talk to him out my open passenger window.

"So far," I say, trying for a smile. He doesn't smile back.

"Thought maybe you'd be gone by now."

"Me too. But I need to know what happened to Allegra."

Charlie nods, spits into the dirt. "Like I said before, might be we never know, Lane. Not a good enough reason for you to stay." His eyes are phlegmy. Old man's eyes, but their gaze is keen. He picks up one of the kittens, rubs his big, scarred fingers under its tiny chin.

"I'm doing okay," I tell him, but my trembling hands, my whiskey-sour stomach and aching head make a liar out of me.

"You sure?" Charlie asks.

I nod, take my foot off the brake, and coast away. There are things I can't talk about, even with Charlie, who holds all the same secrets I do.

I don't really have a particular destination in mind. The Eat is out, unless I want to share a meal with my grandparents. And Ronnie Joe's is off-limits, the risk Cooper might be there too great. I stop at the grocery for some beer and then drive around town aimlessly, find myself at the park without making any conscious decision to stop. It's almost full dark now, and the park is deserted. As I get out, a car passes, momentarily blinding me with its headlights.

The air is even thicker than usual, making it difficult to inhale a full breath. My lungs turn to sponges and my hair takes on weight, sweat bubbling to the surface of my skin only five steps into the park. Heat lightning streaks across the sky. I head for the carousel, slide in through the gap in the chain link, snagging the back of my shirt on the ragged end of the fence. The only sounds are the rustling of leaves in the huge trees surrounding the carousel, the ever-present cicadas, and a lone rumble of thunder in the distance. I clamber up onto the wooden deck of the carousel and give thanks to the full moon, otherwise I'd be slamming my shins into horses as I move around the circle searching for my favorite, the black one with the aqua mane and the eyes rolling back in her head.

"I knew you'd go for that one." Tommy's voice slides out of the darkness behind me, and I whirl around, smacking the horse on the head with the six-pack of beer in my hand.

"Scared the shit out of me," I inform him as I swing a leg up, settle myself onto the horse's back. "And I always pick this one. I like her."

"Her?" Tommy's next to me now, pulling himself up onto the palomino on my left. It's missing its tail, and someone has keyed a long streak down the paint on its side, leaving a glinting silver scar in the moonlight.

"I don't know. She always seemed like a girl horse to me." I give her a friendly pat on the head and pull two beers from the six-pack, hang the remaining four from the horse's ear. "Want one?"

"Sure." Tommy takes his beer and pops the tab, holding it out from his body as foam spews.

"What are you doing here?" I ask, opening my own can. I haven't seen Tommy since the silo, have no idea if Sarah's told him about my visit. He's acting like the same old Tommy, but I know better now, know he has secrets he's hiding like everyone else. Maybe I should be nervous, alone in the dark with him, but I can't make myself take seriously the idea that he might hurt me. Which is probably what Allegra thought, too. I hope he isn't playing both of us for fools.

"I was headed home after a late shift. Saw you getting out. You always did love this place. Figured I'd stop and say hello."

"Won't Sarah be wondering where you are?"

"I won't stay long. Things are pretty tense at home right now anyway." He hoists his beer in my direction. "A little liquid fortification before my arrival won't hurt."

"I'm guessing you and Sarah had a talk?"

Tommy nods. "I finally came clean, couldn't hold it inside anymore after I told you. And you were right. She knew about Allegra the whole time."

"Think you're going to be able to work it out?" I ask.

"I don't know." Tommy sighs, belly-deep and heavy. "She wants to. And, really, I do, too. I love my wife." He sucks in air, and I want to shout *Stop! Don't say it!* because I know what's coming. And I don't want to be the keeper of those words, the bearer of his unrequited flame, but he gets them out before I can find a way to deflect them. "But she's not Allegra."

"Oh, Jesus." I sigh. "After everything, Tommy, why would you want her to be?" I lean forward and rest my forehead against the golden pole running through my horse's body. The metal is warm and slightly tacky against my skin. "Allegra's never going to be what you need. Trust me. You want babies and a wife and the whole American Dream. She's never going to be soccer mom material, and I think deep down you've always known it."

"You're probably right," Tommy says after a pause. He lobs his crushed beer can toward the trash barrel near the fence. It makes a loud bang on contact, but in the dark I can't tell if it was a hit or a miss. I pull another beer from the six-pack and hand it to him.

"I never quite understood it," I tell him. "Allegra and you. What the fascination was. She never seemed like your type, like the kind of girl a guy like you would fall for."

"Could say the same about Cooper and you."

"No, you couldn't. Cooper and I were a matched set. So fucked up no one else would want us. We're like the poster children for dysfunction."

"Cooper's dad did a number on him, that's for sure," Tommy says. "But Cooper's come a long way." Exactly what Cooper told me in his kitchen and I didn't want to hear. Maybe I'm jealous that I'm still as messed up as ever while he's evolved into something more than he used to be. Tommy continues, "He's not perfect, don't get me wrong. But he's turned into a good man. A better man than his dad ever was." Tommy reaches over with his foot and snags my horse's stirrup, rattles it to make sure he has my attention. "And I never thought you were that screwed up, for what it's worth. Just young. We were all so damn young."

I laugh, but it's not a happy sound. "We *were* young. But that doesn't excuse anything. The way I treated Cooper . . ." This is more than I've ever admitted out loud, and I can't even bring myself to finish my sentence, don't want to think too hard about the way I left things with Cooper this morning.

"If there's anyone who understands lashing out, it's Cooper," Tommy says. "I think he'd forgive you, Lane, for all of it. But you have to be willing to let him."

I drop my empty beer can at my feet, open another one even

though the ghost of last night's alcohol still lingers on my tongue. "No offense, Tommy, but you're not exactly in a position to be giving relationship advice."

Tommy laughs, the one I recognize, not the sharp-edged version from the silo. "Touché."

"Besides, I thought we were talking about Allegra and you."

"I used to watch her all the time, even in grade school." Tommy shakes his head, a soft smile passing across his face. "She always seemed so fragile, underneath all her crazy bravado."

"She *was* fragile," I say. "She is fragile." Which is the simplest explanation for how Tommy fell in love with her. He was always the boy who wanted to make things better, fix anything broken. And in a world filled with damaged goods, Allegra is the most broken thing of all.

Tommy nods. "When she agreed to go out with me, I thought I was the luckiest son of a bitch in the world. Took me a while to figure out she didn't choose me, she just allowed herself to be chosen. Which isn't the same thing at all. She was never really mine."

"No," I say. "She wasn't." I grip my horse's mane as though I'm about to be bucked off. "What do you think happened to her, Tommy? Not the cop version. The honest version. The guy-who-loves-her version."

Tommy exhales, his breath uneven. "She's dead, Lane. That's what I think. She's gone. It all got to be too much for her and she . . . drifted away."

I close my eyes. It's what I think, too. One way or the other, Allegra is gone. But I can't say it out loud. I've never been superstitious, never believed you can change fate through the power of a wish or a curse. But I'm not willing to risk it on Allegra's life, not willing to voice dark words that might forever seal her fate.

"If I knew anything concrete about what happened to her, I'd tell you," Tommy says, voice quiet in the darkness.

I don't open my eyes. "Even if it made you look bad?"

"Yes."

A strong breeze blows through the trees, cooling my skin and bringing with it the loamy scent of rain. "Even if Sarah had something to do with it?" I ask.

The slightest of pauses. "Even then."

I wish I could believe him.

Then

Even when Allegra sat still she never stopped moving. Some part of her was always in motion, a finger twisting a long wave of hair, a foot tapping a rhythm against her chair, her tongue passing back and forth across her lower lip. But her fidgeting didn't have the same unfocused, sluggish energy I usually associated with people who couldn't hold still. Hers felt frenzied, uncontrollable almost, like something lived beneath her skin and was playing her body like a fiddle. Sometimes being in the same room with her exhausted me.

"How do you spell *abortion*?" Allegra asked.

My head jerked up. Allegra tapped Granddad's pocketknife against her leg, her free hand tracing the wooden arm of the chair where she sat. "Seriously?"

Allegra laughed. "No, not seriously."

I rolled my eyes. "Why are you always carving up stuff?" I asked, my gaze falling to the pocketknife.

Allegra's hand tightened protectively around the knife. "I don't know. I like doing it. Sometimes a word or a feeling is so strong, I have to get it out. It helps me."

"Helps you with what?"

Allegra shrugged with tight shoulders. "Feel normal, I guess.

Calm." She flicked open the pocketknife, ran the blade along the wood.

"So it's kind of like a diary?"

"Yeah." Allegra snorted. "The diary of a person with a super-short attention span."

"And you don't mind people reading what you write?"

Allegra shook her head. "No, sometimes that's the point."

"Like when you left *cunt* on Sharon's cutting board?"

"Exactly," Allegra said, a smile on her face. "You should try it sometime. You could write about how much you and Cooper looooove each other." She mimed writing in the air with the knife. "Lane Sullivan. Mrs. Lane Sullivan." She stuck a finger down her throat so I'd know exactly how she felt about that idea.

"Cooper and I aren't in love." And we weren't. Or at least not the kind Allegra meant. The night of the party and the fight with Nick hadn't ended things between Cooper and me, only reduced us to our lowest common denominator—angry sex that left me hollowed out in the aftermath. We were horrible to each other now, and it felt familiar, safe. Safer by far than whatever it was I'd felt that day in Cooper's bed. Our barbed-wire affection was the type of love I understood.

"Whatever," Allegra huffed. "You two still fuck all over the place."

Now it was my turn to shrug. "Your point?"

"I don't want to talk about Cooper," Allegra said, eyes flashing.

"You brought him up," I reminded her. "And what about you and Tommy? I bet you've got a few *Allegra Kenning*s scrawled around here somewhere."

Allegra looked away from me, her gaze lingering on the view from the library window, endless green prairie rolling into the distance. "I'm not going to marry Tommy," she said.

"He would, though," I said. "In a heartbeat."

"Even if I wanted to someday, Tommy's too nice for me," Allegra said. "Besides, I'll never leave Roanoke."

That stopped me. I shifted from where I'd been lying on the floor, flicking my way through a fashion magazine. "Why not? What are you going to do here your whole life?"

Allegra's eyes snapped back to mine. "You're not staying?"

"Forever?" I laughed. "I seriously doubt it."

"But . . . where would you go?" Allegra's knuckles were white where they gripped the arm of the chair. I forgot sometimes she had been born here, had never seen anyplace but Roanoke and Osage Flats. When I told her stories about New York, I might as well have been describing life on an alien planet.

"I don't know. It's not like I have a specific plan. But I don't picture living here with Gran and Granddad when I'm older. That would be weird."

Allegra was already shaking her head. "I don't think it's weird. They're our family. This is where we belong." She pulled her legs up and hugged her knees to her chest. "I'll never leave here. Not until the day I die."

It was no longer a given that Cooper would be there when Allegra and I met up with Tommy in town. Sometimes he was. Sometimes he wasn't. Sometimes he was there with some other girl on his arm, her tongue swirling inside his mouth while his blank eyes followed me. This was where we were now. And somehow I'd always known it was where we would end up.

But tonight it was only the four of us at the park, sharing a bag of food from the hamburger stand and a bottle of bourbon. At some point Tommy and Allegra disappeared, and Cooper drove me home after a stop at the old silo that left us sweaty and sore. Cooper pulled my hair as he came, jerking my head backward, not gentle, not kind. "No matter what, I had you first," he whispered, his hips bucking, teeth scraping against my throat. "Don't ever forget. I had you first." Lately it felt like we were trying to break each other, see who'd be the first to cry uncle and end it once and for all.

Cooper didn't linger when he dropped me off, didn't kiss me good-bye or touch my cheek with the backs of his fingers. He left me with a *see ya around,* and no backward glance. Roanoke was mostly dark when I let myself in the front door. A faint light glowed from the kitchen, but when I went in, no one was there. I stumbled up the back staircase, drunk on sex and bourbon, the smell of Cooper clinging to me like some exotic perfume. The scent made me feel close to tears, heavy with a melancholy I couldn't explain, and I was anxious to wash it away.

I didn't bother to turn on any lights as I made my way through the dark second floor. Most of the time I showered in the new bathroom down the hall from my bedroom, but sometimes I preferred the old, claw-foot tub at the other end of the house. I picked my way gingerly through the sleeping porch, careful not to snag my toes on the frames of the metal bunk beds. Once in the bathroom, I kept the lights off. The moon peeked in full and bright through the uncovered windows. Allegra hated this bathroom, thought it was old and gross. But I loved how big it was, the wall of windows giving a view of the sky, the cold, white tile floor, the tub with its cracked rubber stopper on a rusted metal chain.

I sank into the lukewarm water and let my hair drift out behind me. Since the bathroom I usually used had been added on after my mom left, I sometimes imagined her floating in this same tub, me growing inside her. The water nudged over my face, and I closed my eyes. Did she ever think of trying to go under? I have to think she did, knowing how she ended up. I let my head sink lower, the water lapping at the edges of my nose.

Someone tapped lightly on the bathroom door, and I bolted

upright as Gran slipped inside. She carried a half-full crystal high-ball glass in her hand. I'd never seen Gran with alcohol before.

"Mind if I join you?" she asked. She didn't turn on the light. Before I could answer, she'd lowered herself onto a tiny wooden chair at the end of the tub by my feet. It was a child's chair, and even Gran's petite frame looked too big for it, her legs bent like a grasshopper's.

"Did you need something?" I asked.

Gran shook her head, took a swallow of her drink. "No. I heard you come in. Thought maybe you wanted to chat. We don't talk enough, you and I."

It took me a second to realize Gran was drunk. Not falling-down, puke-in-a-toilet drunk like Allegra and I got, but definitely not herself. There was a slight slur to her words, and a chunk of her hair had loosened itself from her chignon to lie along her cheek. That's something a sober Gran never would have allowed. I rarely saw Gran at night. She usually made herself scarce after dinner. For all I knew, this was her usual routine. She could spend her evenings getting quietly sloshed and I'd be none the wiser.

"Where's Allegra?" I asked. "Is she home?"

"Who knows?" Gran said. "I never know where Allegra is. Or if I do, I'd rather not."

"She was with Tommy earlier."

"Tommy," Gran scoffed. She waved her arm dismissively, and a bit of alcohol splashed out of her glass, forming a tiny amber puddle on the floor. "He doesn't know the first thing about who Allegra really is. If he did, he'd run away screaming."

I took the bar of soap from where it sat on a metal stand hooked over the side of the tub and lathered my neck and under my arms. I could feel Gran's eyes on me.

"You probably think Cooper Sullivan's always going to be wrapped around your finger, don't you?" she asked.

I hadn't known Gran was aware of Cooper. Until now, Granddad was the only one who'd mentioned him. I finished soaping myself, rinsed with water cupped in my hands. "I don't think that," I said finally. In fact, I thought Cooper was probably about done with me. The sheer relief that thought brought was tempered only by the corresponding ache in my breastbone.

The crystal glass in Gran's hand caught the moonlight as she lifted it up, swirled the liquid inside before taking another sip. "Probably think that body, that face, will always get you what you want. That men will forever be mesmerized by what's between your legs." Her eyes pierced my flesh, probing, judging. "That's what your mother thought. Always so proud of herself."

The girl my gran described was not the woman I knew at all. My mother wore her beauty like a punishment. She couldn't escape it, so she tried to disguise it, decorated her face with tears instead of makeup, wore clothes designed to conceal, rather than flaunt. I think perhaps the worst day of her life was the morning she woke up and discovered I was destined to look exactly like her. Maybe if I'd been ugly instead, she could have found a way to love me.

Gran and I stared at each other, and her face folded in on itself, wrinkles hidden in daylight making an appearance in the near darkness. She closed her eyes, pinched the bridge of her nose. When she opened her eyes, her face was impassive again, as if I'd only imagined her momentary loss of control.

"You be careful, Lane," she said, pointing at me.

"What are you talking about? I don't—"

"You be careful," she repeated, stood on unsteady legs. "I'm just about done raising other people's children."

Now

I've started taking long walks through the fields surrounding Roanoke during the day. I tell myself I'm looking for clues about what happened to Allegra, but really, I don't know what else to do with myself. I was stupid to think I could be the one to help Allegra. It's more obvious every day that I can barely manage to take care of myself. Did I actually think I'd ask a few questions, make people a little uncomfortable, and the truth about Allegra would come tumbling out? I've exhausted my ideas, and the entire town of Osage Flats feels off-limits after my fight with Cooper anyway. It's more his territory than mine, and I don't want to run into him, see that cold, distant look on his face. And Roanoke is just as bad, Granddad weepy-eyed and quiet, Gran drifting from room to room like a ghost.

It was clear and hot when I left the house after lunch, but only an hour later dark clouds are rolling in fast from the western horizon, blotting out the sun. I try to beat the weather back, but I'm soaked through to the skin by the time I reach Roanoke, the rain falling in thick sheets that obscure the ground only steps in front of me. I've never seen it rain anywhere else the way it rains in Kansas, like the sky has something to prove, each thunder crack in a contest to be the loudest, the ground quivering under the aim of angry lightning bolts.

I drip my way up the back stairs and shiver even in the heat. I leave my wet clothes in a heap on my bedroom floor and change into dry shorts and a T-shirt, wrap my soaking hair in one of the plush mint-green towels from the bathroom. The storm has made the house dark as twilight, deep shadows in every corner, and I move through the empty hallway switching on lamps as I go. The sharp tap of hail begins against the window panes like bony fingers trying to find a way inside.

The sound of the rain draws me up to Allegra's turret room. The few times it rained the summer I lived at Roanoke, Allegra and I would sit in her windows and let it blow in on us through the screens. I turn on her bedside lamp and curl up on her unmade bed. The damp towel around my head soaks her pillow, releasing the scent of Allegra's hair, and I close my eyes, breathe her in.

"Help me, Allegra," I whisper. "I can't do this without you." There's no answer, of course, only the sound of rain slamming into the roof and windows. It's like being in a tiny boat, adrift on storm-tossed seas. Sleep overtakes me, and when I wake the rain has stopped, although the sun has yet to make a reappearance. I should probably get up and see what time it is, do something besides sleeping away another wasted afternoon, but I can't make myself rise. I'd forgotten the strange inertia of Roanoke, the way being inside its walls makes you stop caring very much about what goes on outside.

My gaze lands on Allegra's bedside table, and from this angle a double-paned picture frame peeks back at me. I reach out and lift it closer. The photo on the left is of my mother and Allegra's mother, Eleanor. I slide the photo out of the frame, looking for a date or indication when it was taken, but there's nothing written on the back. I would guess they are about fifteen and sixteen in the shot, both of them in bikinis. They stand hip to hip with their arms slung around each other's shoulders. Their dark hair blows in the breeze, Cheshire cat grins stretching across their beautiful faces. There is something faintly seductive in both their smiles, in the come-hither tilt of their slim hips. Which means it was probably my granddad behind the camera. Another day of wholesome family fun at Roanoke.

The second picture is of Allegra and me, taken the summer I lived here. We are both in bikinis, too. Mine red and hers black. We are standing exactly as our mothers did fifteen years earlier, white teeth flashing, coppery highlights in our hair catching the sun. I remember posing for this photograph, Tommy behind the lens, Cooper off to the side, smirking. It had been the only time the four of us had visited the swimming hole together, and Allegra had insisted on this photo, had moved me around like a department store mannequin, trying to get my limbs in exactly the right position. I hadn't known she was attempting to re-create a photograph of our mothers. Maybe she'd hoped we'd be the same girls with a happier outcome.

I remove the back of the frame and pull out the picture of Allegra and me, meaning to take it downstairs, keep it safe until she comes home. Two more photographs fall onto the bed from their hiding spot behind the original picture. The one on top is of Allegra and Tommy, a close-up of their faces, cheeks smooshed together as they grin crazily for the camera. I can't help smiling at the sight of it. Underneath is a photo of Cooper and me. He's lying on a towel spread across the trampled grass near the edge of the swimming hole, one arm hooked behind his head. I'm on my side, my head resting on his chest, my hand starfished on his bare stomach. I don't remember this picture being taken, would probably have objected had I known. We both look relaxed, easy in a way I can't remember ever actually feeling. The image burns my eyes, makes them sting, as Cooper's words whisper in my brain. *I think we had something, Lane, even way back then . . . Something good.*

I take all three photographs and shove them into the back pocket of my shorts, hop off Allegra's bed, and leave the green towel on her pillow. My hair is still wet, and I pile it up on my head using a handful of bobby pins from Allegra's vanity. After a stop in my room to grab my sunglasses and car keys, I race downstairs and out to the garage.

"Hey, Charlie," I call. "If you see Gran or Granddad, tell them I won't be back until later."

Charlie looks up from where he's working inside the barn. "You heading into town?"

"No." I jangle my keys with impatient fingers. "I'm driving out to the old swimming hole." I have no idea why I want to go, what the urgency is, but now that the idea's got ahold of me, it's digging in deep.

Charlie shakes his head, takes a few steps closer to me, out into the slowly returning sunlight. "That hole's about dried up, Lane. Had a few years of bad drought and it never recovered. Not safe to swim in it. Hell, might not have any water in it at all this summer."

My heart sinks, but I say, "That's okay. I just want to see it again." I don't even know why, exactly. It's not as if looking into the swimming hole's weedy depths will bring Allegra home, turn back time to the days when Roanoke held such promise, when I had yet to destroy what was growing between Cooper and me. But I still want to stand on its banks, even if it's no longer the same place. Stand there and remember what might have been.

It takes me a long time to find it. It's been more than ten years, and there's no clear marked path. But finally I spot a familiar withered tree in the distance, discover the hidden ruts through the long grass. My car bounces and rattles over the ground, not meant to cover such rough terrain. I'll be lucky if I don't lose my muffler.

The wind hits me when I get out of the car, whipping across the prairie and tangling around me like vines. The sun has come out again, although clouds still race across the sky, making strange, misshapen shadows slide along the ground. From where I stand, I can see Charlie was mostly right—the swimming hole doesn't live up to its name anymore. But it's not completely dry, the dark, dirty water probably still a good six or seven feet deep. Long cattails grow out of the water's edge, and the sides of the hole are cracked and crumbling, sending tiny avalanches of rock and soil into the water.

I turn in a slow circle, trying to get my bearings and remember exactly where Cooper and I were lying when that photograph was taken. I feel it in my back pocket, but I don't pull it out. Not much has changed out here other than the level of the water and the passage of time, but somehow it's enough to skew my entire perspective. Nothing is the same as I remember it. Or maybe I remember it wrong.

The air smells of dust and decay. I pick my way closer to the edge of the swimming hole, and something splashes into the water, probably a frog or tumble of dirt, marring the surface with a few faint ripples. There's something tangled in the cattails, and my breath snags in my chest as I stumble forward. I sink to my knees, a desolate cry bursting out of me. My eyes catch on a coil of dark hair wrapped around the weeds just beneath the murky surface of the water, and a flash of white bone disappearing into the shallow depths.

"Lane," Tommy says, "why don't you go back to the house? Wait with your gran and granddad."

"No."

Tommy sighs, holds up a finger to the ring of cops waiting behind him. "They could use you there, Lane. They're falling apart."

My eyes don't move from the swimming hole. "I don't care. I'm not leaving. Not until you get her out of there."

"It might not even be Allegra," Tommy says, and I hear the edge of desperate hope in his voice.

I turn my head, finally, to look at him. "It's her, Tommy."

"You stay right here." Tommy draws an invisible line across the ground. "No matter what. You don't cross it. You hear me?"

I nod, back up a step for good measure. I won't leave until she's out of that water. If they try to make me, I will lose my mind, a flush of panic and sorrow already swirling in my chest.

It seems like lifting her out of the swimming hole should be quick and easy, but the minutes tick away and nothing happens. A cluster of county sheriff's deputies talk quietly near their cars, and a few people in black T-shirts crouch down near the edge of the water, one big-boned woman with a camera taking photograph after photograph.

"You didn't touch anything?" a cop with a notebook asks me. It's at least the tenth time I've been asked the same question.

"No. I saw her body and tried to call Tommy, but I couldn't get a connection on my phone, so I drove back toward Roanoke until I could call. Then I came right back here and waited for you to show up. I never touched the water, or her, at all."

The cop's writing down what I say when he glances over my shoulder and his body stiffens. "Excuse me a minute," he says, walks fast to Tommy. I look behind me and see puffs of dust in the near distance, a truck slamming over the ruts toward us. I steel myself for my granddad, his tears and heartbroken eyes, but when the truck finally stops, it's Cooper who jumps out.

"No," Tommy calls as he walks toward Cooper. "Nuh-uh, this isn't a spectator sport. You need to get the hell out of here, Cooper."

Cooper holds up both hands, but doesn't stop walking in my direction. His face is pale and his eyes cut right through me. "I'm not here to gawk, Tommy," he says. "Jesus Christ. I won't get in the way, and I won't say a goddamn word."

Tommy reaches him, and they stand in a tense little huddle. I return my gaze to the swimming hole, and although their voices are low, I still catch a word here or there. *Can't have you . . . She needs . . . Worried . . . Let me . . .*

Cooper must win the argument because Tommy returns to the edge of the swimming hole, and Cooper comes to stand beside me where I'm leaning against my car. His arm brushes mine and he takes my hand, laces our fingers together and squeezes. A few tears overflow and run down my cheeks, as if the pressure of his hand has forced them out of me.

"Hey," he says. "I'm here." All of the bitter anger wedged between us the last time we saw each other has evaporated. Now, Allegra's sodden corpse bridges the space between us.

I don't trust myself to speak, give a quick nod instead. He squeezes my hand again, keeps my fingers tight in his, and I let my head fall onto his shoulder.

It's evening by the time they lift what remains of Allegra from the water, her dark hair clotted with weeds. "Don't look," Cooper says, but I can't look anywhere else. He raises our still-joined hands to his chest, presses my fingers against his thumping heart.

Tommy stays at Roanoke long after everyone else has gone. He sits at the kitchen table with me, both of us staring at a half-empty bottle of vodka, but neither of us making a move to drink it. Gran and Granddad went upstairs after Tommy gave them the news, climbing the main staircase together. Granddad leaned on Gran like he didn't trust his own legs, and she bore his weight all the way to the top. I know their love is twisted and ugly at its roots, but at least they have something. At least they have each other. It hardly seems fair when Allegra is lying alone somewhere in the back of a police van.

"What happens now?" I ask Tommy. My voice is scratchy, like I haven't spoken in weeks. Tears push against my vocal cords, but other than the few I shed at the swimming hole, my eyes have remained dry.

Tommy, on the other hand, is leaking like a broken faucet, a steady stream of tears washing down his face, tripping over his stubble before landing on the tabletop. "We'll be back out there at first light."

"No, I meant with Allegra."

"Oh." Tommy releases a hiccuping breath. "Now there's an autopsy."

I nod, trying not to think about someone piecing Allegra back together, looking for the secrets of her death hidden on her body. "How long will that take?"

"Depends on the backlog, but I wouldn't think more than a few days." He lets out a shaky sigh, wipes both hands down his face. "Why would she have gone way out there to do it?" he asks. "We might never have found her."

"You think she killed herself," I say, my voice as lifeless as Allegra's body.

Tommy cuts his eyes in my direction, swings them back to the bottle of vodka. "Yeah, I do."

For someone who claimed to love Allegra, I don't know how he can be so stupid. I thought it was possible Allegra killed herself, too, before we actually found her. But Allegra would never have chosen to end her life in the dirty water of the swimming hole, hair knotted with weeds, flesh puffy with rot. Someone else left her there, forced that final indignity upon her. But I'm not going to say that to Tommy, who has a lifetime of anger at Allegra barely hidden beneath his love, whose wife despised Allegra with every bone in her second-best body. Or maybe Tommy just wants *me* to believe that Allegra committed suicide.

"I've got to get home, Lane," Tommy says. "When I know something, you'll know something."

After Tommy leaves, I swear I can hear the sound of my granddad weeping, although I know it's not really possible. But the thought of him shedding tears over Allegra makes me want to scream, and I burst out through the screened porch breathing hard, muscles tight with the need to escape.

I arrive at Cooper's dark doorstep without knowing how I got there. I certainly didn't have his house in mind when I sped down the lane away from Roanoke. We'd parted ways at the swimming hole once the cops were done. When he let go of my hand, I could still feel the beat of his heart against my fingertips.

I knock without giving myself time to think about it. From beyond the door I hear the sound of footsteps, and then Cooper is there in the open doorway, the spill of light from his house making me blink.

"Hi," I say and give a ridiculous, halfhearted wave. I have no idea what the fuck I'm doing here.

Cooper says nothing, steps back and waits for me to come inside. I walk into his living room. He's been reading, a book tented on his coffee table, an open beer next to it.

"Sorry. You're busy." My voice catches, and I keep my eyes on his couch, my back to him. "I don't know why I came. I just . . . I should go." His warm hands settle on my shoulders as I speak, and he turns me in to his body, wraps his arms around me, his lips pressing against my hair.

The sobs spill out of me like gushing blood, raw and violent and threatening to tear my chest in two. I was never a girl who cried, grew into a woman who was scared of her own tears, scared of letting them go. Scared of becoming my mother. But now I can't stop. The sounds I'm making, wild animal moans, embarrass me, but there's no way to control them.

Cooper moves toward the couch, pulling me along with him. He sits, and I crawl into his lap, bury my face in his neck. I cry until there's nothing left, my tears gone, and hollow, hiccupy sobs all that remain. My head feels fuzzy and overstuffed, my nose so clogged I can't breathe through it. I push back, off Cooper's lap, although I keep my legs across his, and run my hands over my tear-swollen face.

"God," I say. "I'm sorry. That was . . ."

"It was okay," Cooper says. One of his hands rubs my bare foot. I lost my flip-flops somewhere between his door and couch. "It's okay, Lane."

I drop my hands and look at him, and he doesn't even flinch away from what I know has to be my wreck of a face. "She's dead," I tell him, as if he wasn't standing next to me when they pulled her from the water. "Allegra's dead."

"I know."

"You don't seem surprised."

Cooper sighs. "You're not surprised either. Not really. Allegra was never going to end well, you know that. Whether it was her body in the swimming hole or a handful of pills, a razor blade . . ." His voice trails off.

"She didn't kill herself," I say, before I think about whether I should.

"You think someone hurt her?" Cooper asks. When I don't answer, he traces my foot from big toe to ankle and back again. "What happened inside that house, Lane? What made you run?"

I can't tell him the truth he's asking about. Not yet, maybe not ever. But I can tell him a different truth. One more painful for him, but easier for me. Which, given our history, sounds about right. I slide my hand down to my belly, lift my shirt up slightly. Cooper's gaze follows my movement, his brow furrowed. My fingers find the tiny, smooth marks, like strands of delicate silver thread sewn into my skin. No one else has ever noticed them, not even Cooper these past weeks, when his hands and mouth have roamed over my body endlessly.

"I had a baby," I say. The words slide out of me like air leaving a balloon, gone before I'm able to snatch them back. I don't look at him as I speak. "A little girl."

I feel Cooper's body tense. "You have a kid?"

"No. I gave her up."

His hand shifts against my foot, restless. "When?"

"The spring after I went away."

Cooper's hand leaves my foot. His head falls back against the couch, and he closes his eyes. "Was she mine?" he asks finally.

The question hurts in a way I didn't anticipate, although it's a fair one for him to ask. "Yes," I tell him. She had a dusting of blond hair and lips too plump for her tiny face. She was three days old when I gave her up, and already a single dimple had formed in her cheek, just big enough for me to rest the tip of my pinkie finger in when I held her. I would have named her Elizabeth.

He lifts his head back up, looks at me, and this time I hold his gaze. "Why didn't you tell me?"

I feel something ugly poised right on the end of my tongue. Something designed to injure in the worst possible way. I take a deep breath, fight against the need to damage ingrained in me from birth. "I was scared," I say when I can speak without hurting, or at least not hurting on purpose. "I didn't think it mattered, Cooper. I didn't think you cared anymore. We were like two animals by the end, circling around each other, waiting to see who would die first."

"I would have cared," Cooper says. "I always fucking cared."

"I couldn't . . . I couldn't be a mother." I hold my hands out to him like I'm asking him to understand. When I recognize how pathetic it looks, I let my hands drop. "I didn't know how. I didn't want to raise another girl like us. Another Roanoke girl."

"But she wasn't a Roanoke, Lane, she was a Sullivan."

"Trust me," I say with a cold little laugh, "if she'd been born in this town, she would have been a Roanoke. And you wouldn't want that for your daughter. Not ever."

"That's why you left? Because you were pregnant?"

I nod. And it's not a lie. But it's still only half the truth.

"Are you sorry you gave her up?" he asks.

"No." I take a deep, uneven breath. "But I'm sorry I didn't know how to keep her."

Cooper shifts away from me, pushes my legs off his lap. His bare feet make a hollow slapping sound against the wood floor as he stands. "Well," he says, drawing out the single word until it takes on the weight of a larger declaration. "We would have made shitty parents, anyway."

Here's what I remember: horrible bouts of morning sickness where my stomach curled and rolled like ocean waves, the inside of my mouth left salty and slick; snipping the waistbands of my cheap maternity pants so they would still fit as my stomach grew beyond what I had previously imagined possible; endless nights of no sleep, straining arms and legs crushing my lungs; pain as big as the world, searing, unbearable beats of hell I managed to endure only because I had no other choice; the nurse's eyes, equal measures pity and scorn, as she held my hand in place of someone who actually cared about me; the relief that came when my body was finally rid of her, empty again and free; a cry like winter wind, searing and bare, a lonely howl, when they took her from my arms.

These are all the same things I wish I could forget.

Allegra

(b. 1989, d. 2015)

I f you opened up a dictionary to the word *normal,* you'd find Tommy Kenning's picture there. He was apple pie and football, homecoming king and white teeth, two kids and a minivan. He always claimed he saw Allegra first, when she was in second grade and he was in fifth, noticed her out of all the other girls. Allegra let him believe that, but she'd actually been the one to set her sights on him. Allegra had always known normal wasn't a regular stop on her crazy family train. But when she was next to Tommy she could pretend, if only for a little while, that her world spun in the same orbit as his.

As they grew older, she even entertained thoughts of actually marrying him, the way he always suggested. Occasionally went so far as to talk about it with him, what her dress would look like, where they would live, what they would name their first baby. Tommy's eyes would light up, he'd get that eager, puppy-dog look on his face. She could practically see the wheels working in his head as he tried to figure out how to make it happen before she changed her mind. And then she would dance away from him. Not for good, not too far. But enough to throw a bucket of cold water on his fantasies of the future.

She had to give Tommy credit, though. She didn't think he'd ever actually have the balls to cut her loose. But when he started dating sad little Sarah Fincher, he'd told Allegra they were over, said he wouldn't be coming to see her anymore. He couldn't wait any longer for his life to start. She'd watched him drive away, police cruiser slipping over a sheen of midwinter sleet. She'd had no urge to run after him, sure he'd be back. She'd always had Tommy right where she wanted him, couldn't imagine this time would be any different. She'd carved a notch on the front porch railing every day, waiting. Stopped when she ran out of room. Two hundred and sixteen days and word from town that Sarah Fincher was Sarah Kenning now.

When she heard, Allegra went up to her room and howled. Buried her face in her pillow and writhed against the grief and rage. She couldn't say whether she loved Tommy, had no real idea what that word even meant. But what she did know was that Tommy was hers. *She* got to decide when it was over, not him. Her granddad was right—boys like Tommy couldn't be trusted. They pretended to love you and left you behind.

But she'd shown Tommy who was in charge. It took only one night, her lips on his neck, her hand down his pants, and he'd caved. Like she knew he would, his precious wedding vows so much dust in the wind. It was almost sad how predictable he was. Plain Jane Sarah just an afterthought when he had Allegra Roanoke spread wide in front of him.

She thought such a triumph might ease the gnawing emptiness inside her, but it didn't. Not even a pink plus sign on the pregnancy test could do that. She suspected the baby was Tommy's—somehow it already felt more settled inside her than all the lost babies that had come before. But she doubted the true paternity would matter much to her granddad. Any baby born in this house belonged to Roanoke, simple as that. And a baby would make her granddad so happy after all the disappointments over the years. But she kept putting off telling him the good news. Waiting, maybe, until she could manage to summon some of that happiness for herself.

She considered telling Tommy, but she couldn't picture living in his crappy house, making him casseroles, and changing diapers. And despite Tommy's frantic, and then increasingly angry, phone calls, she wasn't sure he would want that, either. Because if there was one thing Tommy loved as much as he loved Allegra, it was his idea of himself as a decent guy. And dumping sweet Sarah and shacking up with already-pregnant Allegra would shatter that image forever. No more apple-pie Tommy after that.

She found herself longing for Lane in a way she hadn't for years. She fantasized that Lane would walk through the front door again and know exactly what to do. Lane might be able to help Allegra have the strength to leave, to give her child a different kind of life. Or maybe Lane would stay and Allegra wouldn't have to be alone anymore. They could bear it together. But reality always intruded, and she was left with the fact that Lane was gone, like all the rest of the Roanoke girls, and it would take more than a baby in Allegra's belly to bring her back.

So Allegra spent her mornings crouched over the toilet, vomit thick on her tongue. After, she splashed icy cold water on her face, pinched color back into her pale cheeks, set her mouth into a smile. She went downstairs and ate breakfast with her grandparents. Opened her door, and then her legs, when her granddad knocked in the night. Woke up in the morning and did it all again. Watched the days flow by. Told herself this was what she'd always wanted. But the baby hidden inside her felt heavy, a leaden weight out of all proportion to its actual size.

A looming, inevitable disaster.

Then

My hands shook as I tore open the small package, and I told myself to breathe, calm down, get it together. I was locked in the bathroom down the hall from my bedroom, the house silent around me. Gran had gone to Wichita for the day. Allegra was supposed to go with her, but backed out at the last second, making an excuse about seeing Tommy that caused Gran's mouth to pinch up. And Granddad was working in some distant field, having driven off in a cloud of dust and country music not long after the sun rose.

I'd never taken a pregnancy test before, but it didn't take much skill. Just pull out the stick and pee on it. But honestly, I didn't even need the test. I already knew. Had known for the last week every time my sore breasts brushed against Cooper's chest, ever since the morning I woke up and spewed vomit into the toilet before my first bite of breakfast.

Peeing on the stick was only a formality. The question was what I was going to do afterward. Would I have it? Would I find a way to get to Wichita and get rid of it? Would I tell Cooper? I'd had my period since that night with Nick, so I knew the baby was Cooper's even if he might not believe it. What would flash across his face at the news, horror or joy? I wasn't dumb enough to think a baby could fix what I'd broken between us, our relationship already circling the end like water down the drain. But some stupid, childish part of me still hoped, for what I wasn't even sure.

I managed to pee on the stick with only minimal splashing onto my own fingers. I set the test on the back of the toilet, rinsed my hands in the sink. My face in the mirror was ashen, my eyes luminous. I couldn't stand there and count the seconds ticking by.

I opened the bathroom door, and the house breathed around me, old wood settling. Roanoke always felt slightly alive, especially when I was there alone, as if it could lead me astray down unused corridors, whisk me away into the unknown, never to be seen again. I padded down the hall to my room, the wooden floor sticky under my feet. A hint of warm air swirled across my ankles, and I paused, confused. Gran always kept the windows of the unoccupied rooms closed. But air was flowing out from under the door at the end of the long hall. A guest room Allegra'd told me no one had used in years.

I tiptoed to the door, set my hand on the cut-glass knob. My heart slammed against my ribs, agitated in a way that made no sense. At most, someone had left open a window that should've been shut. There was no reason for the clammy touch of fear. No reason more than half of me was screaming to walk away, keep the door closed. Leave well enough alone. Don't look. *Don't look.*

I opened the door, slowly, gently, and it swung inward without a sound. All the room seemed to contain was a bed, although I knew that wasn't the case. But that's where my eyes landed, and after that there was nothing else to see. They were on top of the covers, asleep, tangled together. Naked. Granddad and Allegra. Her head on his chest, his arms wrapped around her, their legs entwined. His pale feet, usually covered by boots, her sun-brown toes, the nails painted bubble-gum pink. The summer-warm breeze wafted the pale blue curtains inward, blew the earthy scent of sex into my face, ruffled the ends of Allegra's hair. Her body looked long and liquid. She was the most peaceful I'd ever seen her.

I stumbled backward, shut the door with barely a click. I ran on silent feet back to the bathroom, closed the door and locked it behind me. My brain roared. *Roanoke girls. Special. You look exactly like your father. I loved him so much. It's supposed to mean that you're his favorite. Your mama was always my favorite. The best and worst secret.* I barely made it to the toilet before I was sick, heaving up ropy strings of bile, slick and acrid. In one corner of my brain I registered the bright pink plus sign on the pregnancy test. But the baby growing inside me felt very far away compared to the memory of Allegra and Granddad, the image of their bodies burned into my closed eyelids like a nightmare vision.

I knelt before the toilet, gasping and sweaty. My knees ached where they pressed against the hard tile. Tears ran into my mouth, and their salt gagged me, another round of nausea threatening. The real horror wasn't seeing them, wasn't finally knowing what deep down in the darkest part of myself I'd suspected all along. The horror came in acknowledging that my initial flush of shock hadn't lasted long, had been overtaken almost immediately by a neon flare of envy. *Why wasn't it me?* I covered my mouth with both hands to hold in the hysterical laughter. *Why hadn't he picked me?* That's how fucked up I was. That's how badly Roanoke twisted us all.

I barged into Charlie's apartment without knocking. He was sitting on the couch watching a soap opera, which might have been funny on a different day. "Lane?" He pushed himself up from the saggy cushion, his brow furrowed.

"Can you drive me to Wichita?" I asked.

Charlie's eyes ran over my face, down my body to my leg. "You're bleeding."

I glanced down. I'd tripped in my haste to get up the stairs to his apartment, smashed my shinbone against the wooden steps. The cut was deep, but I couldn't even feel it. "It's nothing. Please, Charlie, can you drive me?"

"Why're you crying, Lane?" he asked.

I gulped in air. "Please," I said again, scrubbed at my wet cheeks with both hands.

He pulled a handkerchief from his back pocket and handed it to me, waited until I'd wiped my face and handed it back before he spoke. "You running?" That's all he had to say, those two words enough to make the depth of his knowledge clear between us.

I nodded, and Charlie's eyes dropped to the floor. I knew right then he wouldn't help me. But I wanted to make him say the words. "I can't," he said finally. "Your granddad finds out I helped you leave, I'd be out on my ass. And I don't have anywhere else to go."

"How can you sit up here and let it go on?" I asked. "How can you not do anything?"

Charlie's gaze returned to mine. His face was etched with lines, his eyes dim. He shook his head, and I backed away from him. "Wait," Charlie said. "Wait a minute." He raised one finger and crossed the room to a small desk against the wall. He pulled an envelope from the top drawer and held it out to me. "It's all I've got. Five hundred dollars. Won't get you far. But it'll get you somewhere."

"Is that what you gave my mother, too?" I asked. "An envelope of money?"

Charlie didn't answer, thrust the envelope toward me. I thought about not taking it, showing him what I thought of his attempt at help. I could turn my back and make it obvious that what he was offering wasn't near enough after a lifetime of watching what went on at Roanoke and never speaking up. But I needed to get away more than I needed to make a point. I took the money.

Back in my room, I packed my suitcase, stuffed the money down in the bottom of my backpack, and waited. My fingers drummed on the floor where I sat. I felt like Allegra, unable to hold still, my whole body sizzling with nervous energy. When I heard Granddad's heavy tread on the stairs heading down and Allegra's quick steps going up to her room, I went after her. She had her back to me as she dug around in her dresser. I stopped in the doorway for a second, watching her.

"Allegra," I said finally, and she whirled around, a shirt bunched in her hand.

"Oh my God," she breathed. "Don't sneak up on me!" She cocked her head. "You look like hell. What's wrong?"

She most definitely did not look like hell. Her hair was mussed, her cheeks flushed pink, her eyes sparkling. I thought I could see the slightest hint of stubble burn on the tender skin of her neck. My stomach heaved. "I saw you," I said, voice low.

"Saw me what?"

I didn't answer, and the shirt floated out of Allegra's hand, settled on the floor at her feet. "Oh."

"Allegra," I whispered.

She ran to me, grasped my hands in hers, and pulled me to the bed, forcing me down to sit beside her. "It's not a big deal, Lane," she said, looking at my face and laughing a little. "Okay, I mean, it's a big deal, but it's not *bad*. I promise, it's not."

I squeezed her hands, trying to force her to focus on my words. "I'm leaving. Right now. Come with me."

Allegra's mouth opened, then closed. Her hands went limp in mine. "Leaving? You can't!"

"I can't stay here. Not when . . . Allegra, it's wrong. It's *sick*!"

Her smile was sweet, patient, as if I simply didn't understand. "Oh, Lane, it's not like that at all. He loves us so much. And I love him. More than anything. Granddad—"

"He's our father, Allegra!" I practically screamed. Pinpricks of heat bloomed along my neck and chest as my breathing sped up.

"So? That doesn't change anything," Allegra said, a little more agitated now, the pink in her cheeks flaring to red. "And he loves us. We're everything to him." She raised one of my hands and laid it against her hot cheek. "We really are sisters, you know."

"How long has it been going on?" I asked. "Your whole life? Since you were little?"

"Oh my God, no!" Allegra said, eyes wide. "He's not a pervert! Nothing happened until I was fourteen. Old enough to decide for myself." Her words were bad enough, but the worst part was seeing how much she believed them, how easily he put it all back on her.

I shook my head. "I can't stay. I'm leaving." Allegra had never seen the damage years of this life did, but I had. I'd lived it with my mother. I couldn't do it again. I couldn't let it be me. I tried to pull my hands away, but Allegra held on tight, her fingers digging in so that I hissed through my teeth. The calmness in her eyes faded, replaced with a wild desperation.

"Please don't go," she begged. "Please, Lane. Please don't leave me. Please don't leave me." She was crying now, fat, pregnant tears rolling down her flushed cheeks. "We can all stay here and be happy. I won't be jealous anymore. It'll be perfect. I promise."

I didn't know what to say to her. What string of words to put together to make her change her mind and come with me. Maybe no combination would ever work, a lifetime of our granddad's whispered lies stronger than any truth I could ever come up with.

I pulled my hands away from hers as gently as I could, my own tears falling. When I stood, she wrapped her arms around my waist, buried her face in my stomach. I looked down, ran my fingers over her dark hair. My hair. My mother's hair. Our father's hair.

"Please," she whispered. "Don't tell anyone, Lane. If you have to go, then go. But let me stay here. This is where I want to be. I love him. Don't tell anyone. Promise?"

I could hardly speak, breathing a kind of torture under the heavy weight of pain. And God help me, I promised. But not for

Allegra. And not for my granddad. For myself, so no one would ever know where I came from. So I could keep on pretending I didn't know, either.

I went back to my room and grabbed my suitcase, slung my backpack over my shoulder. I took the stairs as quietly as I could, slunk down the front hall and let myself out the screen door with hardly a sound.

"Lane?"

I whirled and found my granddad standing in the doorway, his eyes traveling from my suitcase back to my face. He pushed open the screen and joined me on the porch. "Why don't you come back in, honey," he said. "So we can talk."

I shook my head, tightened my hand on my backpack strap in the hope he wouldn't see it shaking. "Nothing to talk about."

He took a careful step toward me. "Sure there is. We're family. We can work this out. I know we can."

"You're *fucking* her!" I yelled, flinging my backpack toward him. My granddad didn't even flinch. "How do we work that out? And my mother? All of them? *All of them?*"

"We love each other. I've loved every one of them." His voice was soft, reasonable. If I didn't concentrate hard, it would be easy to slip over into believing him.

"And what about Gran? She sits back and what? Tells herself it isn't happening? Or does she not care?"

"Your gran understands," Granddad said.

My laughter was wild and familiar. I sounded like my mother on those days she locked herself in her room, tearing at her own hair. "Understands *what*?"

"That you girls are special. So damn special. And what we have together is special, too. It's worth protecting. It means something,

Lane, the way we all feel about each other. Other people might not understand, but your gran does. She doesn't interfere."

"You're crazy," I whispered. "I always thought my mother was the crazy one. But really, it was you." I felt the weight of my mother's love for me for the first time, there on Roanoke's porch with my whole world crumbling around me. She might not have been able to love me the way a mother should, with kisses, and kind words, and hopes for my future. But she'd done the very best thing for me—she'd taken me away from here and tried her hardest to keep me from ever coming back. It wasn't her fault she'd failed. I understood now that she'd held on as long as she was able. *I tried to wait. I'm sorry.* Discovering the secrets of Roanoke had given my mother back to me, long after the understanding of her pain could do either of us any good.

"Where are you going to go?" my granddad asked. "What will you do? You're only sixteen."

"I don't know. Get a job. I'll figure it out." I couldn't allow myself to think beyond the end of the driveway. Not yet. It was too scary, the world too enormous, and I knew fear would lead me right back into the house if I let it.

My granddad took a step closer. "You know what happens to girls who run away? They end up living on street corners, prostituting themselves for food and—"

"How's that any different than what I'd be doing here?" I demanded. "At least out there I wouldn't be screwing my own father!"

"Please don't," my granddad said like I was stabbing him right in the heart. "Don't make it into something ugly. It's not ugly."

"How can you say that? How can you even *think* that? I thought this place could finally be my home," I said on a cracked whisper. "But my mother was right, it's a nightmare." A nightmare made worse because even with my mother's warning, I fell into it so easily, caught up in the awful Roanoke spell almost from the start.

"Oh, Laney-girl," my granddad said, his own eyes tearing up. "Of course this is your home. You're a Roanoke girl, through and through." He was right in front of me now, and he reached out, put a tentative hand on my elbow. His fingers burned into my skin, and I didn't pull away.

"But you and Allegra . . ."

My granddad's hand glided up my bare arm. "I love Allegra," he said. "But I love you just the same." That hadn't been what I meant when I spoke, but somehow he read the intent below the surface of my words, the shameful truth I didn't want to acknowledge. *Why hadn't he picked me?*

"I was waiting until you were ready, is all," he said. His fingers stroked the back of my neck, under my ponytail. "I wanted you to be sure."

I saw his face moving closer, and still I didn't stop him. He kissed my cheek, the corner of my mouth. He paused, and the world slowed down. I could hear my own harsh breathing, feel the pressure of his fingertips on my neck pulling me closer. His lips against mine were soft, familiar. His kiss tasted of my mother's tears, Allegra's neediness, my own worst impulses. We were all there, all the doomed Roanoke girls, in the touch of his mouth. Something inside me expanded, took flight with dark and twisted wings. It wasn't desire. Nothing that simple. It was more like a recognition. Like he was already swimming through my blood, already inside of me. He was a destiny it was possible to run from, but one I would never escape.

I lurched backward, covered my mouth with one hand. "No," I said. I rubbed hard at my lips, trying to dislodge the feel of him, the slide of his tongue against mine.

"Don't go," he said, voice rough and pleading, the edges of his mouth white with strain. "I love you."

I dropped my hand. "No," I said again, my voice louder. I could tell from the look on his face that it wasn't a word he was used to hearing. He didn't look angry, just confused. I was probably the first one of us to ever say it to him. But it didn't make me feel strong or brave. I only felt abandoned.

I grabbed my backpack, lifted my suitcase, and walked down the porch steps onto the gravel drive. Hot wind howled off the prairie, whistled under the eaves of the house. I walked away, and he didn't try to stop me. He let me go, and I told myself that was how I wanted it.

Tommy was waiting for me at the end of the drive, leaning against the side of his car. "Hey," he said when he saw me. "Why do you have a suitcase?"

"I need a ride to Wichita." When I'd called him, the only person I could think of to ask, I'd just said I needed a ride, left all the details for later.

"Wichita?" Tommy said slowly, like he'd never heard the word before.

"Yeah." I opened the back door and heaved my suitcase inside. "To the bus station."

"Lane." Tommy put his hand on my arm, but I flinched away. I couldn't stand for anyone to touch me, not yet. Not now. "What's going on?"

"Just . . . can you do it or not, Tommy?" I asked, squinting against the brutal sun. "If you can't, I'll hitch a ride."

Tommy stared at me for a second, then nodded. I slid into the passenger seat and waited for him to get in. I took one last look at Roanoke in the distance. For a second, it looked like Allegra was standing on the front porch, as she had on my arrival, but it might have been a trick of the light.

Tommy waited until we were ten miles down the road before he spoke, which was longer than I thought he'd be able to make it. "Does Cooper know about this?"

"No. And you're not going to tell him, either."

Tommy laughed. "How am I supposed to keep this a secret? It's going to be pretty obvious you're gone."

"You can tell him I'm gone. But don't tell him you drove me to Wichita." I took a deep breath. "And don't tell him I'm pregnant."

The car swerved a little, the driver's side tires skating the edge of the double yellow line before Tommy pulled it back. "You can't tell me something like that!" he protested. "You can't tell me you're pregnant and say it's a secret."

Before I'd ever set foot in his car, I'd known Tommy would need an answer, a reason why I was leaving. And I'd promised Allegra I wouldn't say anything about our granddad. Even without that promise, I don't think I could have made my mouth form the words. Not to Tommy, who even if presented with the evidence right in front of his face would probably have tried to find a way to make it into something less horrible, something he could live with. So I told him about the baby instead. And I trusted he wouldn't break my confidence. Tommy might have loved Cooper like a brother, but even he wasn't naïve enough to believe Cooper and I had any business being parents.

"What are you going to do?" Tommy continued. "Are you going to have the baby? Do you have any money?" He fired the questions at me, glancing from the road to me and back again, each word amping up my anxiety. I hadn't given much thought to what came next, my only goal to get away from Roanoke. But if Tommy kept talking, I would panic, beg him to turn the car around and take me back to where at least I knew exactly what the future held.

"Shut up, Tommy!" I said. "I don't know, okay? I don't know." I took a deep breath, closed my eyes, and let the sun seep through my eyelids. "All I know for sure is you can't tell Cooper."

"It's not fair," Tommy said, "to ask that of me."

"Tommy, if you think anything in life is fucking fair, you're an idiot."

He stopped talking to me after that, his mouth set in a thin line, his hands clamped on the wheel. The parking lot of the bus station was deserted when we drove up, only a few cars parked on the outer edges. It could have been the same day I arrived, nothing different except for me. I'd thought I was stepping into a whole new world that day, one that might make up for all the years that had come before. I felt the hot sting of tears and rubbed my temples, willing them away.

Tommy pulled up to the entrance, and I put a hand on his when he started to set the emergency brake. "No. It's okay. Just drop me off."

"I can't leave you here."

I tried to smile. "Sure you can."

"This is going to kill him," Tommy said. "I've known Cooper my whole life, Lane. I know him better than anyone does. And I know how he feels about you, even if you want to pretend like you don't."

I opened the passenger door, sucking in a breath as the heat radiating off the pavement smacked me in the face. "It was one summer, Tommy. Give me a break."

"What does that matter? One summer is enough. Hell, sometimes one day is all it takes to change your life."

He was right. One summer was more than long enough, for a lot of things. Already I knew these one hundred days would be the rotted foundation the whole rest of my life was built upon. "He'll get over it," I said with a nonchalance I didn't feel. "As long as you don't tell him about the baby. That will only make it worse."

"What about Allegra?" Tommy asked. The words rushed out of him as if he was using everything he could think of to try to change my mind.

I couldn't look at him, kept my gaze focused on the tinted doors of the bus station. "She'll be fine, too. She has you." My throat ached as I swallowed. "And Roanoke." I got out of the car and pulled my suitcase from the backseat. "She'll be fine."

Tommy leaned over, braced his hand on the passenger seat, and looked out at me. "Are you sure about this?"

I nodded. "Yeah." I slammed the back door. "Thanks for the ride."

Tommy shook his head, blew out a defeated breath. "Good luck, Lane." I stood on the uneven pavement and watched him drive away. Stayed there until his silver car turned into a tiny glimmering speck in the distance.

When the woman at the ticket counter asked me where I was headed, I looked over at the big map of the United States, crisscrossed with bus routes, and picked the farthest point. If I was lucky, nothing in California would remind me of Cooper. I would have my baby and give her to a family who would raise her under mild, sunny skies and watchful smiles. My granddad would never lay eyes on her. I would stand in the ocean and let it wash Roanoke away, leaving me clean and new. I would start again.

Apparently, Tommy wasn't the only idiot.

Now

The hyoid bone is small. Most people have never heard of it. I never had before Tommy called and told us the news. Now I'm sitting in front of Granddad's computer, my gaze fastened on an image of the U-shaped bone at the base of the throat. The single bone coroners examine to determine if someone has been strangled. A lot of times it doesn't break, even when a person's life is throttled out of her. But Allegra's did break, before her body disappeared into the dank water of the swimming hole. Allegra was murdered, strangled, her hyoid bone snapped. They found it tangled in the rotted skeins of her hair. Tommy was professional on the phone. His voice broke only once, near the very end.

I'm going to be late to her funeral if I don't pull it together and find something to wear. Gran laid out a plain black dress on my bed this morning, one culled from her own closet. But I don't want to look like a version of Gran. All I can focus on is Allegra, her flare for the dramatic, her love of making an entrance. I want to honor her memory. I want to make my grandparents uncomfortable, punish them a little, and a sensible cotton-silk blend won't cut it.

So here I am, standing in Allegra's closet, fingers flipping through her collection of clothes. They aren't much different from when we were teenagers, most of them too tight, too short, too *much.* I lean forward and bury my face in a handful of her shirts, breathe in the faint smell of her skin. My shoulders shake and my throat burns, but I don't cry, can't afford to give in to tears. She wouldn't approve of puffy eyes and blotchy cheeks.

In her collection of dresses, I find the perfect one. Black, short, low-cut so my boobs threaten to spill out of the neckline. I pull my hair up on top of my head, slip a pair of Allegra's giant gold hoops into my ears. I sit at her vanity table and slick my mouth with a tube of her red lipstick, dab her perfume behind my ears. My reflection in the mirror isn't my own, it's Allegra's, and I smile, already relishing the pain I will cause. I run my fingers across her message to me, RUN LANE, before I stand. "Just a little longer," I promise her.

Gran sucks in a startled breath when I appear at the top of the stairs, and Granddad turns away. I've never seen him in a suit before, and he looks more dashing than he has a right to. "Oh, Lane," Gran says as I sweep past them toward the car on a pair of Allegra's stiletto heels.

"What?" I say, light, mocking. "You don't like it?"

Gran doesn't answer me, just gives her head a swift shake.

"Well, Allegra would like it. And since it's her funeral, I figured what the hell." I wrench open the back door of Gran's Mercedes and slip inside. Charlie has already turned on the car, the air-conditioning running full blast, and the cool leather makes goose bumps crawl along my bare arms and legs.

The funeral is taking place at the Methodist church in Osage Flats. The summer I lived here we went to church exactly twice. Just enough to keep the Bible thumpers from condemning us, not so much that people actually started expecting us to show up regularly. I'm surprised my grandparents had the nerve to go at all. The walls should have crumbled the second we walked through the wide double doors, all of us dead in a hail of fire and brimstone. But I guess God likes to dole out his punishment slowly instead, the better to really make it hurt.

The church is already full as we walk down the center aisle. I think it's more a case of gawking, the news of Allegra's murder already having made the rounds, than from any genuine love for her. No one can resist being part of the excitement now, the chance to pull out the fake pearls and the button-down shirts and share stories of the last time they saw her. To pretend they're sorry she's gone. I keep my eyes straight ahead, my shoulders back, and think about Allegra, how much she would love the shocked murmurs my appearance is causing, how hard she'd laugh about it later.

"Interesting choice," Cooper says under his breath, eyes on my dress, when I ease in next to him on the pew behind my grandparents.

I give him a half smile. "Thanks."

He folds my hand into his, rests it on his leg, and I let him. Tommy and Sarah are on his opposite side, and Tommy glances at me before his eyes dart away, barely able to make eye contact. He is wearing his police uniform, freshly starched, his hat balanced on his knee. Sarah doesn't even look in my direction. I feel a momentary stab of regret. I didn't consider how hard it would be on Tommy to see me this way—a version of Allegra who's still breathing.

The service is banal and boring, has nothing at all to do with who Allegra was. Of course, no one in the entire church would want to know her true story. How the love of her life was the sixty-something man sitting in front of me. The man who groomed her to be his lover from probably the time she could talk. Her father. Her grandfather. Two for the price of one. A sob that sounds dangerously close to a laugh spills out of me, and Cooper squeezes my hand, pulling me back from an edge he doesn't even know I'm teetering on.

When it's over, everyone shuffles down to the church basement, cinder-block walls and flickering fluorescent lights. The overpowering smell of Pine-Sol from the freshly mopped linoleum starts a headache beating right behind my eyes. Someone has pushed a few long folding tables against the far wall, and they are already burdened under dozens of cheese-and-mayonnaise-clogged casseroles and platters of gooey desserts. My grandparents are standing together in the center of it all. A flock of sympathizers hover around them, offering food and drink, a few quick pats to their shoulders, but nothing more familiar than that.

"Can we get out of here?" I ask Cooper.

He doesn't ask questions, just nods and follows me up the stairs, his hand on the small of my back.

"Are they coming here after?" he asks me once we've turned down the lane to Roanoke.

I nod. "To bury her."

Cooper clears his throat. "You want me to stay?"

"No, that's okay. Only family for this part, I think." A party of three forming a gothic little tableau around Allegra's grave.

Cooper pulls over in front of the house. "You'll be all right?"

I look at him. "I'll be fine." I don't make any move to get out of the car, though.

Cooper takes a toothpick from the stash in his ashtray and pops it between his teeth. "Has Tommy said anything about leads?"

"He hasn't talked to me about that," I say. But I don't need to speak with Tommy to know some random stranger didn't kill Allegra, to know the answer is probably very close to home. I think of Allegra's slender neck, her delicate hyoid bone. And my granddad's strong and capable hands.

After Cooper leaves, I bypass the house and head straight for the tiny family cemetery, let myself in through the wrought-iron gate. There's a Bobcat parked in the distance, not close enough to be vulgar, but its purpose is obvious given the yawning rectangle of Allegra's soon-to-be grave and the mound of fresh earth next to it covered with a blue tarp, which flaps lightly in the wind.

My high heels sink into the ground as I walk, not toward Allegra's grave but to my mother's. There are pink roses in a small vase at the base of her tombstone. CAMILLA EVELYN ROANOKE. HOME AT LAST. B: 11–15–71 D: 4–22–04. It's the first time I've ever visited her grave.

"Hey, Mom," I say, run my fingers over the shiny stone. "Sorry it took me so long." A hot tear rolls down my cheek. "Sorry I was such a shitty daughter." I wrap my arms around my stomach, trying to hold myself together. "Sorry for all of it, really. This whole fucked-up mess of a life." Roanoke looms behind me, its shadow falling across my back. I hate that this is where she ended up, stuck forever in the one place she tried so hard to escape. Entombed where he can visit her every day if he wants, sit on the ground above her bones and touch the grass growing there. Water her flowers with his tears.

"I wish I'd known the truth," I tell my long-dead mother. "Back then. Maybe we could have helped each other." The vibrant prairie sun bakes the skin of my neck, burns through the black fabric of my dress. "It wasn't your fault," I whisper, "what happened to you. And it was all right that you loved him. That wasn't your fault, either. I hope you know that."

I doubt she ever did know that, but I want to say the words anyway. I wish once upon a time someone had said them to me.

Tommy waits a decent interval after the burial before he comes knocking. I've managed to choke down a bit of food and changed out of Allegra's dress, back into jean shorts and a tank top that feel more familiar but make Allegra seem farther away. Tommy isn't alone when he shows up. He's flanked by an overweight edge-of-retirement type who flashes a badge in my direction and introduces himself as County Sheriff Mills as he lumbers inside. They both follow me toward the living room, where Gran and Granddad have already gathered.

"I know we talked about this on the phone," Tommy says, stiff inside his uniform as he sits on the couch where Gran points him. "But I thought I should swing by, see if you all had any questions."

"I have questions," I say from my spot in the doorway. "Questions like: Who killed her? When? Why?"

"Yes, Lane," Gran says. "Those are the same questions we all have."

Tommy takes a deep breath, and I imagine he's slipping on his cop persona like a set of clothes, covering up the Tommy who loved Allegra and setting him aside. "First off, I wanted to let you know the county sheriff's office is taking over from here on out." Tommy gives Sheriff Mills a quick nod. "We're not equipped for this type of investigation, and it's probably better this way, considering my past relationship with Allegra."

I can't tell if he's simply referring to all the years he dated Allegra or if he's told Mills the entire story, and Tommy's refusing to meet my eyes, not giving anything away.

Sheriff Mills shifts forward from his position on the couch. "From the condition of Allegra's body, the medical examiner is fairly confident that she was killed around the time she disappeared, and her body put in the swimming hole almost immediately."

"So she wasn't . . . kept somewhere before she died?" Gran asks.

"No, there's no evidence of that," Mills says.

"Was she pregnant?" my granddad asks, voice scratchy. He's taken off his tie and suit coat, undone the top button of his white dress shirt and rolled up the sleeves. He's hunched over, forearms balanced on his knees, his eyes on the glass of scotch between his hands. He looks so goddamn handsome, like some portrait of grief from an old black-and-white movie. I want to go over and punch him in the face, rip him to shreds with my bare hands.

"She was," Tommy says, his voice remarkably steady. "Yes."

My granddad still doesn't look at anyone, just nods and throws his head back. Drains his drink in one gulp.

"How do you know?" I ask. "Her body, it was . . ." I wish I'd listened to Cooper and not looked, because now when I think of Allegra, all I can see are slimy bones and tattered, rotten flesh. From that one quick, horrifying glimpse, I'd assumed her body wouldn't have much left to tell us. Which is maybe what the person who dumped her was counting on, too.

Sheriff Mills clears his throat. "We drained the pond and found a length of chain at the bottom, still wrapped around her left tibia. We're working on the assumption she was weighted down when she was put into the water. That kept her below the surface long enough that it delayed decomposition. Partial kidney, most of her uterus, some skin and ligaments were intact, along with her bones, of course."

No one speaks, and Tommy shifts uncomfortably on the too-soft couch, sinking back into the cushions against his will.

"Can you figure out who the father is?" I ask. "From the fetus, I mean."

"Not yet," Mills says. "The fetal remains might be too compromised for any sort of DNA testing. But it's a possibility if we get a lead on who the father might be, have his DNA to test against the fetus. Was she seeing anyone?" Mills continues. "A boyfriend? Any ideas about the father?"

Tommy looks at me, white lines of strain bracketing his mouth, begging me with his eyes. I stare back at him, waiting to see how deep his cowardice runs, until he drops his gaze to the floor.

"No," Gran says, "no recent boyfriend that we know of. But Allegra wasn't the type to bring men here to meet us."

Mills nods, scratches something into a tattered notebook.

"Is that what we're thinking?" I ask. "Her murder had something to do with the pregnancy?" That gets everyone's attention, both

Tommy and my granddad snapping their heads in my direction. Even Gran stiffens against her chair. I feel like we're all balancing on a house of cards, no one quite brave enough to say *fuck it,* and topple the whole thing to the ground. Not even me.

Mills looks up from his notebook, and I can practically see the question mark forming over his head. "We're not thinking anything at this point," he says. "Still gathering facts. I'm sure you all would have mentioned it already, but was she scared of anyone? Had she been feeling threatened?"

Gran frowns. "No. She never said anything like that."

I picture Sarah and Allegra standing on the front porch. What did Sarah really say to Allegra that day? How far was she willing to go to protect her marriage? My eyes dig into the top of Tommy's skull, but he's returned his gaze to the floor.

"How was her mood in the days before she disappeared?" Mills asks.

"She was perfectly happy," my granddad says.

I snort out a laugh, and Tommy's eyes finally fly to mine. But now it's my turn to look away. I duck my head and count to ten. "Aren't most murder victims killed by people they know?" I ask, once I have myself under control.

"Well, I don't know the exact statistics," Mills says, brow furrowed. "But yes, plenty of murders are committed by people the victim knows." There is so much subtext bouncing around the room, just out of his reach, it's no wonder he looks confused.

"Why don't you leave asking the questions up to the professionals?" my granddad says to me. "Let the man do his job."

"I *am* letting him do his job. But I want to help."

Tommy shakes his head. "Not sure there's much you can do."

I hate it that I can't take a single word out of Tommy's mouth at face value now, always wondering if he's protecting himself, protecting Sarah. I knew I couldn't trust my grandparents, but it hurts to have to add Tommy's name to the list. "I want to keep looking around," I find myself saying. My granddad stares at me for a second before he speaks. When he does, his voice is very gentle. "I thought you already did that. And you didn't find anything."

Run Lane. "I stopped. I should have kept looking, I should—"

"Lane," Tommy interrupts. "There's probably no point."

"I have to do something," I say, my voice breaking. I'm holding on to the doorjamb behind me with both hands, white-knuckling my way through this entire conversation. If I were smart, this is where I'd vomit out everything I know, about Tommy, Sarah, my grandparents, this whole fucked-up family. Leave the whole sordid mess for Mills to sift through. But I've lost whatever shred of faith I had that anyone in this room really cares about what happened to Allegra. For Mills, she's just one more case, a number on the top of a file. Would he be dogged enough to see through my grand-dad's manipulations, to look beyond my gran's self-serving view of Allegra? And covering his own ass is clearly Tommy's priority, deflecting suspicion from himself and Sarah, even at the expense of Allegra. Or maybe it's a mix of guilt and hubris that keeps me from opening my mouth, the belief that solving Allegra's murder is the way I can finally make amends to her, that I'm the only one who can figure it out. The only one she trusted. But whatever the reason, I'm not ready to give up yet, my gut urging me to keep Allegra's secrets a little while longer.

I spend two days literally tearing Roanoke apart, room by room. I look everywhere, even places I know Allegra would never carve. She favored wood, but I look on all the appliances, the undersides of toilet lids, upholstered furniture. When I'm done with the house, I concentrate on the barn, pulling aside hay bales with my bare hands until my fingers are bloody and Charlie leads me away.

Tommy calls a couple of times to check in, but I barely speak to him. I'm too focused, too single-minded, to hold a competing thought in my mind. Cooper gets ahold of me on the third day, after Tommy fills him in, to see if I've had any luck.

"You don't think I'm nuts?" I ask him.

"No," he says. "I'm not saying I'm convinced she left any sort of message. But it makes a crazy Allegra sort of sense. And if she did, I would think she hid it for you to find."

I pause in my frantic search of the linen closet shelves. "Why would you say that?"

"If she suspected something bad was about to happen, she would've known you'd come back if it did. She would have wanted you to be the one to figure it out."

A cold breath whispers down my spine. "How could she have known I would come back?"

"Because she understood the power of Roanoke," Cooper says. "The hold it has over all of you. She probably knew it would draw you home."

"You make it sound like a cult." I try too hard for a laugh and end up with a shaky cough instead.

"Isn't it?" Cooper says, voice so quiet I have to push the phone against my ear to hear him.

I pinch the bridge of my nose, suck in a shuddering breath through my mouth. We are silent for a long moment, listening to each other breathe. "Are you ever going to tell me what goes on out there, Lane?" He already knows. It's there in his voice. Maybe not the ugly specifics, but the general outline, which is bleak enough.

"I don't know."

I tilt the phone up, away from my face, to keep him from hearing the ragged sound of my tears. "Allegra e-mailed me, right before she disappeared. She wanted to talk to me. And I didn't even write her back." I swipe the flat of my hand against my wet cheek. "I didn't help her."

Cooper hesitates. "Why not?"

"I don't know. I didn't like thinking about Roanoke. I wanted to pretend that summer never happened. Allegra was a reminder, of so many things. I just . . . I didn't know how to make room for her in my life. It's not exactly like I have my shit together."

"Even if you'd called her back, it might not have changed anything."

"I guess we'll never know, though, will we?"

"No." Cooper sighs. "I guess we won't. But I think you need to give yourself a break."

I slide down the wall until my butt hits the floor, rest my forehead against my bent knees. "Cooper?"

"Yeah?"

"Thanks for listening to me. And for not pushing."

I hear his smile through the phone. "Anytime."

My skin feels raw. My heart throbs a mournful tune against my ribs. "So where do you think I should look?"

"Hell, I have no idea," Cooper says with another sigh. "Maybe you should be looking in places you'd think to hide something. Your favorite spots, instead of hers."

"I don't have any favorite spots. Not here."

"I'm spitting into the wind, Lane. Just throwing shit up to see if anything sticks, that's all. Your guess is as good as mine."

"You don't think it was random, do you? Her murder?"

This time Cooper doesn't pause. "No. Do you?"

"No." My voice is barely a whisper now. "What are the odds some stranger knew about the swimming hole? I had trouble finding it, and I knew it was there."

I hear his mouth moving, and despite the subject matter I smile into the phone. "Toothpick?" I ask.

"Yep. Sorry. Trying to give up cigarettes." Before I can get a word in, he continues, "And no, it's not because you told me only stupid people smoke."

I laugh and it feels good, a lightness in my chest that somehow burns like a flame. "I should go. I have to keep looking."

"Be careful," Cooper says. "I'm here if you need me."

I've searched every square inch of Roanoke, run my fingers and eyes over every soft-enough-to-carve surface. Even gone so far as to venture up into the attic with a flashlight, netting me only sweaty limbs coated with cobwebs and stray bits of insulation. I've found plenty of Allegra's words—ᛋᚢN, HEART, WEDDING, WHORE, DISASTER— but none of them mean anything within the context of her death. Or at least nothing that I can decipher.

Eventually, I give up on Roanoke and drive aimlessly around Osage Flats instead, desperate for a change of scenery. I stop at the hamburger stand for a lime slush and sit at one of the empty picnic tables in the parking lot to drink it. This was never a place Allegra liked to hang out, but I take the time to check the tables anyway, make sure she hasn't left anything carved into their worn surfaces. Nothing. My slush is too sweet, with not enough ice, and I end up tossing it in the trash can on the way to my car. I don't want to let go of Allegra, hate the thought of turning my back on her again. But I'm running out of ideas. There's only one place left I can think to look.

The afternoon air is sluggish, but not as brutal as it has been, and a cluster of children brave the heat to play on the slides at the park. Their shrieking laughter slices through my skull as I approach. Two mothers watch me with narrow-eyed vigilance as I make my way around the slides, still searching for any sign of Allegra. I can't remember if I ever told her this was the spot of my first kiss with Cooper, but she and I did our fair share of sliding down these slides over the course of that summer. But none of the graffiti here is hers. When I walk away, I wave to the kids, now bunched into silent knots at the top of the slides as they wait for me to finish my strange er- rand. No one waves back.

I head toward the carousel, wiping the sweat from my forehead when I reach the shade of the trees. The gate is open, but all the horses are empty. A lanky teenage boy with a face full of acne lounges on the bench nearby. "You wanna ride?" he asks, barely looking up from his phone.

"No, not really. Is it okay if I go sit for a minute?"

He waves me toward the carousel, probably glad he doesn't have to move his ass. "Sure. Whatever."

I find Allegra's horse. The white one with the pink mane. I walk around it slowly, taking in every scratch and mark of graffiti, but as with the slides, none of them are Allegra's. I pull myself astride the horse, touch the chipped paint of its ears and hold the cracked reins in my hand. If Allegra tried to leave me any sort of message, I have failed her. Just like I failed her when I left her behind. I should have tried harder. Broken her promise. Somehow undone the chains that bound her, even if she claimed to love them.

All these years, she'd stayed at Roanoke, given her life away to the man who ruined her. And in the end, what did she have to show for it? I'm not sure there's a single person who is unselfishly grieving the loss of her, no one whose heart is truly broken. Certainly not Sarah, who probably ran a victory lap when she heard the news, Sharon right on her heels. As for Tommy, he claims to love Allegra, but her absence from the world makes his whole white-picket-fence life easier. Now he can convince himself the baby was never his anyway, move on with a wife who adores him, and finally forget about the troubled girl who smashed his heart between her hands. Gran can't be anything but happy that Allegra is out of the picture. One less Roanoke girl for her to compete against. And Granddad. He lost his Allegra, but he has me, instead. The only one he never completely controlled. I'm not dumb enough to think that's because I'm stronger than the rest of them. It's only because he ran out of time to work the full extent of his awful magic on me. But now he has a second chance. All the time in the world. And if I'm being honest,

I can't exempt myself from the list. Because even as I've tried to avoid my granddad since I've been back—telling myself I hate him, willing myself to believe it—isn't there a part of me that craves his undivided attention? That basks in the glory of being the only one left? After all I know, after all I've seen, there remains a small, rotten-to-the-core piece of me that wants what Allegra had. God, I make myself sick.

I slide off Allegra's horse, my own failure, my own shame, clotting my throat. There's nothing left for me to do but give up. I turn to step off the carousel, and my eyes are pulled to the black, aqua-maned horse. My favorite. A stillness overtakes me. I am suddenly very aware of the tiny hairs standing up on my skin, the blood pumping through my veins. *Maybe you should be looking in places you'd think to hide something. Your favorite spots, instead of hers.* I told Cooper I didn't have a favorite spot here, but maybe I was wrong.

The carousel operator calls out, asking me if I want to go for a spin, but I can't shift my focus enough to respond. I approach my horse, run a hand down her warm metal back, already searching. The side facing me reveals only a smattering of wear-and-tear scratches and the emphatic exclamation that AMBER IS A SLUT! I move around to the far side, my heart thumping like a relentless fist against my rib cage. A strip of missing paint. PUSSY on the flank. JACK WAS HERE along the tail. And below that, down near the hoof: GRAN.

It's like taking a punch to the stomach. A direct hit that pummels the air from my lungs. I drop to one knee, heart worming its way into my throat. I run my suddenly sweat-slick fingers over the word. GRAN. No rust around the letters, the exposed metal clean and fresh. I know it's Allegra's work, have seen enough of her word treasures to recognize the slant of the writing, the exact shape of the capital letters. It's hers. It's recent. And she left it here for me to find.

Gran is in the kitchen when I return to Roanoke, pouring herself a glass of wine. I guess she does her drinking out in the open now. She holds up the bottle as I come through the back door. "Would you like a glass?"

"Allegra left me a message."

Gran doesn't even flinch. She sets the bottle down on the counter, picks up her glass, and takes a sip. "Where was it?"

"Somewhere you never would've looked."

Gran toasts the empty air with her wineglass, a wry smile skating across her face. "Sounds like Allegra." She sinks down into a chair at the kitchen table, runs her finger around the rim of her wineglass. The setting sun bathes her face with red and pink. She nods toward the chair beside her. "Come here. Sit down."

I'm not afraid of her. Although I probably should be. I feel electric with rage and sorrow. Steel running through my veins instead of blood. If she tries to hurt me, I will hurt her back. I pull out the chair next to her and sit, my hands knotted on the table in front of me. "What?"

"Let me tell you a story," Gran says. "It starts out nice, but it ends . . . badly." Another tiny sip of wine. "When I met your grand-dad, I thought he was all my dreams come true, dreams I didn't even know I had until he walked into my life. He was the type of man who was impossible to resist. Kind. Rich. Handsome. So handsome it actually hurt me sometimes to look at him. A little twinge in my heart." She shakes her head at the memory. A bead of condensation gathers at the bottom of her glass, slides down the delicate stem to land on her finger. "But I'd known handsome men before your granddad. Rich ones, too. That wasn't enough to win me over. It was how your grand-dad made me feel when I was with him that did the trick. Alive, like I'd woken up from a long sleep. Wanted. Special." Her mouth thins into a bitter smile. "You know exactly what I mean, don't you?"

I nod, unable to speak. That's always been his most powerful gift. Making each one of us feel like we're the one he can't live without.

"His younger sister Jane was gone before we ever met. Left her daughter, Penelope, as a parting gift. I didn't even mind, although being a mother wasn't something I particularly cared about. But it was important to your granddad, to have a family. So I pretended like it was important to me. And maybe it would have worked out, but his youngest sister, Sophia, lived here, too. Always floating around, on the edge of everything, waiting for her chance. Sometimes I think things might have been all right if not for Sophia. Maybe without her here he would have forgotten what he had before me."

I seriously doubt that. Magical thinking was never going to change this family's hellish destiny. I wonder if my granddad had Gran pegged right from the start, recognized that she was the kind of woman who would always put him first. Maybe that's why he chose her, because he somehow knew she would allow him to have his Roanoke girls and love him anyway.

Gran takes another swallow of wine, bigger this time. "I hated Sophia, right from the start. She was a jealous, spiteful thing, always finding ways to hurt me, to try and turn your granddad against me. At first, I had no idea why. Not until I caught them." Gran's throat works and she pauses, stiffening her spine. "In my own bed. Can you imagine?" She doesn't wait for me to respond. "Sophia drowned a few years later. I still think she did it on purpose, couldn't stand sharing him."

"Why didn't you leave?" I whisper. "Why on earth would you stay?"

"I loved him," Gran says, like it's the most simple explanation in the world. But it's not simple, what she's saying. She loved her husband more than her children, cared more about keeping him than protecting her own daughters. Perhaps that's my granddad's real power, making the women in his life do terrible things to one another.

Gran goes on: "I loved him enough to keep trying, and after

Sophia died, I thought it would stop. But Penelope grew up, and every day she looked more and more like her mother." Gran reaches over, and I flinch back, but she just waves her fingers toward my hair. "That hair. Those eyes. That body. That *face*. How could he resist? It was like screwing a version of himself." I've never heard Gran curse before, and it scares me more than anything else she's said, shows how much her control has slipped. "He told me later he couldn't help falling in love with her," Gran continues. "He stumbled into it like falling into a hole." She laughs, a harsh rasp. "How could I argue with that? It's the same way I fell in love with him."

It takes me a second to find my voice. "One phone call, that's all it would have taken to end it."

Gran's perfectly plucked eyebrows shoot up. "Like the call you made after you left here? Don't lecture me, Lane. You're no better."

Guilt, I'm discovering, is an emotion that's almost impossible to kill. It's like a poisonous weed that keeps on growing, burrowing into every vulnerable spot. Always reminding you of all the ways you've failed. "I was sixteen and scared. But you were a grown woman. They were your daughters."

"They were never mine. They were always his. From the second they were born. I nursed them, held them, rocked them, but from the first breath they always belonged to him. By the time Emmeline was born, I knew what was coming. He'd started disappearing with Eleanor, both of them showing up to dinner with flushed cheeks and shared smiles. There wasn't any way I could stop it from happening with all of them, one after the other." Gran pauses. "No easy way," she amends.

For a second I don't dare breathe, the confession so delicate one wrong move would shatter it into nothing, render it mere words with no admission behind it. "You killed Emmeline?" I say finally.

Gran's eyes slip closed, just for a moment. "It was fast. It didn't hurt her. It was better that way. At least she died before I started hating her. She was the only one I cared about until the end." Gran's mouth twists up into a mean little bow. "Not like the rest of you. Always hanging all over him, batting those long eyelashes and crawling into his lap. Baiting him. Even you. Before you got here, I'd hoped you'd be different, that maybe you wouldn't even be his. But one look at you killed that dream. And you went and acted like all the rest of them, prancing around in those short shorts." Gran's voice turns high and girlish. *"Granddad, will you teach me to drive? Granddad, let me help you feed the horses."*

My fury leaves me breathless. My limbs shake with rage. "I can't believe you're blaming us!"

Gran goes on like I haven't even spoken. "Your mother was the worst. She practically drove him to it. She worshipped him, wouldn't let him out of her sight even after I told her to stay away. I tried to warn her, but she did what she wanted, and look where it got her. Every last one of you made your own beds."

I wonder how long she's been telling herself this version of the story, skewing the facts so she can live with what happened right under her roof, sloughing off any responsibility like shedding a second skin. "And Allegra's punishment was death?"

"I couldn't do it again, not again," Gran says. "Forty years I've lived this life. Watched your bellies grow fat with babies. I couldn't do it, not even one more time." Gran's lips tremble, and I think she's going to cry, finally, but her hand lashes out instead, knocks her wineglass off the table to where it shatters against the floor.

"You told me you didn't hurt Allegra, that you could handle her."

Gran huffs out a laugh. "I could. Allegra was easy. All I had to do was wait her out. Eventually she would have run or killed herself. Allegra wasn't made to last." Her voice is indifferent, as if Allegra is a piece of trash to be discarded instead of the girl she raised from birth. "But that *baby.* That baby would have ruined everything, right when it was so close to finally being over. Allegra'd never been able to stay pregnant, always lost them early. But this time . . . I kept waiting for her to miscarry, but she didn't. This one was going to stick." Gran shakes her head. "Which means it probably wasn't even his. Not that it would've made a difference to him. It would still have been his baby, no matter who the actual father was."

"How did you even know she was pregnant?" I feel sick, like I might have to vomit into my cupped palms before I can go on speaking.

"Sharon found the pregnancy test in the trash and brought it to me."

Good old Sharon. Still Gran's lapdog after all these years. "So you threatened Allegra?" And Allegra felt the danger. Enough that she tried to contact me, left Gran's name carved into my horse in case the worst happened.

"I didn't *threaten* her," Gran says, as if I've accused her of some social faux pas. "I simply told her no more. No more babies. But Allegra wouldn't listen. She never did. Always so goddamn stubborn. I told her I wouldn't have another baby in this house. *I told her.*"

My body is tense with fear and anticipation, ready if she reaches for me. "What did you do? Get her drunk so you'd have an easier time killing her?"

"She got drunk all on her own. She was drunk most of the time, this last year." Gran eyes me with a little smirk. "Sound familiar?"

My cheeks flame, but I hold Gran's gaze. "If anybody had a reason to drink, it was Allegra. I won't fault her for that."

"No," Gran says, "you wouldn't. You girls always did stick together. Not one of you ever thought of me. What it was doing to me. Just spread your legs and didn't care that it broke my heart."

"You have no idea, do you?" I ask. "What a horrible person you are."

Gran shakes her head. "I'm *loyal,* something you girls have never been. I made promises to him and I've kept them."

"Does he know?" I ask. "What you did?"

Gran's hands shift restlessly on the tabletop. "No. He had nothing to do with it."

I choke out a laugh. "He had *everything* to do with it." I'm bone weary. So tired of this conversation, this place, this life. I close my eyes, cover them with my hands. "I can't believe you killed her. I can't believe you would do that to her."

"She didn't fight me, Lane."

I lower my hands slowly, gaze swinging back to Gran. "Are you seriously going to sit there and act like you did her a *favor*?"

Gran gives an elegant little shrug of her shoulders. "I'm not act-ing like anything. I'm telling you Allegra wanted to die. I could see it all over her face. She was happy to be done with it."

I try to fight the vision, but I can picture it clearly. Allegra sprawled on the floor, dark hair spilling across the wood like wine. Gran crouched over her, thin fingers pulling the sash of Allegra's bathrobe tight around her neck, twisting harder and harder. And Allegra not resisting, blue eyes slowly clouding over, a last breath sliding between purple-tinged lips. Finally able to let go, leave Roanoke behind, save her unborn baby from living her life all over again. It may have been what Allegra wanted, but only because she didn't know any other way to be free.

"You're not going to get away with it," I say. "I'm done keeping secrets about this place. I'm done pretending." I pause, thinking of what words will hurt her the most. "You're going to lose him anyway."

I barely have the words out when Gran pushes back from the table fast, lunges toward me, and catches me in the middle of the chest with her shoulder. My chair tips backward, and I go with it, head smacking against the floor, bright fireworks exploding across my field of vision. I can't breathe, the wind knocked out of me. I roll sideways, telling myself not to panic. My breath will come back, the same as it did all the times I took a fall off the jungle gym in school, but the lack of air makes my hands spasm on the floor, my neck straining and mouth gasping.

Through blurred vision, I see Gran reach down for a piece of her shattered wineglass. I throw my arm out, wrap it around her ankle, and yank. Gran cries out, hits the floor next to me with a thud. After several seconds that feel more like minutes, I'm able to breathe again, my lungs filling on a whooping gasp. Before I have a chance to even catch my breath completely, I'm flipped onto my back and Gran straddles my stomach. Her hands claw against my neck, banging my already tender head against the floor.

There is a part of me, even after the revelation about Allegra's death, that can't believe this is happening. That wants to howl with disbelieving laughter. How can Gran, who is always in control, who has lived with this awful reality for all of her adult life and never lifted a finger to stop it, be trying to kill me now? But I look into her wild eyes, lips pulled back over bared teeth, and know this is deadly serious.

"Get off me!" I manage to rasp. I grab hold of her right hand and bend her fingers back. The pop of bone triggers a wail from Gran. "Not so easy, is it?" I pant. "When you're trying to hurt someone who isn't drunk?"

"Shut up!" Gran screams in my face, spit flecking my cheeks like rain. I try to wrench out from underneath her, but the grip of her legs around my torso doesn't loosen. Gran isn't big, but she's wiry, surprisingly strong. And the blows to my head have left me weakened, my vision watery and limbs trembling. Gran leans down toward me, her forearm cutting into my windpipe. For a second I think she means to bite me as her face moves closer, and then I realize she is groping along the floor with her left hand. I manage to turn my head and see a long sliver of glass, barely beyond the reach of Gran's searching fingers.

I thrust my right hip up, hoping to dislodge her, but she doesn't budge, hangs on like I'm a bucking bronco she's trying to tame. Twisting my head to the side, I snap at her hand. My teeth make contact with her skin but don't sink in. But it's enough for her to bring her left hand back toward me, punching me on the side of the head.

We are both breathing hard. Sweat runs down Gran's neck, and moisture gathers near my ears. But whether it's my own sweat or tears, I don't know. What I do know is I have only a few seconds left, probably, to make some kind of move. Gran shifts slightly, and I grab her upper arm and yank as hard as I can, catching her off guard. When she tips forward, I slam my forehead into hers and shove her sideways with all the strength left in my shaking arms.

The force of our skulls colliding brings the fireworks back to my vision, but because I anticipated the contact, I recover faster. I slither out from under Gran's legs and roll over, belly-crawling toward the glass. She grabs my legs from behind me, climbing my body like a vine, and I scream out in frustration as she snags the ends of my hair and wrenches my head backward.

Now we're locked in the same battle as only a few moments ago, only this time I'm the one straining for the glass while Gran struggles to keep me contained. Over the sound of our breathing, I hear the door open behind us, but I can't turn my head to see, my hair still tangled in Gran's fist.

"Yates!" Gran screams. "Help me! Get the glass!" She digs her fingers into my scalp. "Get the glass!"

I fishtail along the floor, my fingers closing around the glass at the exact moment my granddad's booted heel lands on top of it. Gran lets go of my hair, and I twist my face up to his.

Granddad and I stare at each other. His face is unreadable. For an endless moment I don't know what he will do. And even worse, I don't know what I want him to do. If Allegra did long to die, I understand why. Sometimes even one more breath feels too hard. Granddad kicks the shard of glass away, sends it flying across the kitchen.

"No!" Gran wails. She brings both fists down on my lower back, hard and fast. I convulse under her, trying to bring my knees up underneath me.

"Stop it!" my granddad yells. "Jesus Christ!" He shoves Gran off me, and she cries out when her hip smacks against the floor. "What the hell's gotten into you? Have you lost your mind?"

I push myself to sitting, but that's as far as I get. My head swims, and there's a ringing in my ears that makes it hard for me to hear, words reaching my brain about a half second behind schedule. I scoot backward until I'm leaning against the wall.

My granddad crouches next to me, his eyes roaming over my face from hairline to chin. I flinch when he reaches his hand out, but he only smooths my hair back, runs one finger along my cheekbone. "You okay, Laney-girl?"

"I think so," I say. "My head took a couple of good whacks." I tilt my face away from his hand. "She killed Allegra."

My granddad goes completely still, his hand frozen in midair. Over his shoulder, Gran has heaved herself to her feet, one hand braced on the edge of the kitchen table. "Is it true?" he asks, eyes on me.

"Yates," Gran says.

"*Is it true?*"

"Yes," Gran says on a whisper.

My granddad sinks down to the floor, landing heavily next to me. He buries his face in his hands. His shoulders slump. I hate that my first instinct is to comfort him.

"I'm sorry," Gran says, moving closer. Tears trickle down her cheeks. "I couldn't do it anymore, Yates. Not again. Please forgive me." She kneels next to him, loops her arms around his neck, and leans her forehead against the side of his head. "Forgive me."

I push away from the wall, desperate to get some distance from both of them. I use one of the kitchen chairs to pull myself to standing. I hear the cicadas from outside, worked up into a frenzy, so loud it makes my ears ache. I look back at my grandparents, still tangled together on the floor. My granddad has uncovered his eyes, wrapped one arm around Gran's back. His gaze finds mine, captures and locks.

"I wanted it to be you," I tell him. The cicadas scream. I rip my eyes away and limp out into the hallway to call Tommy.

Lillian

(b. 1951)

She played it over and over in her head like a movie on the nights he didn't come to their bed, the nights he spent with one of *them*. In the movie version of her memory, she was as gorgeous as a movie star. A young Grace Kelly, perhaps. The truth wasn't far off, really. She'd always been lovely, still was, even now that time had begun to do its worst to her. She remembered turning in the hotel lobby—it hadn't happened in slow motion, naturally, but it played that way inside her head—and he was standing there, one elbow perched on the marble check-in counter, his eyes trailing over her head to toe. He smiled, and her whole body flushed with prickly warmth, her stomach transformed into a seething coil of snakes and the lace between her legs soaked through.

It was the first time in her life she could recall feeling something beyond polite interest, familial obligation. She'd grown used to her mother's sharp elbow in her side, the hissed reminders to *smile!* when they ran into eligible bachelors at the country club. She lived always with the memory of the day she'd overheard her father and a cluster of his golf buddies on the veranda discussing what a pretty girl Lillian had grown into. Her father's deep, dismissive laugh. *Too bad a face like that is wasted on such a cold fish.*

It was true she'd never been a girl of strong emotion, but she didn't know how to be any different. She watched other girls her own age with their flirting and bell-peal giggles and wondered what reservoir of feeling they possessed that she was unable to find within herself. Nothing made her heart race or her stomach flip. Nothing excited her. Until the stranger in the hotel lobby. He kindled something inside her with a single look, a flame that once discovered she was loath to extinguish, curious to see how hot it might burn.

So she smiled back, let him take her to dinner over her mother's protests and, a few days later, to the courthouse over her father's. And after that first dinner she let him lead her up to his hotel room and peel off her clothes. She'd always assumed sex was something to be tolerated, counting down the minutes until it was over. *Cold fish.* But sex with Yates was all fire and mad, wild hunger. Every touch of his hands was like a magician's scarf trick, pulling more and more feeling from her unresisting flesh. Anything he wanted she was willing to give him, just, please God, let it keep going, let it never end. Afterward, they sprawled across the bed, breathless and sweaty, and Lillian laughed and laughed, limbs so light she felt effervescent, only his big, warm hand on her belly keeping her tethered to earth.

The next morning she told her parents that she loved him. He was the one she wanted. They tried to talk her out of it, first with reason and then with threats. She knew her happiness was only a secondary concern, what they really cared about was her ability to snag some stuffed-shirt Boston blue blood whose old family money and connections would help to prop up their own. Her father warned her she'd regret it. Her mother wept and said she couldn't believe Lillian was throwing away her whole life. She couldn't actually be willing to move to some farm in godforsaken Kansas for a man. I'd do anything for him, Lillian told her mother, felt the truth of the words in the tenderness at the juncture of her thighs, the hot rush of joy when she thought of him. Anything. Her mother looked up then, and Lillian turned, saw Yates watching them from the doorway, his eyes sparking with possessive pride. He proposed that very day.

They married before the week was over. She became the wife of a man who adored her, lavished her with gifts, made her moan in bed and laugh outside of it. He was perfect, and she thought their life would be, too. But like everyone the world over, he had a flaw. Except his wasn't a penchant for fights or a tendency to drink, nothing that easy. His flaw devastated her, tore open her chest, and scoured her heart raw.

Oh, she thought about leaving him at first. When it was only Sophia and Penelope, and Eleanor still a bump under her dress. She told herself she stayed because she had no family to go back to. True to their word, they'd washed their hands of her before the ink dried on the marriage license. She could have left anyway, but she had no money and knew herself well enough to know she couldn't survive without it. She'd put up with almost anything to avoid a low-paying job, some dirty apartment, thrift store clothes, and government assistance. But really, she stayed because she wanted to. Her words to her mother—*I'd do anything for him*—remained true. She stayed because she didn't want to leave him. That was *her* flaw.

So she took a page from her mother's marriage playbook, the tactic used every time Lillian's father had another in a never-ending string of dalliances. Lillian looked the other way. Made a meal of the crumbs of time Yates spent with her—never enough, always leaving her hungry for more. She consoled herself with the ring on her finger. She was his *wife*, the one who would never leave him, and that had to count for something. To his credit, Yates made it as easy on her as he could. He never flaunted what went on out of her eyesight, tried his best not to rub her face in it. And, as he always reminded her, he needed her. He loved her. But he didn't love *only* her.

She outlasted needy Sophia and stupid, careless Penelope. She gave birth to daughters and understood, from the second she held them, that she was never meant to be a mother. She looked into their scrunched faces, stroked their downy heads, and felt nothing beyond a pale kind of duty. Except for Emmeline. For some reason, the smell of her skin, perhaps, or the way her mouth twisted to the side before she cried, she managed to extract at least a hint of maternal instinct from Lillian. Enough that Lillian couldn't stand to watch it happen. Couldn't bear the thought of Emmeline breaking her own mother's heart. Occasionally she wondered which came first: her lack of feeling for her girls or the knowledge she was destined to hate them. Her very own chicken-or-the-egg riddle.

Sometimes, especially at the beginning, she clung to the idea that she could always leave later if it got to be too much. Gave herself an out in some distant future. But the more time passed, the more his secret became her secret, too. Her burden. Because if she told, if she exposed him, she also exposed herself. And she knew who people would blame. They might gossip under their breath about Yates Roanoke, the pervert. But Lillian would be the one they'd crucify. The mother who didn't protect her children, who was too cold to love them. Never mind that the children didn't want to be protected, were complicit in their own destruction. The unfairness of it rankled. The girls had made their own choices, the same way Lillian had made hers, but no one would care about that. The shame, the fault, would land at Lillian's feet because she was the one who birthed them.

But what it boiled down to, after the excuses and explanations, was the simple fact that she loved him. More than her daughters. More than her granddaughters. More than anything in the entire world. He made her come alive, still, with a smile or a tender touch. She would burn cities to the ground for him, if that's what he wanted. His precious Roanoke girls always abandoned him, one way or another. But not her. She stayed. That's what it meant to love. Never letting go. Never giving up. Never giving in. And when it was all over, she would be the last one standing.

The only one left for him to love.

Now

I spend the night in the police station being questioned by Sheriff Mills, who can't control his facial tics every time I mention my granddad and Allegra's sexual relationship. I know they've brought my grandparents in, too, because Tommy tells me when he hands me a stale cup of coffee around three in the morning.

"Is my granddad being charged with anything?" I ask. The ice pack Tommy gave me for my head has melted to lukewarm slush, and the over-the-counter painkillers aren't touching the pounding heartbeat inside my skull.

Tommy can barely look at me, his eyes bouncing around the small room like pinballs. "We don't know yet. The incest stuff . . ." His voice breaks and he clears his throat, fist at his mouth. "With Allegra gone and no one underage still in the house, I'm not sure what they'll do with that."

"Are they going to test the baby's DNA?" I ask.

Tommy shakes his head. "It's a moot point now. Your gran confessed, and they don't need to establish paternity to make a case against her. Everyone's assuming the baby was your granddad's, anyway."

"Lucky you," I say, but my voice is gentle.

"Yeah." Tommy lets out a choked sound. "Lucky me." His usually bright eyes are dim. The skin on his face hangs slack. Allegra's death, the truth about her life, has taken something from him. The belief, maybe, that things can always be put right. Some things, it turns out, are beyond even Tommy's ability to fix. "Your granddad says he didn't know anything about Allegra's murder, and your gran says the same. But it's kind of hard to believe she could move the body herself. Any thoughts on that?"

"Talk to Sharon," I say. "If there's anyone who would've helped Gran, it would've been her."

"She knew?" he asks. "They all knew?"

I nod, and Tommy's shoulders slump. "I don't understand why Allegra never said anything. Why she never left."

There's no point trying to explain it to Tommy, a boy who grew up in a house where his parents loved him, where at the end of a shitty, no-good day, he could always look around the ring of faces at his dinner table and be sure of his family's love for him. That's a gift he took for granted and one Allegra never had. One I never had, either. And into that void stepped our granddad. Handsome and kind and doting. He created the perfect cycle of victims: motherless, unloved, and ripe for his sick devotion. We didn't have any defense against him, especially not Allegra, who'd been with him since birth. He became the sun she revolved around, the only light in her whole world. And she couldn't bear to live in darkness, even as the shadows of her life consumed her.

Tommy shakes his head. "How did I not know? All these years and I never had a clue."

The one person I think might've had a clue picks me up at the police station at dawn, the sun just beginning its peach-colored ascent into the hazy morning sky.

"Hey," Cooper says as I sink into the passenger side of his truck. "Rough night." It's not a question, so I don't bother answering.

"Thanks for picking me up."

"Anytime."

I turn my head without lifting it from the headrest and smile at him through wobbly lips. His fingers glide through my hair, the backs of them feather down my cheek. "You did good, Lane." He makes no move to put the truck in gear.

"Did you know?" I ask. "Back then?"

"No," he says. "Not for sure. My dad had heard a few rumors. Small-town bullshit. I thought, for a long time, it was sour grapes. People jealous because your granddad was so rich. But you left and Allegra got worse and worse." His hand falls away, and he looks out the windshield. A muscle works in his jaw. "I should have said something. Done something."

"Don't," I say. "She wouldn't have left him. No matter what you said or who you told. So just, don't."

Cooper keeps his eyes straight ahead. The tips of his eyelashes glow gold in the gentle sunlight. "Did he ever, with you?"

I close my eyes. Sometimes when I'm tired or my defenses are down, I can still feel the touch of my granddad's lips on mine, the rough rasp of his stubble and the taste of his tongue. It's not even close to what happened to Allegra or my own mother. But it's enough. "Not what you're thinking," I say eventually, when the sun hits my neck, pushes the words out of my throat with warm fingers. "He kissed me once, that's all. But I let him. I let him."

The admission hangs in the silence between us, and I don't open my eyes. Can't bear it if Cooper's mouth is tight with disgust or his eyes dark with disdain. Cooper's hand finds mine on the seat between us. His thumb rubs against my palm. "You didn't *let him,* Lane. You were a kid. And he was your granddad. It's on him. None of it was your fault."

My breath shudders out of me, and Cooper leans over, whispers it again, right in the tender shell of my ear. "It wasn't your fault." I grab onto him blindly, fingers scrabbling against his shirt. I bury my face in his neck and hold on tight.

———

"I'm not leaving you here."

"What about my car?"

"Fuck your car," Cooper says. "Tommy and I will come back and get it later. Or you can follow me once you're done. But no way am I driving away from here without you."

"Okay," I say. "Do you want to come in?"

Cooper rounds the end of his truck and sits down on the front steps of Roanoke. "I'll wait here. If I see him, I may kill him. This is probably safer."

The house echoes when I step inside, all the life force drained away. I walk on careful feet up the front stairs and down the hall to my room. I pack everything back into my mother's old suitcase. The same one I brought to Roanoke all those years ago and took away with me again when I fled. I double-check to make sure I have the pictures from the frame in Allegra's room. On my way back out the bedroom door I take a moment, knowing I will never return to this house again. No matter what else happened inside these walls, this was a good room, with its gauzy white curtains and crisp, clean linens. I was happy here, for a very short while, a long time ago.

I grab my suitcase and start down the hall, anxious to be gone.

"Lane?"

I pause, slowly turn toward the sound of my granddad's voice. He's in the doorway leading up to Allegra's room, one hand against the doorjamb as if for balance. I wonder if he's been keeping vigil up there, mourning Allegra. The idea of it eats away at me, the same way the thought of him standing over my mother's grave chafes. He shouldn't be allowed to mourn, not when he's the cause of all the grief.

"I'm leaving," I tell him. "Cooper's waiting for me downstairs."

He nods, his face drawn, eyes sorrow-heavy. "They arrested your gran."

"They should have arrested you, too."

"What for?" he asks, genuinely puzzled. "All I ever wanted was for you girls to be happy. To do right by all of you."

"Well, you did a shitty job." I drop my suitcase with a hard bang. "You're the reason so many of them are dead. Sophia, my mom, Allegra, Emmeline. Probably Penelope, too. You ruined us all. Even Gran."

"That's not true. I love you girls, more than you know."

"That's the part that kills me," I tell him. "The thing that keeps me up at night. I think you do love us. Love me. And you're the only person who ever has." My voice breaks, and I look away. "Do you know what it's like living with that?"

From downstairs I hear footsteps, and I know Cooper is at the base of the stairs, listening, waiting, making sure I'm safe.

"I never stopped missing you after you left," my granddad says. "Of all of them, you were the one I couldn't let go of. Never did get you out from under my skin." The floor creaks, and I know he's taken a step closer to me. My skin ripples with dread. "You could stay," he says, hope threading through his voice. "We could still make it work. You and me." I don't know whether to laugh or cry. Whether to slap his face or run away screaming.

I turn my head and meet his eyes. "All I've ever wanted is to get away from here. I'm not staying."

He takes the final step separating us, only a few inches left between our bodies. "Then why did you come back, Lane?" he asks, so quiet I have to lean forward to hear him.

"For Allegra," I say. But my voice doesn't sound as strong as it did only a moment ago.

My granddad shakes his head, brings one hand up, and yanks lightly on the end of my ponytail. I feel the contact all the way to my toes. "Allegra is gone. But you're still here. There's a reason for that. You know there is." His voice is soft, sliding over me like warm sunshine, like mornings in the barn, like a promise of the future.

Run Lane. I hear the words clearly, as if Allegra is standing right next to me, shouting them into my ear. *Run Lane.* I look up at my granddad, the warmth in his eyes. It would be so easy. To give in to this life he's made for me. No more being alone. No more worrying about money or what to do next. No more thinking about anything at all. He will love me forever if I let him. But his love kills from the inside out. Chews through girls and spits them out, already hungry again. Over and over. It never ends. Because as much as he loves us, he loves himself most of all. Each one of us a reflection of his own bloated ego. Every time he calls us *special*, every time we smile at him, offer him our bodies and our devotion, we prove how powerful he is, reinforce how much he deserves what he's been given.

Allegra may have carved Gran's name into the carousel horse, but her vanity table warning was always about him. Gran was the one to take Allegra's life, the one who tried to end mine with a shard of jagged glass. But she has never been the real danger inside these walls. The real danger has always lived in my granddad's kind voice, his soft caresses. All of it masquerading as innocent, but really just a gateway drug for girls starved for affection, desperate for someone to love them. He doesn't force us with a heavy hand. He manipulates with a gentle touch, guides us exactly where he wants us to go. So in the end, we blame only ourselves.

I wrench away from him. "There is nothing that will ever make me stay here with you. I won't be one of your Roanoke girls."

I pick up my suitcase, and my granddad staggers forward. "What do I do now?" he asks, voice plaintive. He is such a child underneath all his alpha male bravado. A selfish child who thinks everything in the whole wide world is meant for him.

I shrug, head for the stairs. "I have no idea. I guess you find a way to live with yourself. The same as all the rest of us."

At the bottom of the stairs, Cooper takes my suitcase and follows me out to his truck. The front yard is quiet, no noises from the barn, either. If he hasn't already, I hope Charlie will take this opportunity to leave, get out from under my granddad's control. It is better to be rootless and alone than caged in here. I've lived that lesson. I know its hard truth.

"Do you have something sharp?" I ask Cooper. "Like a knife?"

He raises his eyebrows at me, but produces a scuffed pocketknife from his glove compartment without question. I pull out the blade and work it into the top porch step, dragging the pointed end along the wood, dig in deep. FREE. When I'm done, I slide the blade back into the case and close my eyes. Say a little prayer for Allegra, ask for her forgiveness. *I'm sorry. I love you,* I tell her. *It's over.*

When we drive away, I twist on the seat to look out the dust-streaked back window. Roanoke rises up against the blue sky, clouds pillowing above its high roof. The house looks bigger than ever, cavernous and strange. I imagine my granddad roaming the endless halls and echoing rooms, spending the rest of his days longing for a glimpse of all his vanished girls. I'd rather him be in Roanoke than in prison somewhere, if given the choice. It seems more fitting. A lost and broken king alone in his empty castle.

Later, on Cooper's back deck, a cold beer in my hand and the night sky sprawled above me, the tears come. This time he doesn't hold me. Just sits next to me and lets the warmth of his forearm against mine ground me. The trill of night insects and deep thrum of a bullfrog soothe me instead of murmured words.

"I wish there was some way to wash it all away," I say. "Clean slate." I already know that's not possible. I tried once before, when I ran to California. The ocean was colder than I expected, sandy and rough. And its wet caress didn't change a damn thing.

"I don't think it works that way," Cooper says, echoing my thoughts. "I wish it did. But I think all the shitty stuff stays with you. Like my dad's stayed with me. You just find ways to maneuver around it."

"I'm not sure I know how," I say, while the tears slip down my cheeks. I've gone from a woman who never cries to one who can't turn off the waterworks, my tear ducts making up for lost time.

"Sure you do. You've kept going all these years, right?"

I shake my head. "Not well."

"I think you did the best you could, Lane. About Allegra. About a lot of things."

I know, without him having to say it, that he's talking about the baby. She is the invisible point in the triangle that is Cooper and me. "I'm sorry about the baby," I whisper. I've never been good with apologies. And this makes two in one day. There's something freeing in saying the words.

"I know you are," Cooper says. "And I'm not trying to make you feel guilty or worse, but I wish I could have held her. Just once."

I look up at the stars again, swear I can feel their cool light cutting through the hot night air. "She was beautiful. She looked exactly like you. Nothing like me." That's the first thing I checked after she was born, whether she looked like a Roanoke girl. And I remember staring at her tiny face and thinking, *Thank God, Thank God*.

"If it helps, I think you did the right thing. We were kids, screwed-up kids. And you got her away from here, from him. You gave her a chance." Cooper shifts in his chair, and his shoulder bumps against mine. "I heard you today. When you said your granddad was the only person who ever loved you. That's not true, you know." I turn my tear-drenched face to his, find him already watching me. "Other people have loved you, still love you. Your mother. Allegra." His warm fingers slide between mine. "Me."

I wonder when Cooper got so strong, strong enough he'll risk saying words I could easily throw back at him like knives. He knows me, how awful I'm capable of being, and he trusts me anyway. For the first time, the changes in Cooper give me something akin to hope. Hope that I can be more than the sum of all my miserable parts.

The breath I take feels like it's burning all the way down, the hand I raise to smooth back his hair trembles. I could hurt him now and he might still forgive me, but I wouldn't forgive myself. Not this time, not again. Not for taking something good, the one good thing I've finally found in this fucked-up world, and twisting it into something ugly. Enough things turn to shit all on their own without me adding to the pile.

"That morning in your kitchen when I was such a bitch?" I say, speaking around a mouthful of tears. My heart is trying to push its way out of my chest, battering against bone, and I grab harder onto Cooper's hand to steady myself. I tell myself if he can be brave, so can I.

"Yeah?"

"Can we try that again?"

Cooper nods, a smile winking at the corners of his mouth. "We could start over," he says, the same words he spoke in his kitchen. "Couldn't we?"

"I thought there were no clean slates," I remind him.

"Not a clean slate." He grips the back of my neck with a firm hand that still somehow feels gentle. "A second chance."

Before his mouth reaches mine, I stop him with a hand against his chest. "I'm going to fuck this up sometimes," I say.

He doesn't hesitate. "I think that's pretty much a given. For both of us."

His kiss doesn't erase the ache inside of me. It doesn't miraculously heal me, make everything all right. But it's a start. A damn good start.

I help Cooper load the last box into the back of the U-Haul trailer and slam the door. "That's it?"

"Yep." He smiles at me, and I smile back. "Ready?"

I nod and climb into the truck. Punk, already inside, greets me with a face-full of doggie breath and a juicy kiss. I watch as Cooper locks his front door, slips the key back through the mail slot. Once he's behind the wheel, he looks at me over the top of Punk's head. Anticipation curls in my stomach, stretches out into my limbs, and pulses at the tips of my fingers. I'm not used to this feeling, of looking forward to what comes next.

"So, where to?" Cooper's decision to sell the garage, pick up stakes, and leave Osage Flats with me came fast. But we've never actually decided on our final destination. Somewhere other than here, somewhere new to both of us, is as far as we've gotten. "West?" Cooper says. "East? North? South?"

"Those are all the directions," I say and squirm away when he flicks my thigh. I lean back in my seat with a smile. "Surprise me."

A grin stretches across Cooper's face. "Yeah?"

"Yeah." I look over at him. "God knows it won't be the first time."

Cooper laughs, puts the truck in gear, and pulls out onto the highway. I close my eyes. I don't need to know which direction we're going or where we might end up. It's enough to know I'm leaving Roanoke behind for good, although part of it will always be with me in the memory of Allegra's smile, my mother's tears, my grand-dad's fierce and unspeakable love. In the faces of all the Roanoke girls I see every time I look in a mirror. But this time I'm not running. I know running doesn't get you anywhere. You can't outrun what's inside of you. You can only acknowledge it, work around it, try to turn it into something better. I may not know exactly where I'm headed, but this time I'm choosing my own destiny. I stick my arm out of the open window and ride the warm breeze with my outstretched hand.

Acknowledgements

Thank you to my amazing agent, Jodi Reamer. You were always my "dream agent," but I never thought that dream would one day turn into reality. Or that the dream would be as great as my imaginings. You are the very best advocate, cheerleader, and occasional therapist (all writers are neurotic, right?!) I could ask for, and I'm so thankful I have you by my side. And a special thanks to Alec Shane, who ensured this book made its way into Jodi's hands.

A huge thank-you to my editor, Hilary Teeman, who believed in and "got" this book from the very first read. Working with you has been such a joy. You showed me the road and then took your hands off the wheel and let me steer, which is exactly what I needed. Thank you to Rose Fox, for your fine editing skills and for answering my endless e-mails without ever losing your patience. To Molly Stern, Lance Fitzgerald, Rachel Rokicki, Sarah Breivogel, Jillian Buckley, Danielle Crabtree, and everyone at Crown, thank you for all your hard work on behalf of this book. And a special thank-you to Emily Kitchin in the United Kingdom, who has worked with me on three books now and isn't sick of me yet.

These acknowledgments would not be complete without a heartfelt thank-you to Tal Goretsky, who is responsible for the gorgeous cover, and Anna Thompson, who designed the beautiful interior pages. You both did incredible work and I'm so thankful for your patience, vision, and creativity. And to all the librarians, bloggers, booksellers, and readers, thank you so much for all you've done to support my books. No writer could make it without you.

During the writing of *The Roanoke Girls,* I called upon the expertise of several people to make sure I had my facts straight. First and foremost, a huge thank-you to Dr. Adam Wineinger who answered my endless questions with both patience and good humor (I think at one point I sent five e-mails in the space of as many minutes). A thank-you also to Deputy Sheriff Devin Phillips of the Clay County, Missouri, Sheriff's Department and retired Deputy Coroner John Zieren for the insight and information they provided. Any mistakes (or liberties taken with the facts provided) are my own.

Holly, thank you for reading this book (multiple times) and always remaining as enthusiastic as the very first time. But more important, thank you for being who you are to me. I couldn't make it through this crazy life without you. Thank you to Meshelle, Michelle, and Trish, for being my steadfast, funny, always-have-my-back crew. I feel lucky to have found "my people." Thank you to my mom, Mary Anne, my dad, Rod, and my in-laws, Fran and Larry, for your support and love and for never asking when I was going to get a "real job." And to my stepdad, Bob, I know you'd be cheering loudest of all. I miss you every day. To all my other family and friends, near and far, thank you for believing in and loving me. You make my world a brighter place.

Thank you to my children, Graham and Quinn. The two of you are the best things I've ever had a hand in creating, and watching you grow into kind, smart, interesting, opinionated people is the great joy of my life. And thank you to Brian, the only person I could live with every day and not want to smother with a pillow. You still, after all this time, make my heart beat a little faster. And much gratitude to Larry the cat, who uses my legs as a pillow and makes sure I never get lonely while writing.

And finally, thank you to my Stevenson and Stafford grandparents and great-grandparents. You introduced me to small-town Kansas life (which was, thankfully, much sunnier than what's portrayed in this book): homemade ice cream, trips uptown, carousels in the park, Fourth of July parades. They are a part of my story, and when I sat down to write this book I knew they needed to be a part of Lane's story, too. Thank you for showing me the way.

Reading Group questions

- The novel is split between two different time periods: 'then' and 'now'. How does the dual timeline work to create suspense?

- 'Roanoke girls never last long round here. In the end, we either run or we die.' Discuss how Amy Engel portrays the fate of the Roanoke girls as a mystery or curse. What effect does this have?

- The Roanoke farmhouse is described as 'equal parts horrifying and mesmerizing'. Do you think this description applies to the novel as a whole?

- The 'secret' of Roanoke is revealed abruptly and shockingly quite early on in the novel. Were you surprised by this? How does this affect the rest of the book?

- Do you think Gran is right when she says mothers are judged more harshly than fathers? Why do you think that might be? Is it a fair standard?

- What were your responses to Lane and Allegra? How did they differ?

- The Roanoke Girls is a 'sweat-soaked, sultry tale full of shadows and lurking dread'. How does Amy Engel create atmosphere in the novel?

- Do you feel that any of the past Roanoke girls could have broken the curse? Or were they fated to run or die?